No Chance
in Hell

PROLOGUE

North Riverview, Texas
Two years ago

A sense of pride washed over him. So he gave in to vanity and took a moment to bask in the glow of a job well done. A few adjustments to the focus on his camera improved clarity and provided brilliant shots of his latest masterpiece. He concentrated on highlighting her cold, dead eyes.

He repositioned her arm, closed her hand, resting it on her stomach. Yes. That was much better. Of course, he was uncompromising in his work, a demanding perfectionist.

After all, death was an art.

And he was the DaVinci of the twenty-first century.

DaVinci brushed her long blond hair off her shoulder and then straightened her legs out in front of her. At last, this was the money shot. He lifted the camera, taking multiple pictures.

A loud knock startled him. Damn it, interruptions would not be tolerated. Too much time and effort had been invested in locating her.

The pounding grew louder.

"Chelsea," a woman called out. "Open up. I didn't come this far for you to shut me out."

DaVinci moved to the window, lifted a slat on the blinds, and took a peek. The last rays of the sun washed over the blonde at the door. The hair on the back of his neck rose. She could not be here. She was going to ruin everything.

The knob jiggled as she tried to enter. She stepped back and angled her shoulder toward the door. Son of a bitch. She was going to break in.

Anger boiled through his veins. He took a cleansing breath. A cool head in this situation was critical. If she crossed the threshold, she'd have to die today. There was too much at stake.

DaVinci quickly moved to stand behind the door. He unbuckled his belt, slid it out of his pant loops, and then wrapped the ends around his hands. Not his favorite method of killing, but it would suffice if she crossed that threshold. Please, don't come inside. Go away.

A loud bump and the door pushed open. The intruder stormed into the house. "Chels..."

Without hesitation, he dropped the makeshift garrote over her head and tightened it around her neck. Her scream morphed into a gurgle.

She elbowed him in his ribs. The move caught him off guard. She rolled her shoulders forward, and damn if she didn't stomp his foot. He usually loved it when they struggled, but this was different. She couldn't be allowed to break free. The possibility she'd see his face was too great.

The woman whipped her head back, barely missing his nose but solidly connecting with his chin. The belt fell free, and the intruder spun around on him. He grabbed her neck. Their gazes locked for a split second. The bitch looked directly into his eyes and never flinched. Anger blinded him for a second, but he pushed all emotion to the side and squeezed tighter.

He would dance around her dead body.

His groin exploded into a raging fire. Her knee had connected with his balls. Nausea rushed him. Blinded by excruciating pain, he folded like a broken kite. He dropped to his knees, and involuntary tears flooded his eyes. The darkness called, but he struggled against it. He could not lose consciousness.

The bitch ran screaming out the front door, her footsteps hitting the wooden porch rapidly. A surge of panic gave him a badly needed burst of energy, but she was already banging on a neighbor's front door. He grabbed his camera, stumbled out the back, and hobbled to his own vehicle. The burning sensation radiating from his groin blurred his vision with every step.

Damn her. They would meet again, he vowed. And she would be his greatest masterpiece.

CHAPTER 1

Dallas, Texas
Present day

Chris Holland's eyes flew open. The room was pitch black. She always left the light in the kitchen on. It should have been burning brightly. Her muscles tightened, coiled, ready for her to spring out of bed. She slipped her hand under her pillow, reaching for the cool butt of her gun. She found nothing. Before she could react, something hard pressed into her temple.

"Looking for this?" a male voice whispered.

A wave of terror washed through her, filling her with emotions she'd never experienced. She didn't think for one second that he was a burglar. This was the murdering bastard who'd butchered Chelsea.

"You'd better use it now. If I get out of this bed, I won't be as easy to kill as my sister."

He made a low-pitched sound that filled her veins with ice. Had he actually chuckled? The tip of the pistol pressed deeper into her skin.

"Calm down. I didn't come to kill you. But it's time we talked."

"You mean like over a cup of coffee?" Chris did her best to keep her voice steady. No doubt, he'd heard the tremble in her words. "Put down the gun, and I'll go put on a pot."

He wouldn't accept her offer, and she knew it. But it might buy her some time. If she could get to the kitchen, she might get to the weapon hidden in the back of a drawer of utensils. Chris lifted her shoulders, as if trying to rise.

"You really didn't think I'd fall for that." A gloved hand stroked her cheek, sending her into a full-body shiver. "Your sense of humor is refreshing."

Chris strained to see some part of him in the dark. Anything that might wake up her memory would be helpful. "How'd you get in?"

"I can't give away all my secrets, but I found you again, didn't I? Suffice it to say, I'm a great deal smarter than you think. The only reason you're still alive is because I want you that way."

"Oh. I get it. You're a god. Deciding who lives and dies must weigh heavily."

"Do not push me. You think you're so much better than I am. Growing up in the lap of luxury, you never had to worry about your next meal. Some of us were lucky to eat once a day." His soft tone had turned hard, menacing. "I'll be back. When depends on you. If you make new friends over here in your new neighborhood, let them hang around you, I will kill them. It would be a mistake to bring them into your home."

The pressure eased on her temple, and icy lips brushed her forehead. Something covered her nose and mouth. "Breathe."

She fought his command, holding her breath. A sharp blow landed to her abdomen, and she gasped, inhaling deeply.

****

A steady and annoying *beep beep beep* forced Chris awake. Her brain was foggy, but she managed to hit the off button on her alarm clock. A second later reality hit and fear rocketed through her system. She sat up on the side of her bed, but the room spun, forcing her back down.

Last night's visitor slammed into her memory. The killer had been in her bedroom. Jesus, she'd actually talked with him. She pieced their conversation together while willing away a bout of nausea. Whatever he'd used to drug her had to be responsible for her upset stomach. Frantic, she slipped her hand under her pillow. Relief eased the pain as she wrapped her fingers around the grip and pulled her pistol into view. She stared at her cell. Should she grab it and call for help?

Was he still in the house? She felt sure her stalker had left by now, but no way was she taking chances.

Chris forced herself out of bed. Holding the Glock exactly like the instructor had taught her, she flattened herself against the wall. She checked the bedroom across the hall, took a quick look in the bathroom, and then made her way to the living room.

She paused and let her unsteady feet catch up with her racing mind. Why hadn't he hurt her? The sicko bastard had broken into her home in the middle of the night and issued warnings about how she should behave. The next time he just might fulfill his threat.

Her hand hovered over the phone. Should she call the police or take the advice of an FBI agent she'd met recently? She'd tried the cops, but they couldn't protect her all the time.

Decision made, she dressed, grabbed her purse, and walked to her front door. Her fingers trembled as she gripped the cool knob and turned. Gathering her courage, she stepped out into the sunshine and headed for her car.

The hair on Chris's arms stood on end. The sensation of ants crawling under her skin sent a shudder down her spine. She'd worked extra hard to cover her tracks. Now, her latest attempt to find a safe haven had failed. Was he out there this morning, watching her?

This time was different. Until last night, he'd never contacted her in person. She'd never feel safe until he was locked away somewhere.

It took all her strength not to scream to the heavens. The cowardly bastard didn't want to face her in the daylight. Two years ago, he'd learned firsthand that she had the skills to fight back. He'd had to sneak up on her.

Next time he might kill her just as he'd murdered Chelsea.

Chris gritted her teeth and kept walking. She shifted her purse to her right side and slipped her hand inside, welcoming the feel of the pistol grip. Silently, she thanked Texas for the gun law that allowed private citizens to carry a concealed weapon. She slid behind the steering wheel of her car, started the engine, and drove away as if she didn't know he was just out of sight.

She'd given up her job and her friends. Heck, she'd turned her back on everything except the Big Sisters program and the Animal Shelter. Abandoned as a child herself, Chris's commitment to mentor foster kids meant a lot to her. She'd bought a town house in Plano using her mother's maiden name. Breaking off with her contacts hadn't helped for long.

The bastard would not make her run anymore. Something had to be done before he killed her.

While in Georgia to volunteer on an animal rescue project, one of the FBI agents who'd been working the dog-fighting side of the case had suggested a company that could help. Even his glowing recommendation hadn't filled her with optimism, but after last night, she'd decided to talk with the people who ran it.

She parked in front of the office of Lost and Found, Inc. and debated whether this was a good idea or a waste of time. Why had Dalton thought she should talk to these people? Could they really help her? The police department hadn't been able to. She got out of the car, still unsure. She turned, paced a few steps, and then reversed direction.

"If you need help, you're at the right place."

She jammed her hand inside her purse, locked her fingers around the butt of her Glock, and whirled toward the male voice.

A mountain of a man smiled down at her. "Sorry, I didn't mean to surprise you."

He stood too close, so Chris stepped backward. Something moved at her feet, and her gaze homed in on the dog looking up at her.

"Are you okay?" The tall stranger moved closer, reaching out as if to touch her arm.

"I'm fine."

He dropped his hand, and she breathed a little easier. The beautiful dog lay down at her feet.

The man motioned with his hand. The dog immediately moved and stood at his master's side. "Good dog."

"Does he bite?" She kept a close eye on the animal.

"Not unless told to. Offer him the back of your hand and let him get your scent." The man leaned down and scratched the dog's ears. "Go ahead."

Chris cautiously did as he suggested. The dog sniffed briefly and then rewarded her gesture with a lick. Her heart melted a little. "Aren't you handsome?" She sank her fingers into the brown and white scruff around his neck. "What's his name?"

"Diablo. And you are?"

"Not sure I should go in." Chris still had second thoughts about bringing strangers into her problem. She hoped Dalton was right about this organization.

"Well, Not Sure, you won't know unless you go inside."

Tall, tan, and broad-shouldered, he reached around her and pushed the door open. His muscles flexed, stretching his white shirt sleeve to the max. Cool air caressed her face. His scent, clean and masculine, filled her senses.

"Coming?" he asked. A smile lifted the corners of his mouth. Head and shoulders taller than Chris, he looked down at her with warm brown eyes. A lock of chestnut-colored hair fell onto his forehead, and he raked it back with a large hand.

"You work here?" She hoped his answer would be yes. His eyes projected a quiet confidence, and the way he carried himself left no doubt that he feared no man.

"Yes, ma'am."

There was only one way to find out if Dalton had been right about Lost and Found, Inc. "Then let's do this," she said.

****

Marcus Ricci held the door open to allow the woman to enter the office first.

"Thank you." She nodded, never taking her gaze off him.

"No problem." That he even noticed a hint of citrus trailing behind her surprised him. He sometimes imagined Lynne's perfume on the pillow, but that was late at night when he was alone and thoughts of her sneaked up on him.

He followed the blond-haired woman inside, pushing away his memories. If the faint circles under her eyes were any indication, the lady hadn't slept well in a while. Even looking exhausted, she'd stop traffic with her creamy complexion and that body. Her eyes had been full of defiance when she'd backed away from him. Yet, behind that bravado, he'd seen an underlying fear. That troubled him. She had the look of a woman who was losing hope while clinging desperately to her pride. She exuded mystery, and Marcus loved nothing better.

He paused just inside while she stopped and looked around the office. The work space was laid out much like a police station bullpen. Everyone had a desk and chair, a couple of filing cabinets, and no privacy. Few of their cases functioned as a one-man operation. Even if the help came from one of these desks, backup was always available. The only way to describe their work space was "organized clutter."

Except for Ty Castillo's area. Now that he lived in and worked out of Colombia, his desk had turned into a wasteland. Nate was probably holding that spot open for Jake Donovan, the fourth male in a friendship that had formed in college. Ten years later, three of Wolfe's Pack, as Nate's wife, Kay, had called them, had joined forces when her life had been threatened. After the crisis had ended, Nate and Kay had married. Marcus and Ty had joined the newlyweds at the agency, mainly because each one carried their own personal guilt for something. Maybe helping others would atone in some small way.

"Nate," Kay called over her shoulder. Her eyes were wide and full of curiosity. She came out from behind her desk with a silly smile plastered on her face. "Marcus is back, and he brought a friend."

"No." He squashed that idea quickly. No point in getting Kay started down the wrong path. "She's a lady who's not sure she should've come inside."

"Then let's figure it out together." Nate Wolfe walked out of the break room holding a cup. "Black? Cream and sugar?" he asked the woman.

"Black, please."

"Come in." Kay took over while her husband went for the coffee. She introduced herself and then Nate when he returned. "You've met Marcus Ricci?"

"Not officially," Marcus said as he disconnected Diablo's leash and then extended his hand.

"Christine Holland." Her grip was strong for such a small-boned woman. "I prefer Chris."

Her hand fit his as if made from a smaller mold. Heat traveled from her fingers up his arm, forcing Marcus to release her.

"You okay with a group meeting?" Nate asked.

"That's fine," Chris agreed.

Kay escorted their guest to the small room they used as command central. Diablo followed Kay, dropping at her feet when she sat. Marcus, figuring Chris would feel more comfortable next to another woman, parked himself next to Nate on the opposite side of the table.

"So what brings you to Lost and Found?" Nate went straight to business.

"My sister was murdered...no, slaughtered, two years ago this month." A deep crease formed between her eyes. "I need help."

Marcus liked that she was quick and to the point. He also picked up on an underlying bitterness in her voice. "I take it no arrests have been made."

"None. No suspects have been identified, either."

"You're not satisfied with how the police are handling the case?"

"I'm sure they did their best. I'm told the case has gone cold."

She removed a file from her oversize handbag, placed it on the conference table, and then laid her hand on top of it. She set her purse on the floor. The muffled thud it made caught his attention. He glanced at Nate, whose eyebrows rose toward the ceiling. He'd heard it, too.

The lady carried a gun.

"You have a license to carry?" Marcus asked.

"Of course." Chris blinked a couple of times, as if surprised by the question.

"Tell us how we can help."

"Maybe I'd better start from the beginning. My sister, Chelsea, had a lot of problems. Drugs, to be specific. When she started stealing from our family, things really got bad between her and our parents. They'd paid for her rehab a number of times, but nothing worked. When our father died and the will was read, we learned he'd had her name removed from all bequests. He'd divided everything between our mother and me. Chelsea went off the deep end. She blamed us. Accused us of turning Dad against her. Soon after, she disappeared, breaking all ties."

"Did you try to locate her?" Kay asked.

"Yes. I'm pretty savvy with a computer, so I regularly searched online for her. Called the few friends of hers I knew, but she'd vanished." Chris paused and sipped her coffee. "Our mother couldn't survive without Dad. She overdosed in February. The last thing she asked me to do was find Chelsea."

"You've lost a lot." Kay's tone was soft and full of sympathy.

Chris nodded. "Mother's part of the estate was placed in a trust for Chelsea. As executor, I was to ensure she successfully completed a six-month stint in rehab before half of the funds were made available to her. If she stayed clean for one year, my instructions were to give her the balance. I'd failed in my attempt to find her, so I hired a private detective. He located her living just outside of Dallas in North Riverview. She hadn't been but twenty-five miles away from us the whole time."

"I'm guessing it was too late," Marcus said.

"Yes." Her words were a whisper, but he heard the pain in her voice.

"With your sister's death, you inherited everything?" Nate asked.

"I'm the only living relative, so that would be a yes." Her eyes darkened to a chilling blue. "If I'd arrived at my sister's house one day sooner or even an hour earlier, we wouldn't be having this conversation."

"How so?" Marcus asked. She'd piqued his interest.

"Because Chelsea might still be alive and living with me in Dallas." Chris closed her eyes as if to gather herself. "Her wounds were fresh when I got there. According to the medical examiner, she probably died a few minutes before I pushed my way inside."

"Wait," Marcus interrupted. "Are you saying the killer was there when you broke in?"

"Yes. I still have nightmares."

"That's a tough image to carry around." He'd seen death, knew the mark it left on you. Guilt for not being there when a loved one needed you could eat at a person. It hadn't helped when people told him it wasn't his fault, so he wouldn't waste time telling her. "Sorry for the interruption. I wanted to be sure I understood. Please, go on."

Chris nodded and said, "Her car was home and a light was on. Given her drug history, when she didn't answer, I forced the door open. Her murderer attacked me from behind, but I fought back and got away."

"Did you get a good look at him?" Nate asked. He leaned forward in his chair, and Marcus recognized the expression. They had a new case.

"Yes." Her hand went to her neck. "I saw his face when he choked me, but when the police arrived and questioned me, I couldn't describe him. My doctor diagnosed it as a kind of retrograde amnesia."

"I've heard that's not uncommon when someone goes through something that traumatic. The fact you escaped is incredible." Kay's tone was sincere. She knew all about escaping a killer.

"And the police didn't turn up any clues?" Marcus asked.

"None were ever found. Well, that I know of." Chris pushed the file to the center of the table. "Like I said, her case is considered cold."

"You want us to find your sister's killer?" Nate asked.

Marcus rested his hand on top of the folder. No doubt, it contained painful memories, and he saw no need to open it in front of Chris.

"Yes. If he's not caught and locked away, you'll be looking for my killer." She paled at her own words. Her back was stiff, and her hands, curled into fists, rested on the table. Her chest rose and fell unsteadily as if the simple act of breathing exhausted her. "Sooner or later, Chelsea's murderer will kill me, too."

"What makes you think the killer has come back for you after all this time?" Marcus asked. He was glad he'd helped her decide to come in and talk.

"He never went away. I move and he finds me. He's stalking me," she said.

"How did you come across Lost and Found?" Nate asked.

"Dalton Murphy said you were the best in the business when it came to helping people."

"You're a fed?" Marcus formed a quick image in his head of her wearing dark pants, a white blouse, and low-heeled boots. It didn't work. Sitting there in front of him in a silky blue blouse over crisp white slacks, she looked more like a model. She was maybe five-foot-eight, trim, and sexy right down to her red toenails peeking through her strappy sandals.

"No." She smiled, and he was struck by her beauty. "I volunteer at Dallas Animal Services. We received word the FBI had busted a dog-fighting ring, and the shelter in Atlanta needed extra hands."

"I remember him busting that operation," Marcus said.

"I didn't work directly with him. Hundreds of dogs needed medical attention. I helped crate and load many of them."

Kay leaned down and put her hand on Diablo's head. "Sheesh. That had to be a heart-breaking assignment."

"It was tragic. I still worry about those poor animals." Chris shook her head, as if pushing away images best forgotten. "Anyway, during a few minutes of downtime, I caught myself spilling my guts to Dalton."

Nate huffed out a breath. "It's a talent of his. Nobody can keep a secret around him."

"Do you have any family here?" Marcus pressed.

"I have no one anywhere." Chris was silent for a minute, as if weighing what to say. "I'm the last Holland."

"Let's get back to your sister's killer and how you know he's after you." Nate looked up from his legal pad.

"Up until last night his only contact with me was to send me flowers with cryptic messages. He knew where I lived in Dallas, and now he knows exactly where I moved to in North Dallas. He was in my town house last night. He covered my mouth with a rag. Something was on it that knocked me out."

"What did he say?" Marcus asked. Damn, the woman's story was intriguing.

"He warned me that I couldn't have new friends." She rubbed her forehead with her fingertips.

"That's it?" Kay asked.

"I remember him rattling on about me being privileged and never having to wonder about my next meal."

"Tell me you got a look at him," Marcus said.

"It was too dark. I tried to pick up on something, anything that would help but couldn't."

"What else happened? Did he get personal? Touch you?"

"Not in the way I think you're thinking. He kissed me." She placed her finger on the spot. "Here."

"The son of a bitch is brazen," Marcus said.

Chris unclenched her fists and dropped her hands to her lap. Marcus couldn't tell if it meant she was relaxing or about to run.

"I know my story is bizarre. I swear that I'm not some silly, high-strung female who cries wolf every time the wind rattles the windows. Sometimes, flowers just show up on my doorstep. The card sends a direct message, like, 'You saw what I did to your sister. Wait till you find out what I'm going to do to you.' Or, 'Flowers like these will look good on your grave.' Occasionally, a florist shop delivers them. Those cards are more cryptic. 'See you soon.' or 'Can't wait to see you again.'"

"How long have you lived in Dallas?" Marcus understood why she'd been skittish when he'd startled her outside. Someone was out to get her, and she was wary of any stranger.

"Dallas has been home since I was adopted. I moved to the North side of town a little over six months ago."

"Where do you work?" Nate asked.

"I used to work for Patterson Marketing, but since my parents' deaths, I've concentrated on volunteer work."

Nate looked up from his notepad. Marcus recognized the expression. They needed more information. "Go on," Marcus prompted.

"I'm not rich by any means. But my parents' estate left me in a good financial position, which allowed me to purchase a town house using my mother's maiden name. I've kept to myself, lived simply, and have been careful not to do anything that would reveal my whereabouts." She paused. "I could leave the country, hide on some tropical island, but I'm not going to turn my back on my commitments. After last night, I'll have to reduce my contacts with two girls in the Big Sisters program. I'm hoping to maintain our relationship through phone calls and texts until this is over."

"It's a smart decision to separate yourself from the girls," Marcus said.

"I'm betting we can figure out a way for you to see them if necessary." Kay shot Marcus a don't argue look. Thank God, they had her around to be the heart of the organization.

"Why doesn't this guy just put a bullet between your eyes?" Marcus refused to look at Kay. No doubt, she'd admonish him for not picking a gentler way to ask that question.

Chris didn't flinch. "You'll have to ask him that question."

Marcus nodded slightly. "I will."

Their new client opened her purse and removed a checkbook. "Then you'll need a retainer."

"We're pretty flexible about that." Nate held up a hand to stop her. "We're in the business of helping people. If you can't—"

"I pay my way." She clicked her ballpoint pen and held it poised.

Kay glanced at her husband, and they exchanged knowing grins. "I gave Nate five thousand as a retainer to protect me. We can start there."

"Looks like he did a good job. You're still alive." The corner of Chris's mouth twitched.

"So good I married him," Kay joked.

"I can't take all the credit. It was a group effort." Nate winked at Kay. "I don't have but a couple of weeks before my next assignment. Marcus is just coming back from a week off, so he's refreshed and ready. Kaycie not only runs the office, she's one hell of a detective. She's always available."

Having Nate's help for any length of time was a bonus in Marcus's opinion. "Let's get a few more facts, and then you'll need to report the break-in. We need to know how he got in your house. While we're there, we'll take a look at your security system. It needs to be a top-of-the-line model."

Why he wanted this case escaped him. Perhaps it was the guilt buried deep behind her blue eyes. Or maybe it was because he'd learned not to question his gut.

CHAPTER 2

The silent vibration from DaVinci's cell phone was an alert. His mentor, Michelangelo, had sent samples of his latest creation. Pictures waited on his laptop. Anticipation put a bead of sweat across his forehead. At last, the elevator dinged, and the doors swished open. His heart raced, and he hurriedly unlocked the door to his apartment.

DaVinci paid little attention to his luxurious surroundings, caring only that the door had locked behind him and he was in the privacy of his living room. His fingers trembled as he shrugged out of his suit coat and then unlocked his private office. Once inside his sanctuary, he sank into the plush executive manager's chair and logged on.

His breathing became labored as he scanned through the different poses. The clarity and beauty of the snapshots were classic. He hated to be bested, but he had to be honest, Michelangelo had created another work of art.

The second time his cell vibrated, a smile crept up his face. No need to wonder who was calling, because only one person had this number. "The final presentation is a masterpiece, my friend. Truly breathtaking."

"I thought you'd like them." Michelangelo's velvety smooth voice slid through the phone. "The work took awhile to accomplish, but the end result was worth the effort."

She'd suffered a lot. DaVinci could see the fear and agony on her face. The bulging veins in her eyes, her slack jaw, and swollen tongue had been captured beautifully. Her legs were spread open so the world could see her overused cunt. What pushed this picture into the winner's circle was how the flesh on her chest hung loose, and that she held a breast implant in each hand.

"Brilliant. Just splendid." DaVinci tamped down the jealousy brewing in his stomach. How could he not love this work of art? "It's new and fresh. Without a doubt, it has never been done." He might as well surrender. "I'll have a check written and waiting."

The laughter drifting through the phone reminded him how much he appreciated his old friend and mentor.

"Thank you. For what it's worth, I feel a bit guilty about taking your money."

"I might have been poor when we met, but I'm not anymore. I pay my debts."

"I wasn't insinuating you didn't. You haven't been at the top of your game for the past couple of months."

Even though he knew it to be a true statement, DaVinci's temper flared. "Are you saying you allowed me to win last time?"

"I'm saying you have been distracted of late." A long moment passed. "I don't understand your continued fascination with the Holland women. Frankly, it's bizarre."

"Keeping tabs on her has gotten much easier now that Christine has moved to Plano." He instantly regretted sharing that tidbit. He clicked off Michelangelo's masterpiece and opened a clear image of Christine's front door.

"You cannot be serious. Next you'll be telling me you're neighbors." Venom dripped from his mentor's words. "How'd you find her?"

"It cost me a bundle, but I needed to know."

"You hired someone to trace her?" Michelangelo's tone was sharp, irritated.

"No worries," DaVinci said, trying to soothe his mentor's angst. "After he located her, he mysteriously disappeared. Forever."

"Fine. You killed one of them already. Now kill this one and be done with it."

"In my own good time. For now, I'm having fun."

"Don't make me do it for you."

"That would be a mistake." He hoped the icy tone in his voice sent a clear message. He had no words to explain how important Christine was to him. She had much suffering to endure before he killed her. Not even his dearest friend and mentor would dictate when or how Christine would die. "I would react poorly to your interference."

"Interfere? I'd be saving you from yourself." Michelangelo's smooth tones had turned hard. "Get her out of your mind. Our clients will not tolerate anything less than perfection. It's time you explained yourself."

"There's nothing to tell," he lied. His reason for letting Christine live was his alone.

"Prove it. Dispose of her and concentrate on business."

"Have you received complaints?" The line remained silent for a heartbeat. "Then the subject is closed."

"You're risking us both. And not just our lives, but also our art and our clients."

"This is something I have to do my way. Please understand."

Michelangelo's deep sigh indicated his surrender. "I have a buyer for your Van Gogh reproduction. I'm leaving for London tomorrow."

"Perfect. I'll start on a replacement piece right away. Have it ready for your next buyer."

"You have a showing next week. The damage to your reputation will be irreparable if you let the artist and the public down."

"I have trained personnel who are capable of receiving and uncrating the paintings. I'm going to the studio after lunch to ensure things are going as planned. The exhibit will be perfect."

"Good. But remember we have other clients, too. If things go well in London, you'll have new orders to fill."

The line went dead, and DaVinci dropped the cell on the desk. He closed his laptop and his eyes, letting his memory wander back to his youth. His mentor had found him on a street corner selling cardboard copies of the great artists made with stolen paint. He was sixteen years old and a runaway, and nobody had given a shit about him. Michelangelo had moved an unknown kid into his home, educated him, and trained him on the finer things in life. His guidance had turned an undisciplined painter into a true artist. For that, DaVinci would always be grateful.

In Michelangelo's position as art buyer, he brushed elbows with the elite. He'd quickly found a lucrative market using DaVinci's ability to clone the great masters.

DaVinci had been twenty-one when he'd killed his first whore. He'd confessed his predilection for torturing blond sluts when Michelangelo had caught him with a white shirt covered in blood. Much to DaVinci's surprise, his mentor had begged to be included the next time.

Over the next few years, they'd worked as a team, perfecting their abilities. Their careers had separated them when DaVinci opened his art gallery in Plano, and Michelangelo had accepted a position as the art director for the Willingdale Museum in Sundance Square over in Fort Worth. Soon after, the competition had begun.

DaVinci had never confided his true motivation to his friend. His plan had taken shape only after his gallery became profitable and he could afford the luxury of taking revenge on Christine and her family. Simply killing her wasn't enough. He wanted her to suffer. Know how it felt to be alone.

He leaned forward and opened the view of her town house. She'd tried to hide after he'd killed Chelsea, but he was way too smart for her. Money had bought many things, including information, so he'd allowed her to run. Much like a rat in a maze, she'd darted from one location to the other, searching for a way out and ultimately failing.

This last move had been her best effort. It had taken a few weeks to locate her. Since then, he'd monitored her movements via the camera he'd paid to have hidden in the tree across from her town house. Now he watched and waited. He'd learn who and what meant the most to her. When the timing was right, he'd systematically take it all away from her.

DaVinci shook his head. For the next few days, he had no time for her. He had to concentrate on the gallery show and his next project. Michelangelo had thrown down the gauntlet with his latest win. It was time to pick it up and meet the challenge.

****

"We didn't call Dalton," Marcus commented as Nate drove out of the parking lot behind their new client.

"I figured we could talk on the way." Nate pushed a button on the steering wheel and dialed Dalton Murphy.

"Hey, Nate. What's up?" The FBI agent's baritone matched his dark suits. All business.

"Marcus and I have you on speaker."

"Okay. How was the vacation, Marcus?"

Marcus took the lead. "Short. Congrats on cracking the dog-fighting ring. Too bad the bastards didn't fight back."

"True enough. How's the dog you brought back from Colombia?"

"He's a fast learner and smarter than most people I know. You got a minute to talk shop?"

"Sure."

"What can you tell us about Chris Holland?" Marcus asked.

"She reached out to you guys for help?"

"Yeah. She asked us to help find her sister's killer."

"I'm glad. Based on what she told me, she needs more than that. She needs protection, too."

"She's going to get both." Marcus thought he'd picked up a softening in Dalton's tone. "It might save time if you'd share your thoughts. What's your take on her?"

"She's not making up any of her story. I'm glad she contacted you guys. Sounds like she's admitted to herself she can't go it alone any longer."

"She told you about her sister's death?" Marcus asked as Nate turned into a neighborhood of well-kept town houses in Plano, which was a suburb in North Dallas.

"Yeah, but not a lot. She stayed busy with the other volunteers. One of her coworkers mentioned the murder. Chris didn't bring it up, but I caught up with her over coffee, and I asked her about her sister. That's when I learned the bastard was terrorizing Chris. After I got back to Atlanta, I checked with Dallas PD. They have a file on both the homicide and Chris being stalked. I pulled some information I can share."

"Good. So you agree that this man is a real threat?" Marcus asked.

"Yes. I do."

Nate had remained silent. To an outsider, it might have looked as if he hadn't been paying attention, but Marcus knew better. The ex-Navy SEAL listened and kept incredibly accurate mental notes.

"So give us your take on the murder," Nate said.

"I think the bastard's a sadist. He's addicted to other people's pain. You'll be shocked when you see the crime-scene photos."

"That brings up the question I asked earlier today. Why doesn't he just kill Chris and be finished with her?" Marcus asked.

"He gets off watching her squirm."

"We're meeting the police at her place now." Marcus gave Dalton a quick update, explaining the killer's visit to Chris. "She said he wore gloves, so fingerprints are out, but we need to figure out how he got past her security system."

"What do you need from me? Dalton asked.

"Send Kaycie everything you can dig up on the sister's murder," Nate said.

"Who?" Dalton asked. "Never mind. You mean Kay."

"That's who I said." Nate shook his head and ended the call.

Marcus had learned long ago that some things never changed, and Kay's grandfather and Nate were going to call her by her full name regardless. Out of habit, Marcus turned to speak to Diablo before letting him out. The seat was empty. "Feels odd not having my dog with me."

"I promise he doesn't miss you."

"No shit. He's getting more petting from Kay than you do."

"As if," Nate snorted, getting out of the SUV.

Marcus stopped and scanned the property. He counted three gardeners working on the landscaping. The grass was lush and freshly cut, the hedges trimmed, and knock-out roses lined the exterior. He and Nate joined Chris, who had waited on the sidewalk with two uniformed Plano police officers.

"This is me, here on the corner." She unlocked the door. "Come in."

"I'll speak with these officers," Nate said, showing his identification.

"Thanks." Marcus introduced himself and Chris. After a brief discussion between Chris and the cops, Marcus followed her into a large entryway.

"What now?" Chris asked.

"You give me the two-dollar tour. When Nate and the officers come inside, we'll stop so you can answer their questions."

"Make yourself at home." Chris extended her arm, indicating he should go ahead of her.

The open floor plan allowed him to easily see the front and back doors. Her decor was a little bleak compared to the lush exterior of the property. Shining hardwood floors reflected the overhead lighting, making the area bright. A brown leather couch was flanked by two brown easy chairs. A smattering of pictures hung on the wall. In a word, he'd describe her place as nondescript. Not at all matching his initial impressions of her.

Except for one particular painting that caught his attention. Hung under a wall-mounted light and over the fireplace, it was a really nice copy of the Mona Lisa.

"This is amazing."

"It's all I have left of my sister. Lord only knows where she got the money to buy such a good reproduction."

He understood that Chris would treasure something that reminded her of her sister. Over time, memories fade and hurts heal. It was good to have something tangible to hold on to.

Marcus moved through the space. Her living area was neat and clean. He explored downstairs and upstairs. One room housed a queen-size bed with a plump white comforter spread across the foot. The faint hint of citrus filled the space, reminding him of Chris.

Of everything he'd seen, her scent in this bedroom and the print in the living room were the only things he could tie to Chris. The answer hit him. She'd filled the place with inexpensive furniture in case she had to move quickly.

Across the hall, he found a second bedroom. The room was quite different from the rest of the town house. A lone desk sat against the wall. A secretary chair and one file cabinet made up the furnishings. On the floor were two cardboard boxes and a number of unframed canvases. No curtains. Stark white blinds covered the windows. No niceties. No luxury, but warmer and more lived in than the rest of the place. He wanted a closer look at the artwork.

"You're an artist? May I?" His hand hovered over the first canvas and waited until she nodded. He dropped down on one knee and carefully looked through the stack of artwork. She painted in watercolor. He was no expert, but the portraits of women standing in open fields were great. The ones depicting nature—trees covered with green leaves, flowers growing under bright sunlight—really caught his attention. A weathered barn nestled in a field of yellow wheat was his favorite.

"Not anymore. I don't know why I haven't trashed them. Since Chelsea's murder, I haven't had the desire."

"It would be a shame if you didn't keep it up. These should be on display in an art gallery."

"Thank you. I've been trying to write Chelsea's book. Even though there is no happy ending, if it keeps one person off drugs and out of prostitution, it will be worth it. But the killer has to be brought to justice or there's no end to the story."

"It's a nice tribute, but it must be difficult."

"More than I can say. There are so many unanswered questions that I keep writing myself into a corner. It's a lot harder than I anticipated."

"Once we find her murderer, maybe you'll get those answers." Marcus finished his inspection, and then followed her to the front room. "You'll need to speak with these guys." He motioned to the officers waiting in her living room. "Nate and I will look around the outside. I can tell you now that your security system needs updating."

"Do you know somebody?"

"Yeah. I'll get the installation expedited."

Marcus and Nate walked outside and did a close inspection of each access to her house. They found no broken windows or locks.

Nate stopped on her front steps and shook his head. "Bastard had to bypass the security system. But how'd he get inside?"

The two officers walked out. Their notebooks were closed and out of sight, leaving Marcus to believe they were satisfied. He and Nate thanked them.

"You go ahead," Nate said. "I'm going to take a second look around."

Marcus joined Chris inside. "They weren't here long."

She sat in a big easy chair. "You think they believed me?"

"I don't see why they wouldn't." The doorbell rang. "You expecting someone?" Marcus asked.

"No." She stood and started toward the door. "It's probably Nate."

"We don't know that for sure." Marcus reached out and caught her arm. "I'll get it. You stay behind me."

She tilted her head and glanced down at his hand. When she looked up at him, a deep scowl pulled her eyebrows together. "Please don't treat me like I'm an idiot. I had no intention of blindly opening the door and exposing myself. I fully intended to let you do it."

"Sorry. Automatic reaction."

"No." Chris caught his arm as he had hers seconds ago. "I apologize. I'm a little nervous. I thought by using my mother's maiden name, I'd have more time to figure out who he is."

The doorbell rang again, and Marcus let the subject drop. He leaned down and looked through the peephole. Nate towered over a young man whose eyes were wide and mouth was moving rapidly. In the kid's hand was a large floral arrangement.

"Delivery boy and Nate," Marcus said over his shoulder. He opened the door. "Come in."

"No, thanks. I'll just drop these off and be gone."

"We insist." Nate rested his hand on the young man's shoulder. "Who sent the flowers?"

"How would I know?" The kid pushed his words out with attitude. "I just deliver them. Maybe you should check the card."

Nate didn't release his grip. "Good idea."

"Who are you people?" the kid demanded.

"Investigators," Marcus answered, allowing the kid to fill in the rest. "Were you at work when the order came in?"

"Yeah. My mom took the call this morning."

Marcus pulled a pair of rubber gloves from his hip pocket and slipped them on. He took the flowers from the young man, set them on the coffee table, and then unpinned the small envelope. "You want to come look?" he asked Chris.

She took a step back and shook her head. "You look. I already know who sent them."

He opened the flap and slid the card out far enough to read aloud, "Thinking about last night. Can't wait to see you."

"No signature?" Nate asked.

Marcus shook his head. "Nope."

Chris backed even farther away. Her lips were pulled into a thin line.

"I need to speak with your mom. Where do you work?" Nate asked the young man. "And what's your name?"

"My family owns Fergus Florist. Call her. The number's on the envelope, ask if her son's name is Derek. She'll tell you."

"This isn't about you. Give me the address," Nate said.

Nate wrote down the address and then escorted the scared young man out the door. He paused. "Marcus, you good here until I get back?"

"Yeah."

"Wait." Chris picked up the vase and carried it to Nate. "Toss these in the dumpster or take them to your wife, but please don't leave them here."

"Will do." The door closed behind Nate.

Marcus turned just as Chris melted onto the couch. Her eyes had turned a chilling deep blue.

"I knew it. I felt his eyes on me this morning when I walked to my car."

"We need to move you someplace where we can better protect you."

"I'm through running. Let him come. If he thinks I won't kill him, he's wrong."

"I'm not talking about running. It's being smart. Won't do you any good if I find him after you're dead."

A soft chuckle escaped from Chris. She studied him for a minute, making him feel like a bug under a microscope. "You don't sugarcoat anything, do you?"

"Life's too short to not speak the truth."

CHAPTER 3

Chris listened to Marcus's husky voice while he spoke with the security company. He ordered door and window alarms. He insisted a panic button be installed next to her bed. His voice was firm and knowledgeable when he requested an expedited installation.

A calm settled in her chest. Not that it meant she could let her guard down, but she was beginning to understand Dalton's faith in the people at Lost and Found. Something about Marcus gave her a sense of security. She respected how he spoke to her and not at her. His soulful brown eyes seemed to miss nothing, yet, at the same time, revealed nothing.

It didn't hurt that he was so easy on the eyes. His broad chest almost invited her to rest her head against it. But it was his self-confidence, the manner in which he carried himself, that gave her hope. Nobody in their right mind would go up against somebody his size.

Marcus ended the call just as the doorbell rang again. Chris immediately reached for her purse, seeking the comfort of the pistol grip in her hand. In floor-covering strides, he crossed to the door. After checking to see who was there, he glanced at her and winked. Her heart fluttered as he opened the door. An odd reaction to his innocent gesture.

She gave herself a mental head-slap. Now wasn't the time to find him or any other male attractive. They had a job to do. One that would take a clear head.

Nate Wolfe had returned. His dark blue eyes seemed to always be on alert. He carried himself with authority, just as Marcus did.

Dalton had mentioned the Lost and Found group had been friends since college. Even with the online research Chris had done before seeking their help, she'd been unsure until she'd met the team. Marcus, Nate, and one other member she hadn't met, Ty Castillo, were all ex-military.

A vague description had piqued her curiosity. Had she hired men trained in black ops? "Did you learn anything from the florist?" Chris prayed that Nate had gathered useful information.

"I spoke with the owner. The order came from an 800 number. She remembered the voice was male, and she gave me the credit card information. Kaycie's trying to get a line on the owner."

"You have the capability to gather that kind of data?"

"As licensed PIs, we can. Nate invested in state-of-the-art information systems. He and Kay are the best at digging up information," Marcus answered. "Kay has good contacts with the Dallas Police Department, too. Then there's Dalton, if we need him."

"His help would be great, but can he get involved?" His connection with Lost and Found was apparently personal. Having him for a friend had to be an asset.

"As long as it's not in an official capacity, I don't see a problem," Nate said.

"What's next?" Chris tried to hide her anger at herself. She should've sought help sooner. Damn that she hadn't been braver and smarter.

"Since Chelsea's killer keeps close tabs on you, it's possible we've already drawn his attention. If he figures out you've hired protection, he could bolt, which we don't want him to do. Our job is to catch him, not drive him away." Marcus sat next to her on the couch. "If we chase him off, he'll just come back when we're gone."

"I agree," Nate chimed in. "Other than the flowers showing up at your home, has he contacted you?"

"No."

"But he wants you to know he's around." Marcus rubbed his temple. "You need continuous protection."

"But how?"

Marcus smiled, and her heart did that fluttery thing. "We'll take Nate back to the office. When I bring you home, I'll park outside. Being inconspicuous will be hard during the daytime, but after dark when your neighbors have come home, I can blend in fairly easily. One of us will be nearby twenty-four/seven. When you leave home, I'll follow. Most of the time, you won't know we're around, but if you go places that require us to be closer, you'll have to introduce us into your circle of friends."

"Like I told you, my 'circle of friends' is made up of my Little Sisters and the abandoned dogs at the rescue shelter."

"When you go to the animal shelter, I'll follow," Marcus said. "We'll pretend we've met and that I'm looking for a bunk mate for Diablo." Marcus glanced at Nate, and they both turned their gazes on her. Was she supposed to comment?

"I sure don't have a better plan," she admitted.

"Just know that we'll be close." Nate stood, moving around the room. "And now that we've made contact with the Plano PD, I'll contact Dallas PD. Everybody will know that we're working for you."

"Won't they push back? Tell you to butt out?" Chris had dealt with the North Riverview police during Chelsea's murder investigation. After moving, Chris had complained to the Dallas cops about her stalker. They'd been polite but hadn't been much help. She wondered just how DPD would react to her hiring someone to find the killer.

"They won't mind that we're looking into a cold case. Plus, we've got a decent relationship with them. Two detectives in particular are good resources." Marcus seemed to notice her reluctance. "They put in a few hours for us from time to time. It's better off-duty work than walking the mall on a Sunday afternoon."

"Have you considered using me as bait?"

"No. We don't dangle our clients out like a carrot." Marcus rolled up the sleeves on his white shirt. "We'll force this bastard out into the open using other methods."

"In the meantime, we'll try not to draw attention," Nate commented. "It's important that you carry on as if nothing has changed."

"He's right," Marcus agreed. "In fact, you should call the facility manager and tell him you're having the alarm system tightened. If he asks why, just act casual. Tell him you like to feel safe. Let him open your town house for the installation while you're at the shelter."

"I'll do that right away. What's next?"

"If you'd rather not stay here, we can move you and call off the alarm upgrade." Marcus glanced at Nate.

"I don't want to hide. It's me he's after. If I disappear, he will, too." Chris rubbed her eyes, wondering why she was suddenly tired.

"We'd like to get back to the office and gather information," Marcus said. "And you shouldn't be alone. In fact, somebody will be nearby for the duration."

"I need to stop by child services. You don't think I'm in danger while out in broad daylight."

"It's best not to take chances," Marcus said. "We'll figure something out. For now, you're with us."

She followed Nate and Marcus out the door, set her alarm, and locked the door. She'd felt safe inside her town house until last night. Now, she didn't care if she ever walked inside it again.

Nate walked next to her with Marcus on the other side. Under different circumstances, having two giant bodyguards might have been funny. Marcus held open the car door for her. He glanced down at her purse.

"You know how to use that gun?"

"Damn right."

If he'd gone through drawers or checked under furniture cushions while inside her town house, he'd have found weapons stashed all over the place. Getting caught at Chelsea's without a means of self-defense had taught her a valuable lesson. Granted, her previous classes in karate had saved her life, but she felt safer with added protection.

****

Marcus opened the door to the Lost and Found office, allowing Nate and Chris to step inside.

"Honey, we're home," Nate called out with a laugh.

Kay jumped out of her chair and rushed toward her husband. A smile the size of the Rio Grande River was spread across her face. Diablo got up, stretched, and trotted to Marcus. His tail worked overtime as Marcus scratched his ears.

"We'll work out of the conference room," he told Chris, starting back and leaving the two lovebirds to do husband and wife stuff.

"Wait." Kay grabbed him by the arm. "I have good news. No, outstanding news."

Nate's eyebrows rose in question. "Well, share it with us."

Kay grabbed Chris by the hand. "I'm sorry to talk about people you don't know, but I have to tell these guys or I'll pop."

"Please, don't worry about me." Obviously uncomfortable, Chris pulled away. "I'll wait for you in the conference room."

"That's not necessary," Kay said.

The warmth in Chris's expression as she waved off Kay hinted at sincerity. But Marcus remembered Chris's earlier comment about not having friends. He'd never have survived without his friends.

"Jake is being released soon." The words tumbled from Kay's mouth at lightning speed.

Her energy lifted to celebration level. Jake Donovan had been the youngest of Wolfe's Pack. He'd been tough as nails on the football field, but had always morphed into a big-hearted kid the minute he took off the uniform. To hear the girls tell it, Jake was a hunk. Marcus had learned early on not to argue with women.

He worried that Jake was being released too soon after surgery. The tumor pressing against his brain had explained his erratic behavior. Thinking the doctors were trying to kill him, he'd escaped the military hospital. The pressure had caused memory loss, and they had found Jake working for a human-trafficking ring.

The surgery to remove it had been almost as life threatening as leaving the damn thing alone. But he'd survived and had gone through intense therapy. Jake had been involved in some nasty shit, including damn near getting Kay and her best friend, Holly Hoffman, killed. Marcus would reserve his judgment for a while.

"All your trips to spend time with him must've worked. Congratulations." Nate gathered Kay to his chest. Beaming down at her, he dropped a kiss on her lips.

They were opposite sides of the same coin, completing each other's personalities. A zing of something like loneliness passed through Marcus, which he quickly shoved away. He'd put the past behind him. Trouble was, his memory hadn't received the memo.

"Enough. I'll have that image burned into my retinas." Marcus mockingly rubbed his eyes, pretending to wipe the sight from his mind. They'd known this day was coming, had waited eagerly for a date. "Give us facts. When? I take it they accepted you as a sponsor."

"They did," Kay responded with a proud smile. The pink that had rushed up her cheeks receded. "No exact date yet. And he'll be required to attend regular sessions with a psychiatrist until he can deal with his actions. And we guaranteed he'd have a job here at Lost and Found, Inc."

"What did they say about his memory?" Marcus asked.

"Most of the past returned. He doesn't remember the last few months before surgery. But he knows what he did. He heard it all at his hearing."

"It's best that he's here with us." Nate walked to Ty's old desk and gave the chair a spin. "We'll find work around here for him." He glanced at his wife. "When he's strong enough, maybe the two of you can get out in the field. You've been itching to get more involved."

"You got that right." Kay wrapped her arms around her husband and hugged him. "I was just about to remind you that I didn't sign on to be a secretary. I hate being cooped up in this office."

Marcus could only nod his support. More than once, she'd reminded him and Nate that her experience as a detective for Child Protective Services more than qualified her for a spot on the team.

"I know. It's hard for me to willingly put you in the field," Nate confessed. "But I will."

"Okay, then. Let's get to work." She marched them into the conference room and then passed out a stack of folders. "I made copies of the information Chris brought us, and then I added the stuff Dalton sent. You'll want to sit before you dig in. The pictures are graphic."

Marcus stopped them both. "Chris needs to stop by the Big Sisters office. Why don't we let Kay escort her?"

"My first assignment outside this office."

"I'm not sure I like that," Nate said.

Kay straightened her shoulders and scowled back at her frowning husband. "You think I can't protect Chris? I'm as good a shot as either of you."

Nate huffed out a breath. "Fine. Let's take a look at the intel you've collected first."

Marcus settled in the chair next to Chris. Diablo dropped at his feet. The first few pages were standard documents. Proof she'd been to the police a number of times. Her complaints hadn't fallen on deaf ears. The cops just hadn't found evidence to track back to who had sent the flowers. A throwaway phone and a prepaid credit card were impossible to trace.

"Holy shit," Marcus muttered, turning to Chris. "You don't have to see these pictures or hear the discussion we're going to have. Kay's going to drive you to your Big Sisters meeting. It might be best for you two to leave now."

"No. I can do this. I've seen the pictures, but was never given copies. Please. Do what you need to."

Marcus took a deep breath and read for a few minutes before speaking. "The medical examiner's report says Chelsea Holland had been tortured for hours prior to having her throat cut. Multiple stab wounds covered her body, gashes deep enough to hurt and make her bleed but not lethal. The body appeared to have been posed. Why would you pose a dead body? Shock value? A message to the cops?"

"Fuck," Nate growled. "Baby, you didn't look at these, did you?"

"I did. You can't shield me from these things. Not if I'm going to work cases with you."

"Marcus," Nate said. "You get to the pictures?"

"Yeah." Marcus slid the glossies from the folder onto his desk. He stared into the face of a thinner, washed-out version of Chris. Stale coffee shot up his esophagus and flooded the back of his throat. "This is one sick bastard."

The pictures confirmed the medical examiner's report. Chelsea Holland's naked, bloody body had been posed. Anger rolled into a knot in Marcus's gut. Even in death, a human being deserved respect, but she'd received just the opposite. Her legs had been spread open, leaving nothing to the imagination. One hand rested on her stomach. Blood had run down her body from the knife wounds into puddles on the floor. Some had pooled between her legs.

He turned the pictures facedown. "Killer took his time."

"He wanted to humiliate her," Kay said. Her tone dripped with disgust.

"Yeah," Nate commented. "The question is why?"

"Track marks on her arms are obvious and multiple." Marcus felt a stab of sympathy for Chris. Discovering her sister in this condition had to have devastated her.

"Chelsea was still using," Chris said, speaking for the first time in minutes.

"You thinking the murder was drug-related?" Nate asked Marcus, turning his copies facedown, too.

"No. It took her a long time to die. This bastard had her death planned out. He stuck around and watched. Probably got off on the suffering he was inflicting. He made a statement. Now we figure out what's he saying and who he's talking to." Marcus feared that they'd just scratched the surface of this case.

"Statement, my ass." Kay stopped pacing and fisted her hands on her hips.

She'd copied and put the files together. Marcus had no doubt that she'd read them. "He's screaming. He's a thrill killer, or he hated this woman a lot."

"I don't disagree. Which is why I think he'll kill again. If he hasn't already." Marcus reread the police report on the murder. "No semen was found at the scene or on the body."

"Read on," Chris said. "The medical examiner's statement says there was no evidence of rape."

Nate scowled. Deep concern was written all over his face. "I don't like exposing you or my wife to this crap. You've both been through enough."

Kay's expression softened. "I love you, too. But you're not shutting me out of this case." She turned to face Chris. "We're going to catch this bastard."

Nate opened his mouth, but Marcus waved him off. "Maybe you and Chris should head downtown before you get caught in rush-hour traffic."

"I'll be right back." Kay stood and left the room. She hurried back, wearing a jacket and, no doubt, her pistol.

"I'll call Tomas and Wayne," Marcus said. "They usually appreciate getting the extra work."

"Tomas volunteers so he can be close to her." Nate winked at Chris and held his hand out to Kay. "But I agree. We can't protect Chris twenty-four/seven and work the case," Nate said.

Marcus nodded. The Lost and Found team had gotten off to a shaky start with DPD homicide detectives Tomas Mendez and Wayne Kerns. After Kay's rescue, they'd been pissed as hell that Nate had kept his plans to himself. Truth be told, it was Dalton who'd smoothed things over. Since then, both Tomas and Wayne had become part-time members of Lost and Found's team. Marcus welcomed their help on this job.

"One more thing," Marcus added while he had everyone together. "Since Dalton's agreed to help, I want him to run the murder through the national database. See if there are any other homicides with these same markers."

Chris stood and joined Kay. "I don't know what to say, except thank you."

CHAPTER 4

DaVinci clenched his fists, ignoring the urge to throw his laptop across the room. Drawing his assistant's attention would pique her curiosity. The poor soul fancied herself an expert in the art world. Her promotion had been a wise choice on his part. She was devoted to him and the gallery, allowing him to concentrate on Chelsea and now Christine.

Satisfied his head wasn't going to explode, he replayed the video, slowing it to a crawl. Christine had allowed not one but two men into her home. Why now? He'd been watching her for months, and not once had she brought anyone home with her.

The young man who'd delivered the flowers had been jerked inside. A few minutes later a man followed the delivery boy out of the parking lot. The jackass had thrown the flowers in the dumpster. Exactly what had she told her new friends?

None of it made sense.

He studied the two men as they exited her house. Both were the size of those fighters who got inside a cage and beat the shit out of each other. Wearing dark slacks and white shirts, they both moved as if they owned the ground under their feet. Just who were her new friends?

His pulse ratcheted up again at the way she lingered at the door until one spoke to her. His lips were easy to read as he issued the order, "Lock up behind us."

If she grew attached to anyone, he'd kill them. And do it without hesitation.

She needed to understand the conditions of staying alive. Rules had to be followed or consequences would be levied.

He closed his laptop and locked it in his briefcase. He'd made plans to drive to Austin. The perfect candidate worked in a strip club just outside of town, but he'd canceled the date. She'd sounded disappointed. Well, so had he been. His plans for her had been really quite creative.

But Christine was his focus. He would not lose sight of the end goal. She thought she'd outsmarted him. Little did she know, he'd just begun to make her squirm. She would not be allowed to make new friends. The two bruisers she'd had in her town house could easily be dealt with. He sighed, straightened his suit jacket, and then walked out to the gallery.

"Here he is now," one of the clerks announced. "I'll let him tell you what inspired this painting."

He plastered a fake smile on his face. "Love to." He strolled to the potential buyer and linked her arm in his. "I'd just returned from a week in California where I'd been overwhelmed by the colors of summer and the feeling of the breeze wafting over the ocean. I had to commit that beauty to canvas." Partially true, the painting had burst from him right after he'd killed Chelsea Holland.

"May I ask the price?"

"I couldn't bear to part with this one. But I do enjoy meeting someone who appreciates and feels the message."

The woman made a soft sigh of approval.

"Message?" An older man spoke from across the room. His cowboy boots clomped as he crossed the distance. "Looks like the paint fairy puked."

"Harold," the woman whined. "Don't be rude."

"It's all right." Swallowing back a harsh retort, DaVinci struggled to keep his cool. "Not everyone understands abstract art."

"That ain't art. Looks more like chicken scratching to me." The man socked his Western hat on his head and started toward the exit.

"Sorry." The customer's face flushed red, but she hustled after him.

DaVinci nodded his dismissal. He hated that he hadn't told the old bastard that his paintings were on display only to be observed and enjoyed. He'd never sell one of his favorite memories.

"Jerk," his assistant, Janet, muttered.

"Exactly." He turned to face her. "Let's take a look around. Show me how you arranged the paintings." He tucked her hand through his arm and allowed her to take the lead.

He'd blessed his lucky stars the day he found this location in Dallas. A heavy-foot-traffic area with lots of high-end eateries that drew in- and out-of-town visitors. His initial investment plus the remodel had cost him a pretty penny, but he'd easily recouped his money.

The offerings in the upcoming show came from a handful of local artists, ones he considered to be worthy of his attention. He had paintings on display for sale, but certain special works were priceless, never to be sold. His first one was particularly stunning. Angry slashes of dark hues against a background of pale blue. His mother had never looked so good.

Janet's voice pulled him from his deep thoughts. "You're displeased?"

"Not at all. The arrangement will pull the traffic through nicely, allowing the customer to pause and enjoy each piece."

Before she could gush and get under his skin, he insisted she leave early and get some rest. Tomorrow was a big day for Janet, as he'd given her total control of the show.

****

Someone pounded on her front door. "Chris," Marcus shouted. "On three, I'm coming in."

Chris jumped out of bed, ran and opened the door. His brown leather boot was raised, and Diablo stood next to him. A low growl came from the dog, hackles raised, the scruff on his neck standing straight up.

"Easy, boy," Marcus said. He took the gun from her hands. "You all right?"

"Yeah." She backed inside, and he followed.

"Then why didn't you answer your phone?" The area around his mouth relaxed, but behind his brooding gaze, Chris saw concern. Even though they were strangers, he cared.

"For the first time in many months, I slept so soundly that I didn't hear anything." That statement alone frightened her. Marcus banging on her door had startled her and, hard as she tried, she couldn't slow down her heart rate. Looking for some normalcy, she started a pot of coffee. "At first, I didn't want to set foot in this place, but knowing you were outside made me feel safe. I didn't wake at every little sound."

"I'll take that as a compliment. But you make a good point, maybe you shouldn't stay here at all. Be easier to protect you in a safe house." His gaze swept across her body, searing her with heat. Then, as if he realized he was staring, he looked away. "We'll wait in here while you change. Come, Diablo."

"Be right back." Her knees wobbled as she darted into her bedroom. How had she forgotten the fact that she wore nothing except a cami and jogging shorts? Mortified, she grabbed a pair of jeans and pulled them on. She followed with a sports bra and a T-shirt. After a splash of water on her face, a quick brush of her teeth, and pulling her hair back in a clip, she attempted to ignore the fact he'd seen her almost naked. She rejoined him and acted as if nothing had happened.

He'd poured the coffee by the time she slid onto one of the stools at her kitchen breakfast bar. Heat burned her cheeks. Thankfully, he made no mention of her earlier state of undress.

"I'm sorry if I scared you by banging on the door. It's my job to keep you safe." Marcus shoved his fingers through his hair. He'd returned to his usual stoic self. "But when you didn't come out ready to go to the shelter, I called."

Chris finally relaxed. "I can't imagine you panic often." Marcus's expression of horror made her laugh out loud.

"I didn't panic," he growled out his answer. His hand covered hers. "I'll admit to being concerned."

His touch was warm and strong, leaving her unable to speak with his hand on her. Marcus jerked his hand away, almost as if he'd startled himself by touching her.

Her cell sang out, and Chris ran to retrieve it. She checked caller ID. It was the shelter. Today was free adoption day, and she'd promised to help. She apologized profusely to the facility manager and went back to the kitchen.

"The manager at the animal shelter is depending on me to show up."

He poured her cold coffee back in the pot and refilled her cup. The aroma put her taste buds on alert. Marcus turned back to face her. "We can follow the original plan. I'll follow you. But we should think about moving you."

"As much as I hate that he was here, I don't want to run. If I disappear, he'll never be caught."

"There's a difference between being brave and being stupid. The difference is often death. We're not using you as a sacrificial lamb."

Chris walked to him. "Is that for me?"

"Yeah." He handed the cup to her. "You need it. Maybe it will clear your head."

"I'm not trying to be brave, and I try not to make stupid decisions."

"Ignore me," he said, pushing a lock of hair off his forehead. "I wasn't insinuating you were stupid."

"But I'm right, I can't disappear. Besides, he'll just find me again."

"And we need to figure out how he does that. He knows a lot about you."

"I can't let the shelter down. They expect to be swamped."

"Hang on." He slid his buzzing cell from his pocket. While he spoke with Nate, Chris grabbed her socks and boots. She returned to find Marcus pacing.

"What's the verdict?" she asked.

"Did you tell the shelter when you'd be there?" The nerves in his jaw had started twitching again.

"We're good until after lunch. Should we check with the police first? They were going to ask the neighbors if they'd seen any suspicious vehicles in the parking lot."

"Nate will do that from the office."

"Then I need to get to the shelter."

"That's not a problem. I'll follow you over. We'll enter the shelter together, and you can introduce me as a neighbor. It will give me an excuse to stay close."

"Help is never turned away. No matter what pretext we use, you hang out for very long and we'll put you to work."

"Let's try something before we go. Come sit down." Marcus patted the back of her easy chair.

Chris did as he asked. "Now what?"

"Close your eyes and take a few deep breaths." He dropped to one knee and took both her hands in his.

Her hands were cold inside his warm and comforting grasp. His thumbs rubbed across her knuckles. How long had it been since a man had demonstrated such tenderness with her? She'd been looking over her shoulder for two years, not allowing anyone to get close.

"Tell me again what you remember about the break-in."

A chill raced up her spine, and she tightened her hold on Marcus. "He seemed really angry that my parents had money. Was bitter I'd grown up in the 'lap of luxury.'" She opened her eyes and looked into Marcus's troubled gaze. "I've already told you that he said I shouldn't make any friends. If I do, he'll kill them."

"Let him try." Marcus released his grip on her hands and stood. "Maybe you remind him of someone who had money and lorded it over him. He's dangerous. Unpredictable."

She walked to the kitchen counter, picked up the pistol, and slid it into her purse. "And he has to pay for killing my sister."

"I'm sorry the law let you down. I won't."

CHAPTER 5

By the time Marcus and Chris arrived at the shelter, the place was crammed with parents and kids, who milled from animal to animal. They asked questions and were allowed hands-on experience with the dogs.

He'd kept Diablo to the side until he was comfortable his animal wouldn't become aggressive. He was pleased with his dog's behavior, because keeping up with Chris in such a crowd was proving to be a challenge. With all this traffic, his radar stayed tuned to high. No one was going to sneak up on her, put a gun to her temple or fucking kiss her on the forehead. Not happening. He would not be caught with his guard down.

Marcus moved closer as Chris removed a mixed-breed puppy from one of the cages and gently placed it in a little girl's arms. She knelt down to the kid's eye level and chatted easily with her. In fact, she'd been amazing with the kids. The girls in the Big Sisters program probably loved spending time with her.

Her gaze lifted and met his. A smile brightened her face, turning her from beautiful to stunning. She motioned him to come over. His heart stirred inside his chest. A weird little twist that he quickly squashed.

"We're closing in about thirty minutes. I have to finish cleaning up before I can leave. I'll tell the manager you're staying in here with me. Okay?"

"I'm not going anywhere. I'll give you a hand. Cleanup will go faster if I help."

"My back will be eternally grateful."

The facility manager and one other helper tackled the last few adoptions of the day while Marcus and Chris put the animals back in their pens and mopped. Diablo stayed right on Marcus's heels. The exposure to other dogs was a good exercise for him.

"Marcus?"

"Yeah?" He secured a cage door and went to help her.

"How long have you lived in Texas?"

"All my life except for a stint in the Army. Why?"

"Just seems fair that I should know more about you. I shared my family's dirty laundry with you, Nate, and Kay. No doubt, you read all about me in my file. Right?"

"I did." Having just met her yesterday, he'd studied everything in her folder. She'd done a good job of collecting data, but Dalton and Nate were in the process of gathering even more information. "Nate and I read your file carefully. As I'm sure you're aware, it left more questions than answers. My office and Dalton are working hard to provide us with more intel. In the meantime, I'd like to hear from you."

"There's not much to tell. My dad was a respected neurosurgeon. He'd traveled all over the world, performing operations no one else had the skill to pull off. My mother never worked. Her life revolved around Dad, Chelsea, and me. I believe she felt she'd failed him by not producing biological children."

"You and Chelsea were adopted. See, I've already learned something I didn't know."

"Chelsea and I were five and seven when the Hollands picked us to be their children. I don't remember that time in my life. To tell you the truth, my first childhood memory is living with them."

"When did you learn they weren't your birth parents?"

"They never kept it from us. Made sure we understood that we were special, and they had chosen us because it was love at first sight.

"What happened to your dad?"

"Three years ago, a State Highway Patrol officer found his car at the bottom of a ravine outside of Carsonville, where he'd been on a consult. He either lost control or went to sleep. Mama couldn't deal with his death. She lost her desire to live."

Chris had an oversize dog that didn't want to cooperate, so Marcus took the leash. Diablo crouched and emitted a low growl. Marcus settled him with a hand signal. Hell, he understood why the dog didn't want to return to his pen. He knelt and spoke calmly to the animal, before walking him inside his wire prison.

"Have you tried to locate your birth mother?" He wanted to keep her talking about her past. The more he learned, the better he could protect her.

"Once, after my parents were gone. A detective located her grave. She'd died a few months before Chelsea. I have no idea who my birth father was."

"You've lost a lot." He couldn't fathom having to shoulder all that weight. His wife's death had almost killed him.

"I took it hard for a while. My dad's philosophy had been 'you can give up or you can go on.' I chose to go on."

"Sounds like you loved your adopted mom and dad."

"They were the best." Chris closed the door on the last pen and turned to face him. One eyebrow arched, and a curious smile lifted one corner of her mouth into a half smile. "Nicely done, Marcus. Did the Army teach you how to be conversationally evasive or does it just come naturally?" The impish grin lit up her eyes.

"Just one of my many talents." Marcus couldn't help but smile back at her. "Ask me anything. I'm an open book."

"You don't wear a wedding ring, but that could mean anything. Let's start with the usual. Married?"

"No." That was all he intended to say about marriage. He motioned for Diablo to heel. "Next question."

"What appealed to you about working for the Lost and Found agency?"

"Other than getting to be the hero? The salary is great."

"So that's the way you're going to play?" She cocked her head and studied him as if looking at a worm under a microscope. Her gaze had turned cold. "I spill my guts, and you tell me nothing."

What was it about a female that drove her to want to know your innermost thoughts? "Long story short, I was between jobs. Had been drifting for a while. Kay was dealing with a human-trafficking ring, and her life was in danger. Nate called me and Ty Castillo. He needed help. No way would I have turned him down. After the job was over, he asked me to stay on. Ty is part of the company, too, but his home base is Bogota, Colombia. End of story."

"Why were you drifting?"

Why he'd wandered like a ship without a rudder wasn't open for discussion. He'd put the past behind him, or at least he'd tried. He was on the verge of telling her not to pry when the shelter manager stepped through the door into the pen area.

"You two battened down the hatches?" The manager chuckled at his own joke, unruffled that neither Marcus nor Chris laughed.

"We're finished," Marcus answered a little too quickly. "And I'd better be going. It was nice to meet you both."

"You, too." Chris shouldered her purse, digging out her keys.

"You decide against getting a companion for your dog?" The manager fell in step with them, pausing to lock the door.

"For the time being." Marcus scratched behind Diablo's ears. "But we'll be back. This one has never been around other dogs. He'll come around."

"Stop by anytime. We can use your help while he finds a friend."

The open invitation he'd just received would be helpful. The day had gone exactly as Marcus had wanted. He put Diablo in the car, buckled up, and watched Chris walk to her car. He'd stall, wait for her to drive away and then fall in behind her.

The distinct crack of a rifle broke the silence, and Chris's rear window exploded. Marcus jumped out of his car. "Stay down," he shouted to the shelter manager. "Call 911."

His heart pounded against his rib cage as he scanned the area for the shooter. There were too many high-rise buildings in the area for him to even speculate as to where the shot came from. He'd dodged bullets in combat, he could do it again. Marcus ran across the open parking spaces between his car and hers.

He dropped to a crouch and then jerked the passenger door open. She lay facedown across the console. Blood spatters on the seat sent his stomach into free fall. "Chris," he said on a prayer.

She lifted her head and stared up at him. Eyes wide and full of shock, her expression tugged at something buried deep inside Marcus. A couple pieces of glass protruded from her cheek. One troublesome shard had wedged in her neck right under her ear. All the blood had drained from her face, leaving her pale as a ghost. Was this a warning? Or a miss?

"My face stings."

"A few pieces of glass managed to find your face." He rocked back on his heels and scanned the buildings again. Where was the bastard?

She lifted her hand, touched her cheek, and grimaced. "How bad?"

"Small slivers. They won't leave a scar, but it's best to let the paramedics remove them." He caught her hand when she reached for her neck. "Don't touch. Listen to me. I need you to stay down and remain calm."

"Calm? I'm scared, bleeding, and in pain. Sure, no problem." The corners of her mouth twitched, and his chest hurt. If he got his hands on the bastard who'd done this, he'd tear him apart with his bare hands.

"One shot makes no sense. The shooter used a rifle." Her eyebrows rose in question. "There's a distinct difference in the sounds. If he really wanted to kill you, why didn't he riddle the car with bullets?" Marcus leaned over her and picked loose glass off her back. "I'm coming around to your side. I'll clear the seat of glass before you sit up."

"No. That puts you out in the open."

"That's my job. Besides, I think that was a warning."

"He said he wouldn't put up with me having friends. So why didn't he shoot at you?"

"Good question. Wish I had an answer." He opened her car door and helped her to her feet, catching her hairclip as it fell off. Loose waves cascaded down her back. He reached for a shard of glass stuck to her blouse, and her entire body trembled. His heart double clutched and for a fleeting moment, he considered pulling her into his arms to comfort her. The arrival of an ambulance, fire truck, and police cruiser ended that thought.

Marcus wrapped an arm around her shoulders and tucked her close to him, using his body as a shield. "Come on, I'll walk you to the paramedics."

The cops were full of questions. Marcus and Chris answered them together. This wasn't a high-crime area, but they called for a couple extra squad cars. They would canvass the area looking for witnesses. The lead officer put in a call to the detectives who'd fielded Chris's original complaint, who responded right away.

Marcus left Chris in the back of the ambulance but kept her in sight. He called Nate, gave him a quick update, and suggested they bring Wayne and Tomas in for some off-duty work.

Chris sat still, her face a mask, showing no pain while the paramedics removed the shards of glass. Marcus liked how she appeared brave and calm to the outside world. Underneath, she was probably a bundle of turmoil.

A few minutes later, she walked away from the ambulance and toward him. She moved with such poise and confidence. No one would have guessed that she'd had her home broken into, a gun held to her head, and had almost been shot, all within the past twenty-four hours. His first impression of her had been right. Chris was one hell of a woman. Not once had she lost her composure.

A news van pulled in and parked. The shelter manager excused himself and rushed to meet them. A reporter caught sight of Chris walking across the parking lot. The jerk broke away from Chris's boss and ran toward her. Marcus started to intercept him, but she waved him off. She shook her head at the reporter and, apparently, refused to be interviewed. She went straight to the manager, got a set of keys from him, and then disappeared inside.

An odd panic slammed into Marcus the minute she was out of sight. He cut off the cop he'd been speaking with midsentence. Whoever was toying with her life would pay dearly.

****

Chris stopped by the front desk and grabbed a rubber band. Once in the restroom, she finger-combed her hair, putting it in a low pony. She leaned over the basin and dabbed cold water on the parts of her face that weren't covered by little round Band-Aids. She stared at herself. The woman in the mirror wanted to run and hide, but she wouldn't allow it. With Marcus's help, they'd figure out what to do. Had this invisible killer just tried to shoot her, maybe he was a bad shot, or had he been warning her? She closed her eyes and tried to make herself remember him. Nothing came.

"Chris." Marcus's voice wrapped around her and gave her strength. She turned to find him standing with the door open, his handsome face drawn tight with worry. "The cops will fish the slug out and run it through ballistics. I called a buddy of mine who owns a wrecker. He'll have the window replaced and then drop your car off at your place."

"Thank you."

"You'll have to ride with me and Diablo."

"Sounds good."

"I'll wait right here."

"Is the TV news crew still out there?"

"Yeah. We'll walk right by them. Diablo will keep them from getting too close."

"Then I'm ready." No way would she succumb to self-pity. Giving in wasn't an option.

Marcus rested his hand on the small of her back and guided her outside. Heat from his touch sizzled, firing nerves best left dormant. They paused on the way out to tell her boss goodbye.

Two men in dress slacks and button-down shirts were looking through her car. Both wore badges clipped to their belts and pistols tucked into holsters. They turned and nodded at Marcus. "Do you know them?" she asked.

"Homicide detectives and friends. We're going to hire them for some part-time work."

"Homicide let Chelsea's case go cold."

"These guys didn't work her case." Marcus moved his hand to rest on her shoulder. "They help us out occasionally. Been there when we needed them, on duty and off." Strong fingers tightened their grip. "Trust me on this."

"Okay."

The red-headed detective crossed the parking lot. He introduced himself as Wayne Kerns, shaking her hand and then Marcus's. A smattering of freckles gave him the look of a much-younger man than the creases around his eyes suggested. His smile was warm, and when he spoke, his slow, comfortable drawl was slightly reminiscent of New Orleans. Chris immediately liked him.

"How can we help?" Wayne asked.

"Nate filled you in on the details?" Marcus spoke to Wayne, but his eyes scanned the buildings across the street.

"He did, but I'd like to hear what you want," Wayne said. Chris couldn't help but smile at the good-ol'-boy sound of his voice.

"Chris's stalker broke into her house last night. Nate and I found where the alarm had been bypassed, but a second pair of eyes might see something we missed. And we'll need extra coverage when I need to pull off surveillance."

"Then we'll start at her place." Wayne's easy manner reassured her that he was interested in helping. "We're done for the day. When you're ready to head home, we'll tag along."

Even when they walked the short distance to his car, Marcus pulled her next to him. She understood and appreciated what he was doing. He wasn't comforting her. He was putting himself in the line of fire. She'd never met anyone willing to give his life for her, and the protected feeling screwed with her emotions. She'd have to be careful not to fall victim to the misunderstanding that his actions were anything other than professional.

His silence during the drive to her house surprised her. Chris turned in the seat and studied his profile. A strong jaw and chin matched the last name of Ricci. The urge to touch his cheek, to run her fingers across the dark stubble was difficult to control.

"You're staring." His lips curled into a smile, sending the temperature of the blood in her veins higher.

"Am I?" She was grateful he couldn't read her mind. "I'm just wondering what's going to happen next."

He reached over and touched her cheek next to one of the small Band-Aids. "I've failed you today. If you want to replace me as lead on your case, you won't get any pushback from me."

"What? How could you have known somebody would take a shot at me? We don't even know for sure I was the target." Chris caught Marcus's hand and held on for one brief moment. His strength wasn't something she wanted to lose. "No way. We started this together. Let's finish it."

"We can't control what the killer does, but we have to stay prepared." He cut a glance sideways. "After Wayne and Tomas check out your house, we'll go to the office. Nate or Dalton will have come up with some additional information by now. We'll dig through every bit of it. The cops must have missed something. It's that something that will lead us to this bastard."

"It's just so weird he would try to shoot me."

"It doesn't fit his preferred method. He brutalized your sister. A gun wouldn't give him the satisfaction that an up, close and personal kill would." Marcus smacked the steering wheel with his hand. "I'm sorry. That descriptive language was too strong."

"The only way to uncover the killer's identity is to talk about him." She didn't understand how she'd so easily grown to trust Marcus, but he made her feel protected. When he'd tucked her under his arm, his pulse had quickened. Was it his nerves or had he felt a spark of interest in her? It was time to get her hormones under control. She wasn't going to be one of those women who developed a crush on every handsome man she met.

"What facts did the investigating detectives share with you about your sister?" Marcus asked.

"That she'd hung around with some pretty bad drug dealers and maybe she'd gotten caught in the middle of a deal gone wrong."

"I wonder just how wide a net they threw." Marcus pushed a button on his steering wheel and asked the monotone recording to dial Dalton Murphy.

"Marcus," the familiar voice said.

"Dalton, Chris Holland is with me. We're on our way to her house. The killer paid her a visit last night. If that wasn't enough, somebody took a shot at her today."

"You hurt, Chris?"

"No. A few scratches."

"I don't get it," Dalton said. "Why didn't he kill you last night?"

"I'm sure I don't know," she answered. "That seems to be everybody's question."

Marcus muttered something under his breath. "It's a damned good one."

"What can I do?" Dalton asked.

"DPD didn't mention any murders that matched Chelsea in Chris's file. You and Nate are looking, but why don't you check across the US for similar murders?"

"You think this bastard doesn't kill the same way twice?"

"You know more about that profiling stuff than I do. But maybe he's just perfecting his style."

"Actually, that does happen. The killer sometimes evolves as he goes. Let me see what I can do. Anything else?"

"That's it for now."

Somehow, Chris felt safer. The call had lasted only a couple of minutes, but she liked that Marcus believed in her and didn't hesitate to ask for additional information. He parked in front of her house. The plain blue car carrying Wayne and his partner followed. Marcus caught her arm, stopping her from getting out. "Give me your keys. Let us take a look around before you get out."

Suddenly too tired to answer, she nodded.

He turned to Diablo and spoke in a low tone. She didn't hear what was said, but the dog crawled over the seatback and joined her. He snuggled against her, his big paw resting on her knee as if to hold her in place. She buried her fingers in the thick fur. "You'll protect me, won't you?"

"That's the idea." Marcus smiled.

Just that lift of his lips generated a coil of heat low in her stomach.

Tomas and Wayne waited at the edge of her sidewalk.

"I'm not sure I ever want to go back in there."

"Then let's move you to a safe house."

"And let that bastard win? No, thanks."

"Then let me check inside first." He held out his hand. "Key?"

"Oh, that." She laughed and handed it over.

Marcus joined the two detectives, and Chris watched as they disappeared inside her house. She wondered about Marcus's life away from work. He'd said there was no wife, but was there a woman? Did he live alone? Chris wouldn't describe him as sullen, but he certainly had a mysterious air about him. While keeping his personal life to himself, he'd allowed her to chatter away about her family history.

The dog put both feet on her leg and stood. He leaned toward her window. His lips pulled back, revealing razor-sharp teeth. A low growl came from deep inside.

CHAPTER 6

"Don't open that door," Marcus shouted. Caught up in her daydreams, Chris hadn't noticed the detective approach the car. If memory served, this was Tomas.

Tomas's hands went up in surrender. "What the hell? That dog knows me."

Marcus crossed her lawn in long strides. "Relax. He's protecting my car and anything inside."

"He's a damn good judge of character, too," Wayne called out, poking fun at his partner. He laughed at his own joke, and ten years disappeared from his face. "Marcus, you should be training police dogs for a living."

"No, thanks. It took a lot of work to break him of his bad habits." Marcus opened the back door, grabbed the dog leash, and clipped it on to Diablo's collar. "You ready, Chris?" At her nod, he let them both out.

"Everything clear?" she asked.

"Inside and out." Tomas spoke to her for the first time. "Marcus was right. There were no signs of forced entry. Bypassing that alarm took a smart guy. It was no easy feat."

Marcus caught her hand and pulled her closer, again positioning himself between her and the street. "Who else has access to your place?"

"The onsite manager has a key," Chris said. "I just remembered something. The killer said he was smart." She closed her eyes. "Damn it. What else did he say that I've forgotten?"

"Don't try to force it." Marcus glanced around the parking lot. "Let's get you inside."

She shifted her purse to her right shoulder and started up the sidewalk. Even with Marcus and two detectives, she felt the hair on the back of her neck stand up. "I'm getting paranoid. It's like I can feel his eyes on me."

Wayne turned and studied the horizon. "I don't see anyone." He followed Marcus inside. "So how else can we help?"

"See if you can get the original case file on Chelsea Holland. Chris has one, but I wonder if they gave her everything. Dalton is pitching in from his side, but can you tell us who did the detective's interview? Contacts, friends, and neighbors? If we duplicate information, it will help verify facts. I'll take anything that might help."

Tomas pulled out his notepad and wrote something down. "I'll take care of it."

"It doesn't take both of us to do that." Wayne sat on the couch, stretching his legs out in front of him. "I'll take a turn here. Give you a break," he said to Marcus.

"Tomas leaves, and you won't have a car," Marcus reasoned. "Besides, I don't need a break. I'll stay with Chris."

"Sure I will." Wayne's tone was that of someone unused to getting pushback. "Tomas can have a patrol car pick him up and haul him to our parking lot."

"Yep." Tomas unclipped his cell and typed something. "Done."

Marcus had spoken highly of these two men. If he trusted them, so would she. She put her hand on his bicep, sending a flash of heat rolling up her arm.

"Wayne can stay with me." Marcus scowled down at her, spreading that heat through her blood. Maybe it was a good idea for them to be apart for a few hours. "Really. You'll be here tonight. Go get a change of clothes."

Marcus's eyebrows pulled together. "I'll swing by the office and pick up everything Kay has dug up. I'm due a shower and that change of clothes, but I won't be gone long." He pressed on. "If you'd feel safer not sleeping here, we can move. All it takes is a phone call to the office."

"I'll do what you think is best," she conceded. No way could she ask him to sleep on her couch. Not with his long legs. The image of him stretched out on her bed flashed vividly in her mind. Her face burned. "If I'm not staying here, should I cancel the security system upgrade?"

"No," Marcus answered quickly. "A woman living alone should take precautions."

"I'll be packed when you get back."

Wayne walked Tomas and Marcus out to their cars, leaving her to dig something out for supper. Cold cuts would have to do. The door behind her opened and closed. The snick of the lock told her they were alone.

"Anything I can do to help?" With Wayne's drawl, the three-letter word "can" had stretched into two syllables.

"Grab that bread. Our gourmet dish for tonight is turkey sandwiches."

"Sounds good to me."

They fixed their plates in silence. "Have a seat anywhere at the table. I have a few bottles of water or I can brew a pot of coffee."

"Water works for me." Wayne moved to the far side of the table, placing his back to the wall and keeping the front and back doors in his line of sight. "So how long have you known Marcus?"

"Since yesterday." He'd asked the question she'd wanted to ask. "You?"

"We crossed swords last year when Nate's wife had a little trouble. Between Nate, Ty, and Marcus, they pushed the boundaries a little." Wayne was quiet for a minute. "I'll just say they tend to take matters into their own hands and leave it at that."

"Yet you work with them."

"In the end, they're helping people. Besides, Tomas and I go way back with Kay. We worked a few cases with her when she was with Child Protective Services."

"She and Nate are so outgoing. Much more so than Marcus."

"He's pretty tight-lipped. Nate says he's been that way since his wife was killed in a car wreck."

Her heart clenched. "That explains why he's all business. He talks, just not about himself."

Wayne finished his sandwich and washed down his last chip with a swallow of water. "Let's see what we can find on television."

Chris took that as his way of ending the conversation.

****

DaVinci drained his drink without blinking. He grabbed the bottle and sloshed another couple of fingers of whiskey into his glass. He turned away from the feed on his laptop for fear he'd hurl the damn thing across the room. Did she think he was stupid? Surrounding herself with men would result only in somebody getting hurt. Judging by the unmarked car, she'd involved the police.

She was alone with one of them. What were they doing? Plotting ways to catch him? The thought was laughable. He had street sense and was savvy to the ways of survival. She'd never been homeless and desperate. Never gone hungry. Never been afraid to go to sleep for fear of being molested. Well, she'd know fear before this was over.

He rubbed his eyes in an effort to clear his head. He moved to his media room and turned on the TV. He grabbed the channel selector, looking for anything to take his mind off Christine.

A local newscaster's lead-in story about a mysterious shooting held no interest. His finger was poised over the button when the camera panned across a parking lot.

The whiskey in his stomach soured. He turned up the volume on the television. Christine slowed long enough to brush off the reporter, but the facility manager was all too eager to spill his guts. A sniper had taken a shot at her. Anger spiked his blood, sending a sharp pain to his temple. She was his to kill. He sprang to his feet and paced back and forth. The answer hit so hard it buckled his knees.

He fished his phone from his pocket. With trembling fingers, he punched in Michelangelo's secret number.

On the third ring, he picked up. "My boy. What a nice surprise."

"Where are you?" The taste of betrayal filled his mouth as he waited for the answer.

"In my room at the Regency. Why?"

"Do not lie to me." His voice quivered with anger. "Just don't."

"I don't like your tone of voice or your accusation. Why are you attacking me?"

"Did you take a shot at Christine today?"

"Considering I don't have access to a long-range missile, I have to ask the question... What the hell are you talking about?"

DaVinci sank into a chair. "Someone tried to kill her today. You insinuated you might try."

"How many drinks have you had?"

The question shocked him. "Two."

"I think more than that. Call me with an apology. When you're sober."

The line went dead. Fuck. His mentor and friend had never lied to him. Had he faked his indignation? Calling the hotel in London to confirm Michelangelo's claim would be a waste of time. He wouldn't have done the deed himself. He'd have ordered one of his minions to kill her.

DaVinci returned to his private office and watched the camera feed. Christine thought she could outsmart him. No cop or bodyguard in the world could keep him from her. She lived at his convenience, a lesson she had yet to learn.

A flash of clarity and resolution came to him. Minutes later, he was dressed in black, his pistol was in the pocket of his windbreaker, and he was walking to his car.

****

"It's Marcus," he called out and knocked at the same time. He'd been gone only a couple of hours, but his nerves were fried. Diablo sensed his stress, the scruff on the back of his neck rising as if the dog watched for imaginary enemies.

Wayne opened the door and stepped back. "You and the dog look like shit. What's up?"

"Nothing. I was in a hurry to get back." Marcus caught Chris's gaze and held it. His breathing leveled off when she smiled. "Everything quiet?"

"Yeah. Chris doesn't even have noisy neighbors."

"We had sandwiches. I left everything out for you." She moved to the kitchen.

"I'm packed and ready, but Wayne's right. You and Diablo look like you could use a meal. We have time for you to eat."

"Better listen to the lady." Wayne walked to the door. "If you need me or Tomas to stand watch, just give us a call."

"Will do," Marcus said.

"Thank you for babysitting me," Chris called out.

"Anytime."

Marcus locked up and joined her at the kitchen counter. Diablo growled at the door. "I'm sorry, big fellow. It's a good thing you reminded me." He clipped the leash to the dog's collar. "If you'll make me a sandwich, I'll take this guy out. We won't go far, but lock the—"

"Door." She finished his sentence with a grin, joining him to do as asked.

"Right."

The crack of gunfire split the night. Marcus dropped the leash. Crouching low, he pulled his Glock and sprinted to Wayne's unmarked car. He jerked open the driver's side door to find Wayne slumped to the right. Blood had already saturated the back of his shirt. A bullet had hit him in the shoulder, behind his left arm.

"I called 911," Chris called out.

"Looks like you took one in the left shoulder blade." Marcus tried not to sound panicked. That was the last thing Wayne needed right now. "I can't tell more than that." He rested his weapon on the top of the car so it would be easy to reach and then jerked off his shirt. "This is gonna hurt." He pressed hard against the wound to slow the flow of blood.

"I was adjusting the rearview mirror. The motherfucker probably aimed for my head." Wayne moaned as Marcus applied pressure.

He placed two fingers on the detective's neck and checked his pulse. An erratic heartbeat could have meant lots of things, but Wayne's heart was pumping too fast. "Breathe for me, buddy. The ambulance is on the way."

"I'm trying." Wayne turned his head. The tight lines around his mouth indi cated he was in great pain. "Did you see anything?" Wayne asked, even as his body folded sideways onto the seat.

Marcus put one foot inside the car, leaning in to keep pressure on the wound. "No. I was inside when Chris and I heard the gunshot."

"Dark car, maybe black or navy, pulled up next to me. I didn't see the shooter. Is Chris okay?"

"She's fine. Let's worry about you."

An ambulance, a fire truck, and two patrol cars sped into the complex. Marcus stepped into the open and waved his hand. Before he could react, four cops were out of their cars with guns drawn and pointed directly at him.

"Down on the ground," one shouted.

"Worry about the man in the car. He's a cop and has been shot," Marcus said as he dropped facedown. He knew the scene looked bad to a stranger. He was naked from the waist up and had blood all over his hands.

"Dude's right, the wounded guy is a Dallas cop," a voice from behind called out. "Says the man on the ground is with him."

A boot toe poked him in the ribs.

"Get up slowly and dig out some identification."

He did as instructed. He wiped his fingers on his jeans and carefully removed his wallet. He handed over his private investigator's license, driver's license, and gun permit.

"My pistol is on the top of his car."

The officer studied the license and checked the picture. Marcus was edging toward the end of his patience.

"Hey," an EMT called out. "This man wants to see his friend."

Marcus turned to go check on Wayne.

"Don't make any sudden moves," the cop said.

"I'm just checking on my friend." He turned his back and walked to the stretcher, where they'd strapped down Wayne.

His face was ghastly pale, his red hair disheveled and his mouth slack. Marcus had seen that expression in Afghanistan. He clasped Wayne's hand as one of the paramedics taped down the needle and started an IV drip. The guy glanced up and lifted one shoulder. Was that his silent way of saying the situation wasn't good?

"I'll be fine," Wayne managed to whisper.

"Load up." The paramedic pushed the stretcher toward the ambulance. He paused by the open doors and lifted his gaze. "We're taking him to Dallas General." The grim expression spoke volumes. Marcus helped lift the gurney.

Wayne's eyelids fluttered closed. The ambulance door slammed shut, but not before Marcus heard words that froze him in place.

"He's coding." The paramedic's voice faded as the ambulance sped off.

Marcus called Tomas and broke the news.

Again, Marcus had left Chris and something had gone wrong. He was supposed to be protecting Chris. It should have been him the paramedics were fighting to keep alive.

The cop returned Marcus's driver's license and gun permit. "You see the shooter?"

"No. I heard the shot and then came outside."

"Too bad."

"Detective Kerns said a dark car pulled up, and somebody inside shot him. Bastard never said a word, just sped off. Son of a bitch was gone before I got over here."

"Was that his family you called?"

"His partner." Marcus sensed Chris's presence. He knew before looking over his shoulder that she and Diablo had come outside. She stood at the edge of the walk, holding a towel in one hand and the leash in the other.

He nodded, holding out his hand to her. Chris and Diablo rushed to his side. The overhead lights cast a shadow across her face. Tension reflected in her eyes. She used the wet end of the towel to wash his hands, the other to dry them. The weight on his shoulders lifted a little. A fierce need to protect her burned through his soul.

"Thanks," he said, unable to find the words to express how her generosity touched him.

She didn't speak. Instead, she wrapped her arms around his waist and leaned against his chest. Something tight and uncomfortable unraveled inside him. Giving or receiving comfort had been absent in his life for a long time. Chris had regenerated that need in him.

"How's Wayne?" She stepped back and cleared her throat. Her gaze traveled across the crime scene. Tears brimmed in her eyes, but she held back, proving her inner strength to him once again.

"I don't know." He dropped down and spoke to Diablo, calming him with words. The bloody towel was still in her hand.

"And you are?" the young cop asked Chris.

"Chris Holland." Her shoulders straightened at the cop's tone of voice. "And you are?"

Damn, Marcus liked her spirit. This was a woman who could hold her own.

"Billy Joe Parson, ma'am. Did you witness what happened?"

"No. I was inside with Marcus."

"If you're finished with my Glock, I'd like it back." Even though Wayne had vouched for him, one of the cops held up Marcus's pistol and sniffed.

"It hasn't been fired," the cop said. "I'll run the serial number. If it comes back registered to you, I'll give it back."

Hell, the shooter could be halfway to Fort Worth by now. Marcus wanted to ask if they had someone canvassing the area. But he was smart enough to know it wouldn't get him anywhere to piss these guys off.

"We've told you everything we know. We need to get to the hospital."

"The gun's his." The cop handed the Glock to Marcus. "You can go."

"Thanks. If you need anything else, call that number on my card." He caught Chris by the elbow. "Let's get your suitcase. We'll have to take Diablo by my house. I can't take him inside, and I don't ever leave him in the car."

"I'm ready." She fell in step with him. Her soft, small hand gripped his arm. "You couldn't have prevented this."

"Yeah?" Damn, she'd read his mind. "And if I hadn't brought Tomas and Wayne in on the case, Wayne wouldn't be on his way to surgery."

Chris came to a fast stop. Her gaze searched his face. "You can't believe you're responsible for Wayne being shot," she exclaimed, her voice jumping an octave higher. "There's more than enough blame to share. If I hadn't involved Lost and Found, Wayne wouldn't have been in my home. If I'd done more to help Chelsea—"

Marcus couldn't let Chris continue. "You're carrying a lot of weight on your shoulders. I'm betting you loved your sister and that more than once you tried to help her kick her addiction. Am I right?" He guided her to the car and held the door for her.

"I tried." Chris buckled her seat belt while Marcus loaded Diablo.

"Go on," he said, as he slid behind the steering wheel.

"I tried the tough-love approach that her counselor suggested. It might have worked on some people, but it drove us further apart. That distance between us might have put her in the killer's path and brought us to today. Wayne has to make it. He has to."

"I hope so, too." Marcus feared the worst, but saw no reason to dash her hopes just yet. "At some point, you have to accept you can't change the past. The only thing you really control is what you do next." They drove in silence as his own words haunted him. How easy it was to give advice. Yet, he clung to his past, hoping that someday the guilt would fade.

The EMT's words kept circling through his mind. *He's coding.*

Marcus pressed the gas pedal harder.

CHAPTER 7

Marcus had been quiet since driving away from the crime scene. No doubt, his mind was on Wayne. Chris said a quick prayer that he'd pull through.

Diablo's front feet came over the back of the seat. One paw came to rest on her shoulder. Chris wondered if she should try to get Marcus to talk. Anything to keep him from blaming himself.

"Is it okay to let Diablo come up here?"

"Sure." Marcus, still shirtless, patted the area between them, and the dog crawled over. Marcus's muscles flexed as he stroked the dog's fur. His body was trim and perfectly defined.

"I think he's a ladies' man." She scratched behind Diablo's ear, wondering if she was doing the right thing to pull Marcus out of his shell. "He seemed to like Kay, too."

"Like you, she spoils him."

"How long have you had him?"

"A few months. I brought him home with me from Colombia. Took him from a young man who'd taught him to kill on command."

Chris burrowed her hand deeper into the dog's silky fur. He rested his head on her thigh. "No way."

"It's true. He understands fluent Spanish, which meant I had to start all over with him. He's smarter than most people I know. And better company."

Chris recoiled at that last statement. "Ouch. Sorry if I ask too many questions."

"What?" Marcus glanced at her, shaking his head. "You're being a little paranoid. I wasn't referring to you."

"First, I lose my family one right after the other, and now a detective who had been protecting me has been shot. I'm a lot paranoid."

Marcus took an exit off the freeway and wound through a well-kept neighborhood. He turned down the driveway of a ranch-style house and killed the engine. "Let me wash up, grab a shirt, and get Diablo situated."

He got out, grabbed her suitcase that he'd loaded for her, and started inside. Again, the rippling muscles in his back drew her attention. Guilt rolled into a knot in her stomach. No more inappropriate thoughts while Wayne was in the hospital.

"Are we staying here?"

"No," he answered quickly.

"You have my suitcase."

"We have to come back so I can throw some clothes together and pick up Diablo. I didn't want to leave your things in the car. Want me to put it in the trunk?"

"No. Leaving it here is fine."

Marcus hesitated on the front porch. Did he not want her to go inside? He unlocked the door, opened it, and stepped back for her to enter first.

"I'll feed Diablo and be right back."

Alone in his living room, Chris looked around. A beige carpet paled under a royal blue couch and chair. A white oak coffee table complemented the pastel blue of the walls. Pictures on the shelves of a bookcase drew her attention. In one, a beautiful brunette stared lovingly at Marcus. Short and petite, she made Chris feel like a giant. Both their expressions spoke volumes. They had been very much in love.

"My wife," Marcus said, standing directly behind Chris. "Lynne."

"She's lovely. So is your home."

"This room is exactly as she left it."

The pain radiating off him because his friend's life was in danger now doubled as he spoke of his wife. "Is Diablo all settled?"

"Yeah." Marcus wasted no time leading her out of the house and hurrying to the car.

He'd washed up and slipped on a tan button-down shirt. She'd thought him handsome that first day at Lost and Found, wearing his crisp white shirt and dark slacks. Then he'd floored her by showing up in Levi's, boots, and an Army green T-shirt. But tonight, her mouth had gone dry as she'd washed the blood from his hands while his bare chest, gigantic shoulders, and bulging biceps had been all she could see. He truly was a work of art, as perfect as if chiseled by one of the great masters.

She kept pace with him, understanding his sense of urgency. Silence between them had returned. Marcus broke speed records getting to the hospital. He maneuvered the parking lot and snagged a spot close to the emergency room entrance.

They hurried inside. Marcus's imposing presence drew the attention of the nurse behind the counter.

"A police detective was brought in earlier. Wayne Kerns?"

"He's in surgery. If you'll wait here for just a moment." She walked to the in-house phone and spoke softly with someone. She turned back to them. "His wife and partner are in the waiting room. You're expected."

"Thanks. I know the way." Marcus looked down at Chris. His dark eyes were hard to read. "His wife? This just keeps getting worse."

"You didn't know Wayne was married?" Chris put her hand on his back, hoping to make both of them feel better. Marcus seemed to have mastered the art of not showing his feelings, but tonight the rigid frown between his eyes said differently.

"No." The lines drew tighter. "The subject never came up."

"Marcus, there was probably no reason for you to ask."

"You're right. We never got that personal." He took her hand in his, turned it over, and stroked her knuckles with his thumb. "Let's go see if there's some way we can help."

His innocent act of holding her hand sent a wave of tenderness straight to her heart. His wife's death had caused him to withdraw, but somewhere under that cold persona Marcus used as a shield, a gentle giant hid from the world.

They caught the elevator, and he punched in a floor number. He really did know his way around this hospital. Was it because his wife had been a patient here? The wife he couldn't let go?

The doors swished open, and he led her to the right. A soft sob came from the room at the end of the hall. Chris's heart fell. Please, she prayed, don't let it be Wayne's wife who's crying. Don't let him have died.

****

Two uniformed officers stood outside the waiting room. A couple more were standing in the hall. One nodded as Marcus and Chris approached. "You Marcus Ricci?"

"Yes."

"You're cleared."

"Thanks." Marcus had never been in this situation, but he wasn't surprised that the police force would close ranks around one of their own. Like the military, they were a close-knit group, brothers for life.

He stopped in the doorway. His gut boiled and clenched. Tomas held a woman in his arms while she sobbed into his shoulder. The slight movement of his head told the story. Wayne was dead.

Marcus felt Chris's weight lean into him. "Please, no," she whispered. "This can't be happening."

He wrapped his arm around her and backed her away from the door. He tucked his thumb under her chin, lifted her head, and stroked her cheek with his thumb. The pain in her blue eyes ripped right through him. "I promise you, I'll find the bastard who did this."

"Don't you see? You can't be around me. Nate, Kay, none of you. You will be killed because you're trying to help me. Go pay your respects."

"I'm not going in without you. Nate and Kay will be here soon, as will half the police department. Let's do this together." He held out his hands, waiting while Chris struggled with her decision.

She stared at his open palms for a few seconds.

"You're right. I have to speak with Mrs. Kerns." Chris straightened her shoulders and wound her fingers through his.

Again, she'd amazed him. Truth was, he'd known only one woman with that kind of strength. No doubt, Lynne and Chris would've been friends if they'd ever met.

They sat next to Tomas and waited until Wayne's wife was ready for introductions. In spite of her red and tear-swollen eyes, Alice Kerns was a pretty woman. She wore tan slacks and a yellow blouse. Her hair was strawberry blond. Her genes mixed with Wayne's must have produced carrot-topped kids. She and Wayne had probably made a striking couple.

Words of sympathy meant as much to the people giving them as to the one who received them. Would Alice Kerns remember anything that was said tonight or even the next few days? Marcus doubted it. But it was important that he and Chris offer their condolences.

The Army had flown him home after Lynne had been killed. During a long, lonely flight, he'd rehashed their last phone conversation, which had ended on a sour note. Still angry because he'd re-enlisted, she'd accused him of caring more for his men than for her. Those words had been spoken in anger. A few comforting and loving expressions from him would've gone a long way. Oh, hell no, he'd clammed up and hadn't told her that she was the most important thing in the world to him.

The next day it had been too late to tell her anything. A drunk had T-boned her car, hitting the driver's side door so hard the steering wheel had bent almost in half.

Lynne's funeral had been a blur. He remembered little of what happened that day. He'd crawled so deep into his misery, he'd refused the comfort that his friends and her family had tried to share.

"Marcus?" Chris's voice pulled him back to the present. She tugged her hand out of his grip and wiggled her fingers.

"Sorry. Did I squeeze too hard?"

"No worries." She leaned closer to him. "Wayne's department captain and the rest of his family will be here soon. Are you ready to go?" Her whispered words brushed across his cheek.

"Yeah. Let's give Mrs. Kerns some privacy." Had he fooled her? Or could she tell his mind had wandered?

After they excused themselves, Tomas walked them to the elevator. Marcus had no idea how long Wayne and Tomas had been partners. Having spent some time with them, Marcus had witnessed a camaraderie that said they were also friends.

"I tried to stop the bleeding—"

"Don't do that," Tomas insisted. "The doctor said nothing could have saved him. The bullet nicked an artery. Wayne was bleeding inside. He died on the operating table."

"You'll let us know if there's anything we can do?" Chris stepped into the elevator and held the door open.

"Will do." Tomas turned to Marcus. "I'll have a courier drop off at your office everything I'd pulled on Chelsea Holland. If this is your guy, he's royally fucked up. He killed one of our own. Every cop in three counties will be looking for him. You understand I won't be available for off-duty work. All my time will be devoted to catching the bastard who shot Wayne."

"Of course," Marcus assured him. "If we learn anything that might help you, I'll call."

He watched Tomas walk away as the doors closed and the elevator started its descent. Marcus replayed Chris's last statement in his mind. She'd said if "we" can help, let "us" know. She'd referred to them as a team or couple. A cold spot buried deep inside his chest warmed.

After he drove away from the hospital, she reached across the seat and squeezed his shoulder. Then she leaned her head back and stared out the window for most of the drive.

Marcus drove down the off-ramp, made a quick turn into a busy shopping center parking area. He took the exit at the far end of the lot and took a tour through a high-end neighborhood. Then he got back on the freeway. Traffic was heavy in this area of Plano, and he intended to ensure no one was tailing them.

Finally, she turned in her seat toward him. "Where are you going?"

"You need some rest. Tomorrow, we'll go to the office and start piecing your sister's life together."

"Marcus—"

"Nothing you say will make me walk away from you. I'm in. Period."

"I know that. I've known that from the beginning. You're a man of honor, and you'll protect me at all costs. That wasn't what I was going to say."

Crap. He'd jumped to conclusions. "Sorry. I won't interrupt again. Go ahead."

"Where are we going?"

"My house."

"Do you know where we're spending the night?"

"Of course. I'll grab a change of clothes, get your bag and my dog, and we'll go straight to the safe house."

"Good. Then we'll do a quick in and out. I don't think you're ready to have another woman in your house." She pulled her hand back. "Not even a business associate."

Marcus was speechless. He hadn't allowed anyone inside until Chris had gone in tonight. The living room was all he had left of Lynne. At first, he'd been upset to find Chris looking at his private memories, but then he'd realized it hadn't bothered him at all.

He'd spoken about Lynne with both Ty and Ana. Assured them that he'd moved on. It had been a lie at the time, told to encourage Ty to let go of the past. Marcus had tried to go down that path with a couple of women at different times. The relationships had failed as soon as they wanted more from him.

Chris's touch had been soft and warm. She intrigued him, kept him on his toes, and man, did she smell good. But she seemed determined to keep everyone at bay. In the long run, that attitude would work out better for them both.

Once he was comfortable no one had followed them, he took the next exit, turned around, and drove to his neighborhood. A few blocks away from home the night sky was blazing. Red and orange flames shot into the air.

He pressed the gas pedal to the floor. His brain screamed as he turned the corner onto his block. Where was Diablo? Was he smart enough to go to the backyard? Fire trucks and patrol cars dotted the street. His home was burning. He'd lost everything once before. He would not lose his dog. If somebody had set this fire intentionally, he'd tear the motherfucker apart with his bare hands.

"Chris, you'll have to come with me. I can't leave you alone."

"Go. I'll be right behind you."

As soon as the car came to a stop, they both were out and running toward the fire trucks.

"That's my house," he said to the firefighter who tried to stop him. "Chris, stay with this guy. Don't move."

A dog barked insanely, as if he were about to rip someone's throat out. To Marcus it was the sweetest sound in the world. It meant Diablo was alive. Marcus ran toward the back of the house.

"My dog!" he yelled. Without thinking, he stepped in front of the cop who'd taken aim at Diablo. "Don't shoot him. He's scared."

In a wild frenzy, the dog charged and snapped his powerful teeth every time the two firefighters tried to open the gate.

"Down, Diablo," Marcus commanded loudly. The dog went down but stood again, growling.

"We have to get in there," one of the firefighters said. "The wind is blowing the fire toward the houses behind yours."

"I'll get him under control." Marcus opened the gate, walked inside, and then fell to his knees. He gave the hand signal to come and then dropped both hands to his sides.

"Come, Diablo. It's okay." He used the most soothing tone he could in spite of the fear racing through him. "Come."

The frightened animal crawled on his belly into Marcus's arms. Seeing no burns, Marcus picked him up and held Diablo's trembling body against his chest. A knot the size of a football had wedged in the back of Marcus's throat. "It's okay, boy. I've got you."

"Take that dog, get to safety." The cop holstered his gun.

"We're going." He carried his dog out of the yard, and the same cop escorted him out.

Heat from the blaze streaked across his face as he crossed to the car. The dog squirmed and tried to bury his head under Marcus's arm. He could feel Diablo's heart racing.

Now if Chris was all right.

She stood next to the fireman, exactly where he'd left her. Tears streamed down her face. She opened her arms wide and came toward him. He and his dog walked straight into her embrace.

CHAPTER 8

"I've never been so scared." Without thinking, Chris cupped Marcus's cheek. The stubble felt good against her hand. The pain behind his eyes ripped at her heart.

"We're okay." Marcus's voice was understandably shaky. His house had burned, and he'd almost lost his dog. No doubt, the things he'd kept to remind him of his wife were lost to him. Gone forever.

"Poor thing, he's had a rough time today."

"Let's wait in the car. This dog needs some quiet time." Marcus shifted the animal in his arms.

His love for Diablo touched her heart. Maybe she even felt a pang of jealousy. Other than her family, she'd never had anyone who loved her that much. Oh, there had been a few near misses, but that was long ago. She hadn't dated since Chelsea's murder.

"Good idea." She tapped the firefighter on the shoulder and told him where he could find them.

A question lay on the tip of her tongue as she joined Marcus in the car. One she didn't want to ask. If her guess was right, he'd never forgive her. No way could he recover the burned memories of his wife.

He leaned over the dog resting on the seat between them and swiped her cheeks with his thumbs. "Were those tears for me or Diablo?"

Chris traced where he'd touched. "I wasn't crying."

"You were." His right eyebrow lifted.

"If that's true, it was for the dog." She couldn't allow herself to admit how terrified she'd been when Marcus had disappeared behind the burning house. Nor could she tell how relieved she'd been to see him lugging the dog in his arms and walking straight toward her.

"I figured." One corner of his mouth lifted. "He can tell you like him. That's why he warmed up to you so quickly."

Marcus had lost so much tonight, yet he hadn't uttered one complaint. No rage, no self-pity, nothing. Except for his love for Diablo, Marcus internalized his emotions, leaving her to wonder what to say or how to console him. In the few moments he'd allowed her to hold him, she'd felt the tension running through his body.

Together, they watched the flames wipe out his past until the firefighters won the battle. Water ran in wide rivers across his yard and out on the street. Neighbors stood on the curb, no doubt glad the fire hadn't spread. When only a few hot spots remained, the crowd dispersed, cops left, and one fire truck remained.

"I'm so sorry this happened." She needed to hang on to something, so she buried her fingers in the dog's fur. If her hunch was right, she'd brought this on Marcus. It was a message for them both.

Without speaking, he nodded and covered her hand with his. Together, they scratched Diablo. Marcus's touch was comforting and reassuring, something she should have been doing for him. But how? She was probably responsible for the fire.

A question burned at her heart. "I have a question."

"Where to now?"

"No. Do you think the killer started the fire?"

"Nothing would surprise me. We won't know for sure until the fire department's investigation is complete."

A news van arrived and parked behind the remaining fire truck. The cameraman hurried to catch the last of the glowing embers while the reporter rushed to one of the firefighters. Chris cringed in disgust when he pointed toward Marcus's car.

The day had been long, hard, and full of tragedy. Neither she nor Marcus needed to be hounded by the media. "Can't we just leave?"

"Probably shouldn't since the fire marshal hasn't spoken with me. I'll take care of the reporter."

"Are you sure you want to speak with him? Let me get rid of them."

"You shouldn't be out in the open." The corners of his mouth lifted slightly, but the pain behind his eyes belied the smile. "But thanks, I'm not used to someone trying to take care of me. Careful, you'll spoil me." Marcus ran his hand over the dog. "He's calmed down. You'll be safe if I leave him with you."

"No doubt." She scratched the dog's head. "We'll be just fine, won't we, boy?"

"Diablo, stay," Marcus said. "If he gets restless, honk the horn. You can try this hand signal." He demonstrated. "I'll try not to be gone long."

She watched him walk away. Strong, brave, and alone. Maybe he needed somebody to take care of him for a little while. No, she shook off that thought. Getting close to Marcus could get him killed.

Marcus said something to the reporter. The man glared her direction, but apparently decided not to argue. Marcus spoke with a cop and then he talked to a man she guessed to be the fire marshal. Marcus turned to the side, took a phone call, and then returned to finish giving his statement.

Diablo growled, and a bright light flashed at the same time. Teeth bared, he stood, placed his front paws on the dashboard, and then leaned toward the windshield. The photographer snapped two more pictures as he backed away. Chris's temper boiled over.

"Stay," she said. She opened the car door and chased the jerk. She had no idea if she had the right to forbid him, but the last thing she needed was publicity. The tension of the day built with each step. By the time she reached him, she was ready to explode. "How dare you sneak up on the car and snap away without thinking? You do not have my permission to use my picture. Do it and you'll hear from my attorney."

"You understood the lady's message. Right?" Marcus's hand rested on her shoulder. He gave her a gentle squeeze. Probably his way of trying to calm her down.

It didn't work.

"Your flash startled an already frightened dog. He'd have taken your arm off if he could've."

"Let's get out of here." Marcus guided her toward the car.

Diablo sat, watching as they approached. "Poor baby, he's been through a lot today," Chris said.

"That's the understatement of the day. Thank you for defending him." Marcus's voice was husky and thick.

"More like he defended me. You should have seen him."

"It's a good thing he didn't get out of the yard. As terrified as he was, there's no telling what would've happened. The cop would've been forced to shoot."

"What? No way."

"Diablo wasn't giving the guy much choice. He was one freaked-out dog. Scared and ready to attack anything that moved."

Chris stopped. Her hand hovered over the door handle. "I wonder what he's thinking," she said as she got in and buckled up.

Marcus didn't hook his seat belt when he slid behind the wheel. Instead, he opened his arms. The big dog crawled onto his lap and rested his head on Marcus's chest. "That I need to do a better job of taking care of him."

"I doubt that. It's obvious he loves you. Had he been treated badly when you got him?"

"I don't think he'd been mistreated, but he hadn't been allowed to be a dog. I wasn't joking when I said he was fluent in Spanish and that he'd been a killer. I've worked hard to help him forget that part of his training."

A chill raced across her arms. Hard to imagine the gentle animal in Marcus's lap killing anyone. "I'm glad you saved him. Working at the shelter taught me just how much a dog can change. I don't believe there are bad dogs, only bad owners."

"Amen. Dogs behave the way they're taught." Marcus had to move Diablo off his lap in order to drive. It was obvious the dog preferred to stay in his owner's arms. "We need to move. Who knows who's watching us?"

"Where are we going?"

"We're heading to the safe house."

"Can we pick up something for Diablo to eat?"

"All three of us could use some food. You don't have to be hungry for your body to need nourishment."

"Then how about drive-through?"

"He loves a good hamburger. No onions." Marcus smiled, and for the first time all day, his eyes sparkled.

Chris's heart did a backflip. The quickest way to help Marcus forget the horrors of the day was to talk about his dog. He needed that downtime. "That sounds as good as a steak right about now."

"I'm not a big believer in feeding him people food, although Kay sneaks him stuff all the time. He's been through a lot today, and I think he's earned a double-meat double cheeseburger."

****

DaVinci paced the length of his living room, stopping to look out his window at the star-filled night sky. He slapped a button and turned his back as the vertical blinds closed off the world behind him. Frustration and anger boiled through him like hot lava.

He'd put a bullet in one of Christine's new friends, but hadn't been able to stick around to enjoy her reaction. No doubt, she'd suffered, but he'd had to scurry off like a thief in the night.

He'd rushed home to his laptop, counting on a front-row seat to her suffering. What a disappointment that had turned out to be. The camera had recorded her protector trying to keep the new friend alive. The ambulance and cop cars had obliterated part of his view. And when the EMTs loaded the stretcher, it was obvious the man wasn't dead. Apparently, DaVinci hadn't shot the bastard in the head.

But the worst part? Christine had stayed indoors most of the time, depriving him of seeing her reactions.

It was her fault he'd torched the house. He'd paid dearly to have the big guy followed and a tracking device placed under his car's fender. When he'd discovered where they'd gone, he'd had no recourse but to take action.

Again, she'd messed up his plans.

By the time he'd arrived, she and her new friend were gone. No matter, he'd tossed his homemade Molotov cocktail through the front window and driven away.

Then he'd received a text from Michelangelo. A challenge. It was indeed DaVinci's turn to create, but who had time? This meant he couldn't keep track of Christine for hours.

He pushed off the couch, called his lady in Austin, and arranged a rendezvous. Michelangelo wanted a masterpiece? Well, he'd get one.

****

Marcus pulled out of the Burger Heaven drive-through and onto the freeway. Neither he nor Chris were hungry, but following his own advice, he'd ordered more than enough.

Traffic was light, but the sun had gone down, which made it difficult to keep an eye on a specific vehicle. As soon as he reached Interstate 30, he took the ramp that dumped them into downtown Fort Worth. Most of the streets were one way, so weaving in and out was easy. He doubled back, cut over to Interstate 35 and headed to the country. The drive was a hell of a lot farther this way, but in this instance, safety outweighed distance.

Chris laughed at something the dog had done. Marcus took a quick glance her direction. God, add a little humor to her expression, and she became stunning. Even after the day they'd had, she could enjoy something funny.

"Dog," she exclaimed. "You are a thief."

He really couldn't blame Diablo for overreacting. The car smelled like greasy food heaven. The dog's nose had started twitching the minute he'd handed Chris the sack of food. Poor mutt started wagging his long tail and whining.

"I warned you not to give in."

"How could I not?" Diablo hung over the seat and slobbered on her arm. "You should have seen him take the burger out of my hand. In two chomps, it was gone."

"I always buy him a couple. One to inhale and the other to enjoy. You might as well give it to him." Marcus surrendered to the moment and laughed at her and his dog.

"You should do that more often." Her tone had softened. This time when he glanced at her, his heart clenched.

"Not much has been funny for a long time." Oddly enough, he didn't feel stupid admitting that to her.

"We'll have to work on that. Won't we, Diablo?" She took a napkin from the sack and wiped her arm before unwrapping the second burger. This time she held it out, open-handed, and let the dog have the whole thing.

"Diablo, down." Marcus spoke in a solemn tone to pull the animal's attention to him. "Stay."

"Wow. I'm impressed."

"With me or the dog?"

"I'd have to say both." Her tone was like sunshine on a chilly day.

Marcus had seldom been stunned into silence, but he didn't know how to respond. He'd asked a leading question, and she answered with honesty. At least, he thought she was sincere.

Even though she'd been his client for only two days, hearing her laugh eased the stress knotting the tendons in his neck. They both could use a little levity.

Time to change the subject. His job was to keep her alive. She'd gone to Lost and Found for help.

"We're almost to the safe house. I asked Kay to drop off a few items of clothing and toiletries for us."

"Thank you. A nice hot shower sounds good."

Nate had recently purchased a small farmhouse, isolated and easy to defend. Their previous hideaway hadn't fared too well. A Colombian drug lord had ordered

Ty's and Ana's deaths. One of his henchmen had strafed the building, shattering windows and leaving multiple holes in the walls. Reconstruction was taking too long, so Nate had bought this place.

Marcus drove down the long driveway and parked behind the house. "Wait here for a second," he said, stopping Chris. He clipped the leash on Diablo, and then he and the dog walked around to the passenger side of the car. He extended his hand, and she got out, grasping him tightly. "Stay close behind me."

"You'll think I'm a shadow." She slipped her purse over her shoulder and stuck her hand inside.

"I think—"

"Don't start. I know how to use a gun, and believe me, I will."

"As I was going to say, I think you'll be more effective if you take your pistol out of your purse and hold it in your hand. That way, if you have to fire your weapon, you'll be more accurate."

"Oh." She sounded a bit sheepish but did as he suggested.

He walked directly to the back door. The two-bedroom brick house wasn't actually in the country, more like the outer edge of a small suburb. Set back from the street and shielded by trees, the area was pitch black. The quicker he got Chris inside, the better he'd feel about the situation.

He handed Chris the key while he kept an eye on their surroundings and his Glock in his hand. "Unlock it and step back. Let me go in first."

"No problem."

Marcus flipped on the overhead lights, flooding the bright yellow kitchen, eliminating the dark shadows. Chris stepped up beside him. The three of them cleared the living room and two bedrooms.

"Kay's already been here." He pointed at the sacks from the local department store sitting in the middle of the bed.

"She bought me clothes?" Chris slid the pistol into the waistband of her jeans and went straight to her new things. "There's a note. She guessed my size perfectly. And she left your things in the room across the hall."

Chris emptied the sack while he checked the window locks. There was nothing fancy about the place. The room held a dresser with a mirror, a nightstand with a lamp and clock and a queen-size bed. The huge white comforter caused images of her cuddled under the fluffy cloud to flip through his mind. The soft blue walls reminded him of her eye color.

He crossed the hall and walked into the other bedroom. Sure enough, two bags waited for him. No doubt, he'd find clean clothes. "I'll let you look through your goodies while I take Diablo outside."

"No, I'll stay close to you." She answered a little too quickly. "If you're going out back, I'll go to the kitchen and put what's left of our supper on plates."

He got it. She was nervous. And maybe more than a little worried about hiding out with a complete stranger. She'd been his client for two days, and he'd been hired to protect her. Other than that, she knew little about him. Best if things stayed that way.

"Your call."

CHAPTER 9

Chris's chest tightened. She spun toward the door and grabbed her gun from the counter. She sighed with relief. Marcus and Diablo were back.

"You startled me." She carefully placed her pistol on the table next to her plate.

"I'm sorry. Next time, I'll call out so you'll know it's me."

"I'm just a little jumpy. Our burgers and fries are cold, but I'm guessing they'll do for sustenance."

"I'd think you were in shock if you weren't."

Chris sat at the table and swirled a fry in catsup. Diablo curled around her feet and stared up at her. "He's even prettier when he begs."

Marcus's eyes sparkled over the rim of his cola. "He's a male. Guys aren't pretty. Besides, he knows he can get to you with that hang-dog look of his."

She smuggled a fry to the dog. "Of course men are pretty. Some I'd even call beautiful."

He grunted. "Well, I can't imagine what a beautiful guy would look like."

Chris decided against clueing him in. Instead, she took a bite of hamburger and chewed. Anything to keep her mouth busy or she was going to tell him the truth. He could be the poster boy for the beautiful guy category. The rugged symmetry of his face, the dark sultry eyes, and sun-kissed dark brown hair placed him right at the top.

They both took sips of their sodas. The ice had melted, watering down the cola. "That's pretty bad," Chris said.

"I've had worse."

"Probably quite often if you were in the military. Were you in Iraq?"

"And Afghanistan." He glanced at her then went back to eating.

Chris almost shivered. His brown eyes had turned cold and forbidding. She wouldn't push. Maybe memories kept him from talking about the war easily. "I didn't mean to pry."

"No worries." He finished off his burger and neatly folded the wrapper.

A day's worth of tension was taking its toll on her neck and back muscles. Marcus, as her dad would've said, had to be wound just as tight. A few hours' sleep would benefit them both. "I think I'll take a shower and call it a night."

He nodded, stood up, and piled the scraps onto his plate. "Here you go, boy."

She closed her bedroom door and emptied the bags onto the bed. Kay had left a change of clothes, underwear, and a handful of welcome toiletries. Washing her hair was going to be a real treat. She held the oversize T-shirt up against her, deciding it and the leggings would be perfect.

"Chris," Marcus said through the closed door. "If you're uncomfortable being alone, Diablo can stay in your room with you."

She swung back the door just as Marcus entered the room across from her. "So you don't think we're safe?"

"I think we're just fine. I don't believe we were followed." His gaze drifted lower, stopping on her chest. Slowly, his eyes strolled up to meet hers. "Nice Dallas Cowboys T-shirt. Blue is your color."

"Thank you." Sheesh, was that disappointment rushing through her? Chris thought he'd been checking out her breasts. Her knees had turned to marshmallows. She'd gripped the door facing to keep from melting into a puddle. "I'll be fine without Diablo sleeping in here. He needs to be close to you."

"Okay. You go head and take your shower. I'll be here if you need something." Then he spun on his heel and retreated.

Chris grabbed her underwear and toiletries and hurried down the hall to the shared facilities. She stripped quickly then jumped under the water while the flow was still too cool, sending her into a full-body shiver. A second later, the warm liquid sluicing over her body felt like heaven. The nerves in her back and neck uncoiled a fraction.

She dressed in her new sleep clothes. After digging through the small cabinet under the sink, she gave up on finding a hairdryer. She combed her hair, leaving it damp and loose. By morning, it would be in little-girl ringlets. Not a good look for her, but so be it. She put the bathroom back in order. No doubt, Marcus was waiting for his turn.

A sliver of light shone from under his bedroom door. Chris stood in the hall, her hand poised to knock. There really was no need to see him, so she decided to let him know she had finished. "Bathroom's open. See you in the morning."

"Thanks."

She closed her door and sat on the side of the bed. The image of Wayne's wife and her gut-wrenching sobs kept running through Chris's mind. Her heart ached for the woman's loss. She'd offered condolences but felt her words had been inadequate. Before she slipped between the cool white sheets and turned off the light, she prayed for Wayne's family.

The sound of running water sent her thoughts back to Marcus. His inner strength amazed her. He'd lost a friend and his wife's mementos today. How would he handle all that now that he was alone with his thoughts? More than once, Chris had stood in the shower, allowing the grief of losing one of her parents or Chelsea to mingle and wash down the drain.

He wouldn't. Not Marcus. If she'd learned anything about him in the past couple of days, she knew he'd hold his pain inside.

****

Chris woke with a start. Her unfamiliar surroundings sent her heart pounding against her ribs. It took a moment to orient herself. The clock on the nightstand glowed, silently showing her it was three in the morning. She'd slept hard for five hours.

The quiet unsettled her. Her mouth was dry. She wished she'd gone after a glass of water before going to bed. Maybe the thirst would pass if she ignored it. It didn't. The more she thought about not thinking about water, the more her tongue felt like a hayfield in the middle of a hot Texas summer.

Surrendering to her thirst, she got out of bed, tiptoed to the door, and opened it. Marcus's door was open, and his room dark, but she wasn't going to look to see if he was asleep. She'd get her glass of water and be back in bed within minutes.

A faint light from the other end of the hallway provided her with the courage to run barefoot toward the kitchen. She'd taken a couple of steps when Diablo rounded the corner and trotted down the hall to her. Chris went down on one knee and shushed the dog. "You have to be quiet. We don't want to wake Marcus."

She followed Diablo toward the living room. She stopped and stared, unable to go forward or back. Sitting on the couch, barefoot and shirtless, Marcus had leaned his head back and closed his eyes. Holy hell, the top button of his jeans was undone. He was magnificent. Even relaxed, his body looked as if one of the mythical gods had come to life. Now her mouth was really dry.

Obviously, the smart thing to do was let him rest. Chris took a step back.

"Never retreat." He opened his eyes, stunning her with his rigid stare. He didn't look to have been asleep. In fact, she felt his sadness fill the space between them. "If you start something, be prepared to finish it."

"Okay." Unsure of the message he was sending, she walked into the room. "I wanted a drink of water."

He waved a hand toward the kitchen. "Help yourself."

Chris poured two glasses and carried one to Marcus.

"Thanks."

She couldn't make her feet move to leave him alone when he looked so sad. To use his words, retreating wasn't an option. She sat on the other end of the couch, expecting him to say something. When he didn't, she took charge. "Want to talk about it?"

"No." He sipped the water while she waited for him to continue.

"Okay. I'll talk."

"I can hardly wait." His eyes brightened a little. Was he teasing?

"Great." She pressed forward. "I'm very sorry about the fire. You lost everything you had left of Lynne. If I hadn't walked into Lost and Found, this probably wouldn't have happened."

"I appreciate that, but if you're trying to take the blame, don't. We don't know what caused the fire. It could have been faulty wiring."

"You don't believe that, do you?" She had no doubts. All of this was because of her.

"No."

"Was your house insured?"

"Sure."

"But there's no insurance that covers memories. You lost everything."

Diablo dropped down next to Marcus and used his feet for a pillow. Marcus leaned down and stroked his fur.

Embarrassed beyond measure for intruding, Chris tried to think of a graceful way to vanish. Coming up with nothing, she scooted to the edge of the couch.

"The last time we talked, my wife was upset that I'd re-enlisted," he said, surprising Chris that he'd made such a personal statement.

An odd circle of gloom wrapped around Chris's chest. Would he ever get over the woman whose ghost he clung to? And why did a pang of jealousy rush over her? Where did the urge to comfort him come from? More than she needed to breathe, she wanted to make him forget the past. The room closed in. The air grew thin. "You'll always have her in your heart."

He nodded, looking at her as if surprised he'd shared that about his wife. "You'd better get some rest."

Had she just been dismissed? Had he embarrassed himself by sharing? "If I oversleep, just bang on my door." Chris took her glass of water with her to her bedroom.

****

Crap, he needed his head examined. Blurting out that comment about Lynne was unacceptable. Frankly, it shocked him that he'd opened up to Chris about something so personal. That had to stop.

He listened until the door to her bedroom closed. Chris was better at gathering information from people than she knew. What was it about her that made him share knowledge that even his friends hadn't heard?

His mind wandered to the burned-out hull that had once been his home. He had nothing left of Lynne except her birth certificate, their marriage license, and her death certificate. Those were in a safe-deposit box, along with his personal documents. His biggest fear had always been forgetting what she looked like, so he'd kept the snapshots on his cell phone and left the printed pictures on display.

He'd waited awhile, watching the hall, half-expecting Chris to wander back into the room. He retrieved his tablet from under the couch, hoping she'd fallen asleep.

Kay had gathered a little more information on Chelsea Holland's death. She'd texted him that she'd emailed it to him. He'd been reading those files when Chris had walked down the hall, so he'd stashed the computer. He wanted to digest the facts before sharing any information with her.

He felt as if everyone else was doing the work. Keeping Chris safe was a priority, but he wanted a hand in bringing the killer to justice. Tomorrow, they'd go to the office. Marcus had to know if Dalton had uncovered something missed by local police.

The reports on Chelsea's murder were long and formal. With intel coming from a number of sources, he'd have a clear picture of her case. Her history of drug use had been well documented. She'd frequented a handful of bars where known pushers hung out, selling their wares and women. If she'd been a prostitute, she must have freelanced. Marcus couldn't find any mention of her having a pimp. Chelsea wouldn't have lived long if she'd tried to work without one.

The autopsy report was gruesome. Chris had seen this in person, which had to have been a hundred times worse than a picture. He could understand that she'd have nightmares. A lot of them.

Marcus had witnessed plenty of nasty shit while in the Army. Nothing as sadistic as what had been done to Chelsea.

He'd totally understood Nate's reaction at the office. He'd been upset Kay had seen the pictures. Marcus hadn't had the time to study them, so tonight, he searched for something others who'd seen them might have missed. The son of a bitch had carved her up little by little. Her blank stare spoke volumes. Why had he posed her? Had the sick fuck taken a souvenir? Something he could look at to relive his deed?

Marcus hated unanswered questions.

He opened the next file and found a picture he hadn't seen before. Chelsea's body had been washed off, cut up, and put back together. Her blond hair had been pulled back, the blood and makeup were gone. A sheet discreetly covered the incision across her chest. There was no doubt whose sister was lying on the medical examiner's table.

Walking in on her sister's death scene must have shaken Chris beyond words. He hoped the cops hadn't kept her at the scene while they questioned her. His heart hurt as if somebody had reached inside his chest and squeezed.

He logged off. Once he was on this bastard's trail, sleep would have to wait. Tonight, he'd try to get a couple hours of shut-eye. That was, if he could get that picture of Chelsea Holland out of his head.

****

DaVinci hated having to hurry. Hated the pressure he felt from his mentor to create. But after he'd gotten started, his creative juices had flowed like a river. She hadn't believed that he would actually cut off her fingers. So he had. Nobody had heard her screams. Not this far out of the city where she was house-sitting for the weekend.

He stuffed a finger in six of her orifices. The four extras, he'd put in her lap.

A little surprise for the cops. No way could he insert one into her anal cavity. Would not go there.

Too many horrific memories of abuse were tied to that part of his anatomy. He'd survived two foster homes where he'd been repeatedly violated. One attacker had been an adult male whose wife thought taking in kids with no parents was a good way to supplement their income. DaVinci had complained to his foster mom. Had she taken action against her husband? Hell, no. She'd had children services come get DaVinci, describing him as an unruly child.

The second home hadn't been any better. The woman who was supposed to protect her charges had had a teenage son. He'd sneak into DaVinci's room late at night and force himself on him. The bastard would never sodomize another foster kid who'd had the misfortune of being sent to that home. In fact, killing the son of a bitch and leaving his body behind the garage was one of the few good memories DaVinci had of his childhood.

He pushed the past from his mind and studied the colossal mess he'd just made. Adrenaline had pumped through his body, the resulting frenzy of slashing wildly instead of stabbing had left blood splattered and streaked across the walls and hardwood floor.

Ignoring the acrid smell of death and taking caution not to step in blood, he studied his creation, adjusted his camera, and took pictures, stopping only when he'd taken what had to be the winning picture.

DaVinci laid a plastic sheet on the floor, stripped naked, and cleaned himself, using wipes he'd brought from home. He changed into his spare set of clothes, wiped down everything he'd touched, focusing on not leaving any DNA behind. When his belongings had been rolled into a ball, he carried them and his bag of tools to the trunk of his car.

He drove away without so much as a glance back and took the long way around to the highway, suffering through the blackness of the night and the winding roads. He drove the speed limit, all the while fighting the desire to push the Mercedes to maximum speed and hurry home.

Christine kept invading his thoughts, making it hard to concentrate. Michelangelo would love this new creation, but the kill had left DaVinci cold inside. Even though she had been blond-haired and blue-eyed like Christine, her suffering hadn't satiated his need.

This kill had convinced him. The time to deal with Christine had come. He'd break her spirit, show her how it felt to be truly alone in this world, and then she'd die.

CHAPTER 10

Marcus took Diablo out for his morning exercise. Without a rubber ball to throw, he broke off a small tree limb and tossed it to the back of the yard. The dog didn't care what he chased. He enjoyed the chance to stretch his legs. Marcus knew this because Diablo hadn't hesitated. He returned, dropped the stick, and watched his master. All the while, his tongue was hanging out and his tail was wagging.

"Good boy." He dropped to one knee and rubbed the big dog's ears, which set Diablo's tail swinging at top speed. "We better wake up Chris."

"She's already up." The voice coming from behind him was warm and pleasant.

He turned to face her. The explosion of blond curls was enough to make a man swallow his tongue. Her hair wasn't pulled off her face today. It was loose, wild, and sexy as hell. The jeans and red blouse she wore fit as if they'd been tailor-made for her.

"Morning. I see you found the coffee," Marcus said, trying not to stare at her. He joined her on the steps, accepting the cup she offered. "Thanks."

"You're welcome." Her eyes sparkled with mischief. "Go ahead and ask."

"Ask what?" He'd never been good at games.

She elbowed him in the ribs. "My hair. It's naturally curly. I not only didn't have a dryer and flatiron, I couldn't find a comb."

"I like it." Marcus found it easier to relax with her. In fact, he'd had more casual conversation with her than he'd had with anyone in a long time. But he couldn't shake the horror of Wayne's death. His focus had to stay on the case. "Did you sleep okay after your drink of water?"

"I didn't. I kept thinking about Wayne's wife. Did you rest at all?"

"I worked for a while after you went to bed, but I caught a couple of hours."

"What was on the tablet you didn't want me to see?" She lifted one eyebrow. "You didn't shove it far enough under the couch."

"I wasn't sure until I'd had a chance to look. Kay sent additional information on your sister. It was pretty much the same information you'd gathered. The cops did interview the neighbors, but they didn't produce any leads."

"What now?"

"As soon as you're ready, we'll go to the office. Kay will send flowers for Wayne's funeral, but I want to send something personally." Diablo pushed his nose against Marcus's hand.

"He worships you." Chris leaned down and patted the dog's back. "Just look at the way he stares, watching your every move."

"He's used to being fed after his morning run. We should go before he decides to drink your coffee."

"Oh no," she said with a laugh, holding her mug high. "I draw the line at sharing my coffee. Let me rinse out the pot, get my stuff, and I'm ready."

Closing up the house took only minutes. Marcus grabbed his tablet, his belongings, and was waiting on the steps when Chris opened the back door, carrying her bag of clothes.

"Funny, the things you don't remember until something triggers a bit of history."

"What's that?"

"Chelsea and I must have lived in a couple different foster homes. When they moved us to a different place, they put our clothes in a bag. Not one of these, but a trash bag."

Marcus loaded Diablo in the back seat and joined Chris in the car. "That had to be rough on a kid. How long were you in foster care before you were adopted?"

Chris's eyebrows dipped. "No one's ever asked me that. I have no idea. It's weird, but I don't remember much before we moved in with the Hollands. The moving and plastic bags just popped into my head. Maybe more will come."

"Did the Hollands have other children?"

"No. They'd tried in vitro fertilization and failed. Dad always said God sent me and Chelsea to them."

Marcus drove the car around to the front of the house. He stopped at the edge of the driveway and scanned the area before driving to the freeway. They'd had a quiet night, meaning the safe house was a viable option for the future. Sequestering Chris might be the only way to keep her safe.

She poked him in the ribs. "How do you do that?"

"Do what? I don't know what you're talking about." He could guess what she meant, because he'd gotten her talking about herself.

"I open up and spill my guts. Yet, I know nothing about you."

"The more I learn about you and your past, the better I can protect you. I'm not only going to keep you safe, I'm catching the bastard who killed your sister and Wayne. And I'll be there when the state puts the needle in his arm."

"Touché. You win this one."

Marcus stopped at the first fast-food joint he spotted. Diablo was hanging over the seat with his tongue hanging out when they drove away.

"Back." He commanded the dog as he eased the car into morning traffic. Chris fed Diablo and then handed Marcus his coffee. The slurping from behind his shoulder gave him a chuckle. "My car will never smell the same again."

"He doesn't usually eat in here?"

"No." A huge paw landed next to Chris. "Wonder if it's like this when you have kids."

"Don't know. I'm not sure I want to know, either," she said flatly.

"Really? I thought all women wanted children."

"What if I couldn't bear the pressure? Or died? I have no family left to step up and take over if they were orphaned."

Marcus clamped his teeth together and kept his eyes on the highway. He could understand her fear, but she'd have a husband someday. He'd be her family.

Marcus parked in front of the Lost and Found office, put the leash on Diablo and escorted Chris inside.

"There you are," Kay said, rising to greet them. She wrapped her arms around his waist and hugged him. "I'm sorry about your house. Did you drive by there this morning and see what it looks like now that the sun's up?"

"No. The fire marshal will release the property when he's through with the investigation. There's a guy I know who will take over salvaging what's left."

"Call him now," she insisted. "Chris and I will talk."

She turned to Chris. "How'd the clothes work out?"

"Perfect fit." Chris turned in a circle. "Thank you."

Marcus unhooked Diablo's leash and left the two women talking clothes. He walked back to his desk, where a thick folder had been placed on the corner. A sticky note from Dalton told him to check email. Marcus sat, cursing himself for not having checked earlier. He retrieved his tablet and located the overview from Dalton.

Before he dug into the reports, he made a call to the fire marshal's office. The inspectors were at the house and had found evidence of arson. Next, he checked in with a friend who'd been in the construction business for years. Turning the job over to someone with his experience took that worry off Marcus's mind.

He thought about telling Chris, then decided against making her feel any worse. Instead, he turned his attention to the information sent by Dalton. No murders had been reported that followed the same MO, so he'd requested all killings containing any torture. Those were the files on Marcus's desk. Kay had made copies.

After looking through the first few cases, he went to the break room and dug around until he located the map of the states that had been left behind by a previous tenant. With that tucked under his arm, he grabbed the thick folder, a box of pushpins, and moved to the small room they used for meetings.

"Marcus?" Chris said, joining him as he affixed the map to the wall. "Have you learned something?"

"I don't know. You want to help?"

"Sure. What do you need?"

He handed her the box. "I'll give you the city name, and you pin it."

"Midland, Texas." He paused, allowing her time to insert the pin.

Her eyebrow rose in question. "Is that it?"

"No. Green Hill, Cali..." She had the city pinned before he'd finished. "How'd you find that so fast?"

"It's outside of Los Angeles. Next?"

Chris hadn't asked why she was sticking pins into a map, she'd just jumped in to help. She was smart and he didn't have to explain the purpose of the exercise. He pulled up each unfamiliar name on a Google map and helped her locate the city on the wall map.

The tension in his neck increased each time she shoved a pin into the map. When he called out the last city and fell silent, she turned. Her blue eyes studied his face.

"You do this for a living. Tell me what you see."

"Nothing yet. But I'm working on it." Marcus rose and stood next to her.

"There are eleven pins. I didn't put one on North Riverview. Is Chelsea's file in that stack?" A manicured finger pointed at the oversize folder.

"No. She makes twelve. Go ahead and add her pin."

"Twelve women have been killed the same way?" She backed up and leaned a hip on the table.

"That's the rub. Except for torture, the murders aren't identical. I'm looking for a pattern to the locations. Right now, they seem random. Some are in this area. Others are spread across the United States. Dalton must've seen something, because he asked me to study them and give him my thoughts."

"May I take a look?"

"I don't think—"

"Please don't try to shelter me. I'm sure Kay saw them."

"No doubt. She's better trained at this sort of thing. All of these women were butchered. I was trying to give you options."

"I'm not a sensationalist. I don't stop at car wrecks to see the blood. But in this instance, I want to help." Her gaze hardened, turning her eyes a deeper blue. "I need to help."

"Then have a seat. I'll split the stack with you. As we finish, we'll swap files. Study each case. Look for commonalities or anything that distinguishes one case from another. Take notes. Dalton made a statement that rang true then, and even more so now."

"What was that?"

"That Chelsea's murderer wasn't about to stop at just one. I've only glanced through each file, but I'm positive he was right."

"Don't tell me anything else. Let's see if I make the connection."

Marcus walked to his desk and returned with legal pads and pencils. He sat directly across from her, resting his hand on top of the folder. "I don't feel good about subjecting you to these pictures."

She covered his hand with hers. Her touch was warm and gentle, meant to assure but failing. It only made him want to protect her from the ugliness.

"It can't be any worse than what I witnessed at Chelsea's house. Nothing could be more horrendous."

"But it can. If this becomes too much, we stop. Deal?"

"You got it." She'd enunciated each word with resolve. Marcus knew in his gut that they were about to put that statement to the test.

He pushed the top file to her and opened the second one for himself. The sharp hiss of her inhale cut right into his heart. She paled, blinked a few times, and then picked up her pencil. He couldn't help but believe she'd missed her calling, because she'd have been a damn good cop.

He bent his head and concentrated on his stack of files, making his own notes as he went. He took an occasional peek at Chris, watching the range of emotions play out on her face.

No two victims had been killed in the same manner, and the women had all come from different towns. They'd been slashed, beaten, stabbed, burned, choked, had their throats cut, or some combination. Bottom line being: They'd all been tortured before death had mercifully ended their nightmare.

He and Chris traded folders and worked through each one. When they'd finished, three things stood out in Marcus's mind.

"You two want some coffee?" Kay asked from the doorway.

Marcus jotted down his final thoughts before responding. "None for me. Thanks."

"I'll pass, too. Thanks." Chris stood. "But I think I'll splash some water on my face."

"Go ahead," Kay said, leaning over his shoulder. "Graphic pictures. I can't image what these women went through."

Marcus looked up at her. "You put these together, which means you studied them. I'd like to get your take," he said, leaning back in his chair. "Stay and let's talk this out."

"Thank you for respecting Chris's intelligence and my experience enough to ask for our help." Kay pulled out a seat and joined him.

"I learned the value of teamwork in the Army. On rare occasions, one soldier becomes a hero. Most of the time, it's a group effort. You hear from Nate?"

"Yeah. As expected, Tomas is pretty shaken up."

Marcus handed over his credit card. "Will you send flowers in my name?"

"Sure thing. Wayne's funeral is tomorrow at ten."

"I'd like to attend," Marcus said. "But I'm not sure it would be safe having Chris out in the open."

"I wouldn't advise it. Even with hundreds of uniforms around, one bullet could—"

Marcus turned in his chair toward Chris. "We ready?"

"You go first." Chris sat and picked up her pencil.

"A couple of things bothered me. The murders are different, yet alike. The fact they were tortured screams serial killer, which is what Dalton had already decided. I'm betting he's already turned this over to his boss. Somebody in the FBI is connecting the dots with the police departments of each of these towns."

"They'll tell us to back off." Chris folded her arms across her chest.

"I followed orders in the Army. As a civilian, I'm less cooperative. This is personal."

The corners of Kay's mouth twitched. She'd obviously misunderstood what he meant, that Chris's case was no longer professional. He had to salvage the conversation before Kay started planning a wedding. "The bastard screwed up Chris's life, killed my friend, and burned my house."

"You got confirmation?" Chris's face flushed. "It was deliberate."

"Yes. I haven't been sent the report, but the inspector found evidence of arson."

"Of course, that's why it's personal." Chris's eyes closed for a second. "What else bothered you?"

"Why'd he pose them?" Marcus continued, grateful she'd moved on. "It's as if he was showing off, but who's he trying to impress? Usually, no one sees these pictures except the first responders, the medical examiner, and the detectives who work each case."

Chris nodded and tapped her pad. "I noted that they all looked posed, too. I also wrote down dates. Looks to me like the killer became more sadistic with each kill."

Marcus was impressed she'd picked up on the dates. "Yeah. The first two murders were months apart, yet the others were separated by only a few days. That's not a known pattern for a serial or spree killer. Maybe Dalton can get a profile put together."

"Spread over different cities and states, I can see why no one connected them," Kay added.

"Picking small towns or rural areas made it even harder." Marcus couldn't sit any longer. He rose and paced. "Half of the women were violently raped. The other half hadn't been sexually violated, but their legs had been positioned to display their genital area. None of this makes sense."

Chris had started sorting through the files again. Her eyebrows were pulled together, and her jaw was set tight. Something had drawn her attention. When she looked up at him and Kay, her expression had shifted to fear.

"What is it?" he asked. Damn that he couldn't remove that panicked look from her eyes.

"Counting my sister, six of these women fit my description. Check it out." She tapped a file. "They have long blond hair and blue eyes; they're around five-foot-eight, and between twenty-eight and thirty-two. Has he been killing Chelsea all along? Then I walked in and disturbed him?"

CHAPTER 11

Chris immediately wanted her words back. Had she just verbally negated the importance of twelve deaths and made it all about her sister? "I'm sorry to be so paranoid. That was a stupid question."

"Not stupid." Marcus stopped pacing. "What if he's been killing you all along? In your situation, paranoia might keep you alive."

"Marcus is right," Kay said, pulling the folder in front of her. "It's not a stupid idea. Let's take another look." She quickly set six files to the side and checked the remaining stack.

Marcus moved to stand behind Kay as she sorted and made notes. Chris leaned closer, trying to see what Kay wrote.

"Interesting," Kay said. Her eyebrows were drawn together. "The six other women were of different races and hair and eye color. It almost seems random."

Marcus reached around Kay and picked up the note pad. He took red pushpins and placed them next to half of the ones Chris had used. Then he repeated the process with green pins. He backed up and studied the map.

Chris couldn't stand the silence. "What do you see?"

"I wish to hell I knew. There has to be a pattern here. What am I missing?" Marcus looked through the files again, writing furiously as he went. He dragged his hand through his hair. "We keep adding facts that tell us nothing. Soon, they start adding up. We just have to keep digging."

"You saw something else?" Chris understood his frustration. All these files, and they were no closer to the killer.

Marcus swept his hand across the map. "The first murdered woman had brown hair and eyes. A couple of months passed before a blonde was killed. A few weeks later, he reversed his pattern and slaughtered both women within days of each other. Yet, they're scattered all over the map." Marcus tapped a pin in Arizona and one in Texas. "The blonde women are all killed inside the Texas state line."

"You're right," Chris said, moving away from the map. "Was he keying on them because of Chelsea? Because he couldn't find her?"

"Doesn't explain the other women," Kay said. "The killer moves around a lot."

"He's got time on his hands," Chris added. "Or he travels for business. Like a truck driver or salesman."

"Could be," Marcus agreed. "Either profession would have the ability to cover a lot of territory."

"So what's next?" Chris blew out a breath.

"I'll call Dalton. Tell him what we found. Maybe he's come up with something." Marcus stood and rolled his shoulders. The muscles in his neck were drawn tight, making her wish she could ease his tension.

"You go ahead." She resisted the urge to touch him. Instead, she remained seated. "I'll hang out with Kay."

"Can you think of anyone in your past who'd like to see you dead?" Kay asked.

"Other than Chelsea's murderer? No. " Chris closed the files. "I don't have any family left. They're all dead. My friends have long ago stopped wondering where I am." The weight of her situation and the truth of the statement slammed into her with the force of a tidal wave. She really had no one to help her except the Lost and Found people.

"You're not alone. We're going to help you." Kay stood, and they walked to her desk together. "Let's call in and order for lunch. There's a Chinese place a couple of blocks away. They make the best almond chicken. You in?"

"It's not too hot. Is it?"

"I'll make sure they keep the spices light."

"Sounds good." Chris sat in the visitor's chair while Kay ordered the food. She pushed her wavy brown hair off her shoulder. Chatting casually with the person on the other end of the line, she agreed a side of eggrolls would be good.

Kay hung up. "While we wait, tell me more about being a Big Sister. How did you get involved?"

"I saw a news report that the Big Sisters program needed volunteers. It was right after Chelsea's murder and I was struggling. Having missed so much work, I'd resigned and was sort of adrift. It just made sense. I don't think anyone shakes off the hurt of being abandoned. When a girl tells me I don't understand, I can honestly tell her that I do."

"Between the two girls you mentor and the animal shelter, it must take a lot of your time," Kay said.

"I'm grateful for every minute I've spent with the girls. The work is very rewarding. When things settle down, I'll rejoin the workforce. Maybe even make some new friends, but not until after the killer is in prison. I hate that I've cut my visits with the girls back to just phone calls, but I can't risk their lives. Now, it seems that if you associate with me, you become a target."

"You're feeling guilty about Wayne." Kay's words were soft and sympathetic. "You're not responsible for his murder." Kay sounded exactly like Marcus. "The bastard who shot him is."

"I spent only a few hours with Wayne. He seemed like a good person, and I loved to listen to him talk."

Kay's eyes watered and Chris took her hand. "I'm sorry. You guys were close, weren't you?"

"He was a great friend and cop," Kay said. "I enjoyed working alongside Wayne. More than once, I witnessed him use that slow, easy drawl of his to pull information out of a suspect. His good-ol'-boy approach was real, and it worked better than any interrogation tactic." Kay blinked rapidly. "You're almost as good as Marcus at deflecting the conversation off yourself. We were talking about you."

Chris gave her the quick overview of her life. How she and Chelsea had been adopted by the Hollands. "That's pretty much it. Other than work. I was the marketing director for Patterson Sports until both my parents died. I took a leave of absence and haven't been back."

"What do you do for fun? Relaxation?"

"I used to paint. Landscapes mostly, old barns, golden fields of wheat. Nothing fancy. But since Chelsea's murder, I haven't been able to muster up any enthusiasm. I started writing her story but decided she wouldn't want the world to know how she died."

"When this is over, we'll take in the art district. My knowledge about the subject is limited, and I'd love to go with someone who can teach me. Have you ever had a show?"

Chris's heart jumped a beat. "No. I'm not that good."

"Not that good at what?" Marcus asked as he moved from his work area to the front desk.

"She's an artist," Kay announced.

"Yes, she is." His thousand-watt smile almost knocked Chris out of her chair. "And she was being modest. She's a hell of a lot better than good."

"I don't know about that, but thank you." Chris wasn't used to praise. In fact, she hadn't shared her paintings with many people. "What did Dalton say?"

"That he wasn't going to waste his breath by telling us to stay out of it. As if I'd leave it to the FBI to sort this out." Marcus huffed a disgusted sound. "He knows that's not going to happen."

"The FBI is involved?"

"They are now that we've tied a dozen murders together. Small towns don't have the wherewithal it takes to run an op like the feds. Local police departments usually ask for help for no other reason than the expense."

"At last." Chris breathed a small sigh of relief.

"Dalton said to add two pins to the map. Three days ago a waitress was slaughtered in Albany. She'd been raped and mutilated. He thinks it ties back to our killer."

"You said two pins. Another woman died." He nodded, and Chris's minute of relief about the FBI getting involved vanished. "Where?"

"This morning a woman's body was found in a suburb outside of Austin. She was house-sitting for a friend. The maid discovered her."

The front door opened, and the smell of food escorted a young man inside. Chris's stomach rolled up and wedged in the back of her throat.

Marcus paid the bill and Kay carried the sacks to the conference table. Marcus put his hand on Chris's arm as they followed.

"You okay?"

"Was the second victim a blonde?"

Marcus hesitated, giving her the answer even before he spoke. "Yes. I mentioned that half of the victims were blond to Dalton." Marcus tightened his grip, squeezed, and silently gave her the assurance she needed.

Kay passed out paper plates and chopsticks. "Could these new deaths mean he's moved on? Gotten tired of tormenting Chris?" Kay held both hands up. "Not that I'm glad they died, but it does sound like he's not even in this area anymore."

"Surely the same person didn't shoot Wayne, torch your house, and then drive to Austin to kill somebody."

Kay leaned forward. "Could you be mistaken and someone other than this butcher is stalking you?"

"We're not taking any chances." Marcus shook his head. He turned and started out the door. "I need a fork. My hands are too big and clumsy to handle chopsticks. Chris, want me to bring you one?"

"I'm fine, thanks." Chris ripped the paper off her chopsticks, thinking that Marcus's hands matched his body perfectly. She doubted he was clumsy.

"You like him." Kay wasn't asking. She'd been firm in her statement.

"Marcus?" Chris almost choked. "I hardly know him."

"Hmm. You were a little dreamy-eyed just now."

Chris couldn't lie. "Who wouldn't be? He's gorgeous."

"You might be just the ticket to bring him out of the shadows." Kay pointed the chopsticks Chris's direction. "Be sure you know what you're doing. 'Cause if you hurt him—"

"You'll kick my ass." Chris wished she had friends like Kay. Close friends who'd watch out for her.

"Something like that, yeah."

With a couple of long strides, Marcus sat at the table and dug his fork into the pile of food Kay had dumped on his plate.

Chris's brain locked down. Had he heard what they'd been talking about when he'd returned? She sneaked a quick glance at Kay only to find her wide-eyed and grinning.

He stopped mid-bite. "What? Did I interrupt something?"

"No. I was venting my frustration," Chris said, winging it. "We've identified all these interesting facts that mean absolutely nothing."

"Not necessarily so. There's a telling thread connecting all those women, one we haven't found."

The phone rang, and Kay returned to her desk, leaving Marcus and Chris to finish eating lunch.

A cool, damp nose nuzzled her hand. "Hey, Diablo. Where have you been?"

"Kay made him a bed in the back corner. He sleeps most of the time when he's here."

Chris pulled a piece of chicken out of the rice and looked to Marcus. "May I give him this?"

One corner of Marcus's mouth lifted, relaxing the tension in his face. "You might as well. You've already established yourself as his go-to human for the good stuff. He's got a bowl of water and some dry dog food in the back, but obviously, he'd just rather eat yours."

"I don't mind sharing."

"The fire freaked him out." Marcus stood. "I'll be right back."

"Here, boy," she said, holding a piece of chicken down to the dog. Diablo was on his third piece when Marcus returned, carrying the leash. Diablo's tail started wagging, and he abandoned her for his master.

"I'd better take him out. He's partial to this nice strip of grass in the alley. If you'll excuse us, we'll be right back."

****

Diablo wasted no time taking care of his business. The minute he was finished, he tugged at the leash, ready to go back inside. Marcus opened the alley door to the office. "You're not fooling me. You want to rejoin the ladies."

The roar of a motorcycle stopped him. Nate drove around the corner onto the narrow road. He geared down his sleek chrome and black Harley to a rumble and made his way to where Marcus waited, who stepped back and waited until the bike's engine was off.

"Rough visit?" Marcus asked, knowing the answer. Wayne's death was hard on everyone who knew him. He and Tomas had become unofficial members of the team when not on duty.

"Yeah. Losing Wayne was tough for everyone who knew him." Nate pushed the Harley through the door and parked it just inside. "I didn't know what the fuck to say. 'Our deepest sympathies' had to suffice."

"It's never enough, but it's all you can do." Marcus unhooked Diablo's leash and watched the dog trot straight to Chris. "Mooch," he muttered.

"He's in a hurry."

"Yeah, to get back to Chris."

"Kay texted she'd ordered Chinese for lunch. Any left?"

"Not if Chris has her way. She's in the conference room, spoiling my dog."

"He likes her." Nate clapped him on the shoulder. "Kay says you like Chris, too."

"Kay needs to stop texting shit she knows nothing about," Marcus ground out.

Nate chuckled. "She's usually right about this stuff. Affairs of the heart fall under her expertise. How's Chris holding up?"

"Good, considering." That was an understatement, and Marcus knew it. Some women would have fallen apart, burst into tears, or withdrawn. Not her. She held her own. "Which is why I let her share lunch with Diablo. After all the data we filtered through so far today, she needed the distraction."

"Dalton's file hadn't come through when I left. What did he find?"

"A dozen murders. It's obvious they're linked, but at the same time..."

"What?"

"They're not." Marcus and Nate joined Chris and Kay at the conference table.

Nate picked up an empty container and peered inside. "I'm guessing I should've grabbed a bite before I came back."

"You are so mistreated," Kay said with a chuckle, shoving a sack toward him. "There's a container of almond chicken for you and fortune cookies for us."

The muffled sound of a phone chimed.

"It's mine." Chris grabbed her purse, fishing out her phone. A frown creased her forehead. "Very few people have this number."

Seeing the tension in her eyes, Marcus sat next to her. "Answer, but put it on speaker until you know who's calling."

Chapter 12

DaVinci turned off the TV. He didn't care that the entire city was outraged. The chief of police had promised to turn over every rock until they had the perpetrator who'd killed Wayne Kerns under lock and key. The cop shouldn't have befriended Christine. It was her fault that she'd suffered another loss.

He rebooted his laptop and pulled up the film, growing angrier by the frame. He fast-forwarded past the part where he'd shot the cop in Christine's parking lot. It was the shared embrace with the big man that DaVinci wanted to see again. It was totally unacceptable.

He watched the hug again and again. He imagined what it would be like to kill the man while she watched.

After she'd ridden off in the bastard's car, Christine hadn't returned. There'd been no sign of her, not during the night, and not this morning. What good was having a camera trained on her town house if she never went home?

Undaunted, he minimized that program and opened the GPS tracker. With a few keystrokes, he found her current location and knew exactly where she'd been. This little tracking device had proved more helpful than he'd expected. He'd identified each stop they'd made, jotted down the address of the house they'd shacked up in last night.

He'd hoped Christine had taken his message to heart. But, no. She was just like her sister.

The tracker on the friend's car showed it parked in its current location for hours. A few additional keystrokes, and Google Earth satisfied his curiosity and provided him with perfect pictures.

What the hell was Lost and Found, Inc.?

He hated research, found it boring, but he needed this information. A laugh burst from him. She'd hired a private eye? To do what? Catch him?

They'd never stop him.

And nobody could save her.

Stupid woman. Did she think she was smarter than he was? She'd forced his hand.

He fished his private cell from his pocket. The one reserved for conversations with Michelangelo. DaVinci had long ago programmed in her number. He'd never actually called her, but it was time she knew he didn't scare easily. The phone rang three times.

"Hello?" The word was a question.

"Do you think me so simple-minded that I would be afraid of a private eye?" Anger he'd been fighting to control flared, burning his flesh from the inside out. Flames he struggled to control turned into words and boiled out.

"Why are you doing this?" Her voice had a hollow sound. As he'd expected, he was speaking to more than just Christine.

"You waste my time with your foolish questions. Ask me something you don't know the answer to."

"You don't have to kill me. Even though I looked you in the face, I can't identify you. Can't remember a thing or you'd already be in prison."

How could she have forgotten? He felt his control slip. "Tell the private eye to stay away, or I'll kill him, too."

"Come tell me yourself." A male voice growled through the speaker. "Or does facing a man not excite you as much as killing helpless women or an unsuspecting cop?"

"Who are you?" DaVinci demanded.

"Marcus Ricci. You pick the time and place."

"You people disappoint me. I won't be goaded into meeting some gorilla in a dark alley." DaVinci struggled to keep his voice calm. Christine should have been pleading for her life, bargaining with him to spare her new friends, not allowing some stranger into their private discussion.

"You'll wish it was a gorilla."

"Christine, this is your fault. Didn't I just warn you not to bring outsiders into this?"

"You're a sick man." Her voice had a tremor. "You need help."

"That train left the station years ago." Goddamn it, he had to control his tongue. "Here's a promise: Before you die, I'll tell you everything."

"But—"

He pressed the end button. Not that groveling would have done her any good. She'd sealed her fate long ago.

His cell rang seconds after he'd hung up on the bitch, startling him. He read the name, and the tension eased and flowed out of his body. Michelangelo was calling. Was he ready to admit defeat?

"Good afternoon," DaVinci said without hesitation. His chest swelled with pride.

"You're chipper today."

"I am now that you've called." DaVinci couldn't hold back. "The pictures were spectacular, weren't they?"

"My boy. This work is strong, bold, and thought out beautifully. I'm very proud of you."

"And?" Excitement shot through his system. His mentor's approval meant everything to him. The only father figure he'd ever known lavishing praise on him sent euphoric warmth wrapping around him. He'd missed this validation.

"How about we meet for dinner? And I'll bring a check."

"Think you could call in a favor and get us into Andre's at seven?"

"Now you're taking advantage of your win." A warm chuckle from Michelangelo filtered through the phone. "Of course, I will. It's good to know your creative juices are flowing again. When will you paint the abstract?"

The question surprised DaVinci. He had to deal with Christine first. "Soon."

"Soon? You usually can't wait to get a brush in your hand and get started. I had hoped this latest creation was an indication that you'd moved on and abandoned your obsession."

"Can we talk about this at dinner?"

"Count on it."

Michelangelo had hung up. They'd ended too many conversations over the past few months this way.

DaVinci stared at the silent phone, half-expecting to find icicles hanging from it.

Christine hadn't suffered enough, not by a long shot. But the time had come to end her life. In his heart, he knew this was right. He'd kill her, not because Michelangelo had pressured him to, but because she deserved to die.

The Lost and Found people created problems. Separating her from her protectors could be difficult. Hiring outside help was dangerous. He'd always picked someone who needed money, and who no one would miss when they disappeared. Perhaps the time had come for him to ask his mentor for help.

One fact still troubled him. He couldn't forget that Michelangelo had lied to him. Who else could be responsible for the shot taken at Christine? That act of betrayal would eventually have to be addressed. He sighed. Every good thing came to an end.

****

Chris's hands trembled when she pushed her phone to Marcus. "I'm guessing it was a burner, and you won't be able to trace the call." Her entire body was in breakdown mode. Her insides felt as if they might liquefy at any moment.

His huge hand covered hers instead of the phone. Frustration overflowed. She stood, paced the floor of the small room, wishing she could vanish into thin air.

"Nate, do you have time to take a look?" Marcus handed him the cell.

"I'm on it." Nate scooted back his chair. The scraping sounded much like fingernails on a blackboard.

"If y'all will excuse me, I'll take care of these leftovers." Kay fished out two fortune cookies and put them on the table. "Yell, if you need anything."

Chris grabbed at the opportunity to do something, anything. "I'll help."

"I've got it," Kay insisted. "You two have work to do."

Chris stood, dumbfounded, as Nate and Kay disappeared. She felt Marcus's presence before she turned around to face him. "Was I that obvious?" An inappropriate, nervous laugh bubbled up and out. "Have you been trained how to handle women who fall apart?"

"I wish." He hooked a finger under her chin and lifted until her gaze met his. "You're one hell of a woman, Chris Holland. A lot of other women would have fallen apart by now."

"Don't you see? I am this far from it." She measured a tiny space with her thumb and forefinger.

"You're wrong." He smiled down at her. "I've never met a woman as strong and determined as you."

"I don't feel very damn strong."

"Anytime you need to punch somebody or just scream bloody hell, I'm here. Let me have it."

Chris's throat clenched, tears she'd refused to shed for years threatened and then vanished. She was fine. Her nerves were steady as a rock, and she knew why. "I can't take credit for being strong. It's you. I draw strength from your quiet, easy way of taking things in stride. How do you do it? Don't you ever just lose it? Go over the—"

He interrupted her with a brush of his lips. Soft, warm, and sexy. She wanted to ask for more, but couldn't find her voice. He leaned his head back, stared into her eyes as if he could see her soul, and then kissed her again. Longer and harder. Deeper and more sensual. Every nerve ending in her body fired like a barrage of Fourth of July bottle rockets.

He ended the kiss, leaving them both breathing hard. "By 'it,' if you're referring to my temper, I try not to 'lose it.' It's not a pretty sight. On the other hand, if you meant my emotions. The answer is, not very often."

Was he saying what she thought? Was she the exception? There was only one way to find out. Chris rose up on her toes and kissed him back. Strong hands cupped her cheeks, cradling her head and pulling her closer. His tongue slid across her bottom lip, and she opened for him. The strength of the kiss deepened, and their tongues warred for control. She clutched his shoulders and held tight, because without something to hold on to she feared her legs would give out.

"I put on a fresh pot... Oh, shit. I'm sorry."

Marcus released Chris from the kiss but not from his embrace. His hand wrapped around her waist and tugged her close. "No problem. We were just taking a break."

Chris fought the blood rushing up her neck to her cheeks. She dislodged Marcus's hand and almost ran from the room. "I'll get the coffee."

She made a quick trip to the restroom and splashed some cool water on her face. Talk about liquefying insides. She'd been kissed many times. None had ever affected her like Marcus's. She'd lost her mind, thought only of her body and its needs. Totally forgotten the circumstances that had brought them together and that she'd known him only a few days.

Chris came out of the restroom to find Kay leaning against the counter. She held up her hand to silence Chris.

"Please, don't apologize. You've nothing to be sorry for. I've seen the way you two look at each other. Especially when you think the other one won't notice."

"Really?" Chris shook off her curiosity. "This is a place of business. It was out of line."

"It's Marcus's business, too. After Tyrell came home from Colombia, he and Marcus bought a third of Lost and Found. Besides, you two aren't the first to kiss in these offices."

"Yes, but you and Nate are married."

"We weren't then. He kissed me right here next to the coffeepot. I was too stupid to admit I was still in love with him at the time. We lost precious time together because of my stubbornness. Marcus of all people knows how quickly fate can change your life."

"He loved her very much. I saw the shrine in his living room. I don't think I could share him with a ghost."

"He probably doesn't know it, but the fire may have set him free." Kay caught Chris by the hand and squeezed. "If you want him, you'll have to fight for him, but I think you can do it."

Kay poured two cups of coffee and handed them to Chris. "Thanks," Chris said, stopping at the door and looking back. "For everything."

A few short steps away, Marcus sat with the notepad in front of him. His hand zipped across the page. What had he heard? Maybe he was just looking for a way to steer the day back to business. Did he regret kissing her? Wish she hadn't initiated a deeper kiss? God, she hoped not. She took a deep breath and marched right into the room.

"Thanks," he said, reaching out to take the cups from her.

"You're welcome," she said.

He patted the chair next to him. "Let's talk about the phone call."

"Other than the jerk is nuts, what did we learn?" Chris dropped next to Marcus. He slid one hand under the seat of her chair and pulled her closer as if she weighed nothing.

"For starters, he knows you came to us. In fact, he knew you were here, and we were listening. Which means we should relocate soon."

"Well, don't I feel stupid."

Marcus hit her with his thousand-watt smile again. "Don't. You talked with him. It's my job to catch and analyze everything that was said."

And wasn't that something for her to remember? She was Marcus's job. "And we need to figure out where he picked up that piece of information."

"Exactly."

"Are we safe staying here?" she asked. "He could set fire to the office."

"He'd be pretty brazen to launch that kind of attack in the daylight. The risk of showing himself is too great. While Nate checks your cell phone, I need to look through your purse. The killer knows too much. Somehow, he put a tracker on you."

Chill bumps raced up her back and across her chest. The thought the crazy bastard had gotten close enough to put something on her phone sent the Chinese food in her stomach to churning. She dumped the contents of her purse on the table and handed it to Marcus.

"Tear it apart if you need to."

He inspected each item carefully. He picked up her billfold, paused, and caught her gaze as if asking permission. Chris nodded. There was nothing he couldn't see. She'd started carrying the bare necessities long ago. The corners of his mouth twitched when he got a look at her driver's license.

"Go ahead and laugh." She gave his shoulder a playful but firm shove. It didn't surprise her when he didn't budge. "It was particularly windy that day."

"I like your hair loose and curly, like it is today."

"I call it the light socket look."

Apparently satisfied a tracer hadn't been hidden in her lip gloss, he rolled every inch of her handbag through his fingers. His gaze was intense as he slowly separated the lining from the leather and inspected it.

Nate rejoined them. "Find anything?"

"Nothing here. You?" Marcus asked.

"The phone is clean." Nate handed her phone back.

"Thanks for checking," Chris said as he sat across from her.

"No problem," Nate said, pulling his notepad in front of him.

"Back to analyzing what we learned from the killer," Marcus said. "The killer believes you know why he wants to kill you. He said Wayne's death was your fault."

"Well, that makes two of us who think that."

"Bullshit," Marcus snapped. "We had this discussion. None of this rests on your shoulders."

Chris thought back over the phone conversation. "He got really upset when I said he needed help. Said that train left a long time ago. What could it mean?"

"To be exact, he said that train left years ago." Marcus's eyes darkened. "Is he saying at some point in his life he needed help but didn't get it?"

"From me?"

"Not necessarily." Marcus lifted his cup to his mouth. He blew on the hot coffee, and a swirl of steam caressed his face. "I'm just looking for something that will give us some insight into this bastard's personality." He took a sip then stared into the dark liquid.

"Could he be someone from your past? Beyond two years ago?" Nate asked.

"No way." She shook her head in denial. "Maybe his mama was a blonde. Maybe she abused him. Maybe he kills her every other time."

"There's definitely a method to his madness," Marcus said. "Our job is to put the puzzle pieces together."

"There's nobody from my past who hates me." Nate's assumption that it might be someone she knew was ludicrous, and her temper flared at his suggestion. "After Chelsea moved to North Riverview, we weren't close enough to have made a mutual enemy."

"Then let's dig a little deeper into the victims' families," Nate continued as if she hadn't disagreed.

"Okay." Chris reached for the files. "What are we looking for?"

"You got me to thinking when you said that everyone you'd ever loved was dead," Marcus said. "Made me wonder if the other women had lost their families, too."

Nate had been staring at her purse. "Not to change the subject, but you searched that handbag thoroughly?"

"I did. But there's a tracker somewhere. He knew we were here, and I don't believe we were followed." Marcus stabbed his fingers through his hair. "There's only one place left."

"Where?" Chris asked.

"My car." He stood and stormed out the door.

CHAPTER 13

Marcus and Nate barely slowed their steps as they passed Kay's desk. Marcus forced his clenched hands to relax. He ignored the tension in his neck.

"We'll be in the parking lot," Nate said, matching him stride for stride.

She nodded. "I'll be here if Chris needs something."

Marcus hit the remote, turning off the alarm. He raised the hood and began his inspection. Nate opened the front door and slid across the seat, checking under the dash. The two of them slowly inspected every inch. "I got nothing," Marcus said.

Nate raised his head. "Me either. I'll take the rear."

Dressed in expensive slacks and a white shirt, Nate didn't hesitate to roll up his sleeves and hit the pavement. Time and again, he'd proved his friendship. A more reliable man had never drawn a breath. If that made Marcus's respect for Nate a bromance, so be it.

Marcus dropped to the pavement and slid under the left wheel well. He ran his hands over every surface, scooted even farther under the car, and found nothing. "Anything?" he called out.

"Not yet," Nate answered.

Marcus moved to the other side. He'd barely slid under when he saw the magnetic tracker. "Got it."

"Don't pull it," Nate said. A second later, he crawled next to Marcus. "Son of a bitch likes to know every move you make. Let's keep him informed."

"What are you thinking?" Marcus and Nate pushed out from under the car.

"That you have things to do. Deal with the fire department, insurance company, and most important, salvage what you can of your belongings. You can't do that and look over your shoulder at the same time."

"I hired someone else to take care of that stuff. I'm not leaving Chris unattended."

"You think I don't know that?" Nate's eyebrows pulled together. "But you can accomplish everything you need to if you leave your car right where it is and take Kaycie's. Tomorrow, I'll drive it to my appointment with the feds and then pick up Kaycie for Wayne's funeral."

"And if the killer decides to take a shot at you?"

Nate's furrowed brow shifted to a slight smirk. "If he shows up, he'll figure out we outsmarted him. He's not going to fuck with me while I'm at the FBI office or the funeral. He's probably monitoring from a distance, and my stops will make him curious as hell."

Marcus thought about it for a minute. "There are things Chris and I need to do without worrying about somebody shooting at us. She's wished for a hairbrush all day."

The corner of Nate's mouth lifted into half a smile. "I heard about the kiss."

"Figures. I don't know what the fuck I was thinking."

"She's a beautiful woman, and for reasons unknown to me, she apparently likes you. Let Kaycie make you a reservation at a hotel for the night. She'll find one with a suite. Take Chris out for a nice dinner. She deserves a break from all the tension, and you could use one, too."

"I'll agree to some of that. She's mentioned needing to get a few personal items from her place. I'd like a team of professionals to scour every inch. If the nervy bastard put a tracer on my car, he might've bugged her house."

"Leave me her key. I'll get somebody over there. If it is bugged, maybe I can do a little tracing of my own. But for the next few days, we'll move you two around. Make it harder to track you. Be good for you to relax and get to know her."

"Don't start playing matchmaker," Marcus warned, hoping to end the conversation.

"I give up." Nate threw both hands in the air. "The only person who's going to drag your ass back into the land of the living is you."

Marcus snarled but made no comment. Nate was hitting too close to home. Truth was, Chris was the first person in years who'd made him think about living again.

"We better get back inside before Kaycie busts out the door." Nate chuckled. "She's never been good at staying out of things."

"And aren't you glad?" Marcus knew how proud Nate was of his wife's strength and independence. "We can swing by here tomorrow afternoon and swap vehicles. Our telephone friend will have figured out by then we found his tracker."

"No hurry. We'll keep Diablo. You concentrate on keeping Chris safe."

"I don't like leaving him."

"He'll be fine with Kaycie and me. It's Chris you should worry about."

"What the hell does that mean?"

"She likes you. So be careful."

"Yes, dear." Marcus ground out the words and led the way back inside. "If I need romance advice, I'll write Dear Abby."

"Hey, I did okay in the romance department," Nate said, closing the door behind them.

"What department?" Kay asked.

"Never mind." Grateful she'd heard only part of Nate's comment, Marcus continued walking toward the conference room. Behind him, he heard Nate ask Kay to pick an extra nice hotel in downtown Dallas and reserve a suite.

He stopped at the doorway, absorbing the scene playing out in front of him. Diablo was sitting in his chair next to Chris. His head was tilted, and he appeared to be in a trance. Chris's hands were buried in the fur behind his ears. Marcus could barely hear her, but the tenderness in her voice was unmistakable. The bond forming between her and his dog filled his lungs with warmth.

The connection pleased him. Yet, in an odd way, he felt left out. Shit. He was too old for schoolboy crushes.

"How'd you get him on the chair?" he asked.

"I patted the seat, and he jumped right up." The smile on her face complemented the sparkle of her eyes. "Tell me the rest of his story."

"There's not much else to say. A drug lord's kid had him attack an old woman. An evil old woman who had sliced me across the chest. Anyway, he'd killed her before I could pull him off. I had to bring him with me. No way was he going to be put down for following orders. So I smuggled him into the country and went to work teaching him to be a dog."

Chris reached up and put her hand on his chest. "She cut you?"

"Not bad. It wasn't deep enough to leave a scar."

"You really are one of the good guys. Not many people would have taken him on."

Marcus had to look away for a second. Her eyes had filled with admiration. Admiration he didn't deserve. "He's not a success story, yet." He motioned for Diablo to get down, and then Marcus sat in the same chair.

"Did you and Nate find anything on your car?"

"Yeah," Marcus said. "Bastard's been tracking our every move." Marcus explained where the tracker had been found. "We're borrowing Kay's car for the night, but first we're going shopping." Her face brightened. Chris's smile was contagious, and he caught himself grinning like a fool.

"Now?" She lifted her eyebrows in question.

"Might as well. Let's find out from Kay where she's putting us for the night. Nate's going to have a crew go through your place to make sure there are no cameras or bugs hidden."

The pink drained from her cheeks. "You think he's been watching and listening to what goes on inside my home?"

Marcus fought back the urge to take her in his arms and offer comfort. He wanted to tell her no, but he'd only be guessing. "There's only one way to be sure. The team Nate's calling will search and, if they find anything, destroy."

She nodded, a slight movement of her head, indicating she understood. "Then I'm ready to go if you are. I've used a lot of excuses to go shopping, but this removes my need to go home."

"I thought any reason worked for a woman." He tried to ease her tension.

"Normally, that's true." She stood and scratched Diablo's head. "What about him?"

"Kay and Nate will keep him. I don't like it, but he'll think he died and went to dog heaven." Marcus gathered the stack of files and shoved them in a briefcase. He knelt in front of Diablo and ruffled the scruff on the back of his neck. The dog looked Marcus in the eyes as if trying to communicate. "I'll see you tomorrow afternoon."

"He's so smart. I'm glad he has you."

"Me, too," Marcus said honestly, following Chris to Kay's desk.

"You be careful with my car. No bullet holes," Kay said then bit off a laugh. "Sorry. Bad joke." She handed him a printout of the hotel reservation and her car keys. "I'd say have fun, but if you're like Nate, I'd be wasting my breath."

"You're right," Marcus agreed. "Shopping is about as much fun as stepping on a rusty nail." He was faced with an unavoidable task, so he straightened his shoulders and walked into the fray. "First, we take care of a little business."

****

The insurance adjuster waved goodbye and drove away, leaving Marcus and Chris standing in front of the pile of brick and charred lumber he'd once called home. Not much was salvageable, but the construction company had people who would sift through the pile of rubble before starting the rebuild. Any memorabilia found would be cleaned, boxed, and saved for Marcus to pick up.

"I'm so sorry this happened. Your things, your memories, they were important." Her blue eyes had clouded with a layer of anguish. She suffered for his loss, and somehow it lessened his pain.

"Sometimes the past is hard to let go." Oddly enough, he was okay if they didn't find a lot of his keepsakes. "It's silly, but I hope my college football team picture survived. Nate, Ty, Jake, and I played for the University of Texas in Austin."

"Not silly at all." Chris pulled away from him. She crossed the yard and hailed the leader of the crew. Minutes later, she returned.

"They'll watch for it."

That simple act of compassion meant a lot to Marcus. "Let's get out of here."

He opened the door to Kay's sports car. Chris slid inside. Marcus paused. He squatted and rocked back on his heels. He owed her an apology and now was as good a time as any to give it. "I'm sorry for back there in the conference room." He hoped she'd see his sincerity.

She frowned for a second. Then her blue eyes frosted over. "The kiss?"

"I let it get out of hand."

She waved him off as if shooing away a fly, but he caught the hint of embarrassment in her eyes. "We kissed. No big deal. Don't give it a second thought. You have your life, and I have mine. The sooner the killer is behind bars, the sooner I can get back to normal. We'll both be happier."

Her feigned indifference didn't fool him. "Don't do that. Don't diminish what happened between us. You felt something, and so did I. You also know it would end badly, and I don't think either of us wants that."

She nodded her agreement but kept her face turned away from him. Marcus stood, walked around, and slid behind the wheel. His diplomacy never had won any praise, but he'd never handled a situation so poorly. Maybe he'd screwed it up, because deep down, he hadn't meant a damn word he'd said.

"You call it," he said, taking one last look at his burned house. "What store do you want to hit first?"

"The nearest drugstore." Chris ran her fingers over her hair. "I'm going to make their cash register sing."

"And then?"

Chris was silent a minute. "Would you mind going to Han's? They're fairly new to Texas, but I like the quality of their merchandise."

"Works for me. You'll have to point me in the right direction."

"It's inside the Galleria."

"Just shoot me now," he muttered to himself. "This can't be a long drawn-out shopping spree." He took the ramp onto the freeway. He hoped she wasn't one of those women who liked to browse. After a few minutes of watching for a tail, getting off I-635 and then back on, he took a side road to a neighborhood drugstore.

He had to admit the stop at the drugstore benefitted them both. But Marcus had picked out and paid for his toiletries long before she'd settled on the right shade of lipstick. Then it was back onto the freeway, headed for one of the largest and busiest malls in the state.

Halfway through the store, Marcus wholeheartedly agreed with Nate that giving Chris a break from the case would help. His decisions had been easy—underwear, jeans, one pair of slacks, and a couple of shirts, and he was good to go.

Chris, on the other hand, had tried on half of the women's department. He'd finally parked his ass in a chair outside the dressing room and watched the show. It wasn't long before he was waiting expectantly for her to come out and show him the next outfit.

Nate always claimed to hate shopping, but that guy was so in love, he'd have gone in the dressing room with Kay to help her. The more Marcus thought about it, helping Chris in and out of those clothes seemed like a great idea. That kind of thinking caused him to shift in his chair and will away a rising erection.

Chris breezed past him, stopping at a full-length mirror.

"Well? What do you think?" she asked, doing a three-sixty.

"Aren't blue jeans just blue jeans? They look the same as the last two pair you tried on." They didn't. In fact, this pair hugged her bottom, curving in just the right places, but he was having too much fun teasing her.

"Men," she huffed with a grin. "I've got enough to last a few days. Let's get out of here."

"Music to my ears." He almost acknowledged his enjoyment at watching her relax and forget her worries for a few minutes. The words rested on the tip of his tongue, but they seemed to be stuck. Probably for a good reason.

At the cash register, he insisted on paying for her new things, gathered her packages, and walked beside her to the parking garage. The scene was too domestic for him. Hell, he'd never spent this much time shopping with a woman.

He'd married Lynne while he'd been on leave, and their two weeks together hadn't been spent in a mall. The few times he'd had a pass, they'd met halfway, usually somewhere with a beach. He'd never taken the time to do the simple things, like watching a beautiful woman try on tight blue jeans.

Chris slipped her hand inside his arm. He glanced down, soaking in the warmth of her smile. Admitting he'd had a good time wasn't an option. His man card might be revoked if he said it out loud. It was best to keep that bit of news quiet.

"Thank you for the clothes."

"My pleasure."

"I'm letting you off the hook. Where to next?" she asked.

"It's a surprise."

The trip into downtown Dallas was pleasant. Chris, it seemed, was the only woman in the world who could leave the word "surprise" alone. Not once had she tried to pry their destination out of him.

"Want to hear something weird? I miss Diablo," she answered her own question without waiting for his response.

"So do I. When we came back from Colombia, I took a few weeks off and spent twenty-four hours a day working with him. Now I feel like something's missing without him along."

"I love how he looks at you as if he understands every word you say."

"He's smart. Teaching him English wasn't as hard as I'd expected."

It occurred to Marcus that he'd been talking a lot, something he never did. He was having a hard time remembering she was his client. A vulnerable and scared client.

He turned into the long driveway of the Grand Herron Hotel, relieved they'd reached their destination.

"What are we doing here?" Chris asked. She leaned closer to the windshield, looking up as if to double-check the name on the marquee.

"We're crashing here tonight." He smiled, enjoying her surprise.

"I'm not going inside dressed like this. My hair looks like...well, like I haven't combed it."

Marcus killed the engine and pushed the trunk-release button. A bellhop rushed to retrieve their bags just as the passenger side door swung open. A man dressed in a navy blue uniform offered Chris his hand.

"Welcome to the Grand Herron," the man said.

Marcus got out and joined her curbside. He reached up and caught her hand to stop her from pushing and patting her hair. "You look gorgeous."

"Easy for you to say. The desk clerks will be too busy staring at your broad shoulders to notice what you're wearing."

"Really?" he teased. "Then stand behind me. Problem solved."

She burst out with a robust laugh. Quickly, she slapped her hand over her mouth. "You made a joke."

Caught up in her charm, he leaned down, brushed her ear with his lips, and said, "Who's joking?" She visibly shivered, so he did it again.

She backed away as pink rushed up her cheeks. "We could've at least put the clothes in our new suitcases."

The bellhop cleared his throat. "If you'll follow me," he said. With a sweep of his hand, he invited them to enter the hotel.

Marcus caught Chris by the elbow and guided her to the front desk. They registered and strolled to the elevator. The doors swished closed, and she let out a deep sigh.

"See? Nobody noticed us," he said.

"You're enjoying this."

"A little."

The corners of her mouth twitched, reminding him how soft her lips had been when they'd kissed. Enough. It would be a long night.

He'd brought Chris to the Herron for a reason. She needed a break from fear, and that included not being afraid he'd make sexual demands. By the time they reached the twenty-fifth floor, he'd adjusted his thinking and was back in work mode.

CHAPTER 14

DaVinci closed his laptop and locked it in the safe. He was wasting time watching the tracking device on the bodyguard's car. The vehicle had made a few stops around town before returning to the Lost and Found office. But it hadn't moved for hours. Were they really still inside? If they were trying to make a fool out of him...well, he'd make sure they regretted it.

Tonight, he and his mentor would figure out how to separate Christine from the people she'd hired to protect her. DaVinci had no qualms when it came to killing the man who'd been with her for days. Excitement rippled through him. He had so much to tell her. So much pain to inflict.

He dressed in preparation to make an appearance at his gallery. Customers loved to meet the owner, and he would never jeopardize his business by not mingling with rich buyers.

The bulk of his fortune resulted from sales of DaVinci's knockoffs of the great masters. He nor Michelangelo made claims that the paintings were authentic. What their clients told their friends was of no concern to him. He'd used a lot of that money to locate and keep tabs on Christine.

He checked himself in the full-length mirror. Michelangelo was picking him up at the gallery at seven for dinner. How would he react when he knew the truth? How much should he be told? After all, DaVinci's trust had wavered when someone had taken a shot at Christine.

How far would Michelangelo go to help?

****

Chris couldn't find the right words to say. The richness of the fabrics, the European-designed furniture, and contemporary paintings in the lobby had been lavish but tasteful. Her stomach had dipped during the ride up in the glass elevator, making her feel like a kid in her favorite theme park.

Nothing had prepared her for the luxury of their suite. The main room was enormous and filled with furniture upholstered in the same beautiful colors as the lobby. She walked to the small wet bar and ran her fingers over the polished wood. The carpet softened each of her steps, eliminating any sound as Marcus pulled the floor-length curtains back, revealing the Dallas skyline.

"It's breathtaking," she said.

Marcus turned and walked to the bar, propping one hip on the edge of a stool. "I'm more of a Fort Worth man myself."

"You'll have to show me your favorite places someday."

"We'll see." His tone had suddenly gone cold.

What had she missed? His personality and demeanor had changed so quickly. The playful flirt, the man who'd sent flashes of lust racing through her system, had disappeared. In his place was the stoic bodyguard.

The desire to push him for details ate at her, but he wasn't the type who'd be pressed. Not Marcus. He'd withdraw even further if she tried to ask him what had changed.

"Why did Kay put us here?" She swept an arm to indicate the room. "This is too much. Too expensive."

"Not really. Nate did some work for the manager a few months ago. We get a substantial discount."

Discount or not, she couldn't allow Lost and Found to absorb the cost for even one night at the Herron. "It's beautiful. But the cost should be added to my bill."

Marcus's right eyebrow rose. "You'll have to take that up with Kay. She's in charge of costs and expenditures." He pointed at the closed double doors. "The sacks and empty suitcases came up ahead of us. Your clothes are in your bedroom."

"My bedroom?" She opened the doors wide to find a king-size bed. The sacks of clothing were on a foot table. "Where's yours?"

"The hotel has only one-bedroom suites. The couch has a foldout."

"Nonsense. Those things will cripple a man your size. You're not sleeping out here with a perfectly good bed in the next room. I'll take the couch. Let me sort out our clothes, take my shower, and then I'll turn the bathroom over to you." With that, she closed the door, eliminating the argument she knew he'd been ready to unleash.

****

Did she really expect him to sleep in there? Her on the couch and him in a king-size bed? "Not fucking likely."

The door opened, and Chris peeked out, just her head appearing. "Did you say something?"

Had he? If so, he hadn't intended to. "Nope. Didn't say a word." He hurried behind the bar and got busy fixing a cup of coffee.

"Are we eating out or ordering in?" she asked.

"Out. Sort of. The hotel has a great steak house."

"Nice."

She vanished behind the closed door, leaving Marcus to wonder if she'd been naked. He grabbed his cup and moved to the couch. Sinking into the thick cushions, he decided she'd been wrong. He could stretch out right here and sleep. He'd get a hell of a lot more rest than he would if he took the bed.

He turned on the television and kicked back, clicking channels until he found the local news. While he listened to the reporter drone on about a traffic jam, he pulled his briefcase onto his lap and opened it. They were missing something, and he had to figure it out.

The killer's pattern troubled him. Why had he selected six blue-eyed blondes?

The other six were a jumbled mix, almost as if they were random. It was almost as if he had a split personality. Or...shit.

He fished out his cell and called Nate.

"How's the hotel?" Nate asked.

"Plush. I've got something to run by you."

"I'm listening."

"What if there are two killers?" Marcus knew it was a reach. He hoped bouncing the idea off Nate would help sort it out.

"What'd you find that makes you think there's two?"

"The differences in the women. Half are almost carbon copies of Chris and her sister. I know it sounds nuts," Marcus said. "Saying it out loud makes me think it's a crazy idea."

"Partners are rare, but there have been more than a few serial killer teams in the past. The two cousins in California come to mind."

Marcus heard a noise. He turned to find Chris perched on a stool. "Gives us something to think about. We'll talk more in the morning."

Jesus. She was stunning. Her blond hair had been tamed and pulled away from her face. Along with a cream-colored pair of slacks and a turquoise blouse, she wore skin-toned high heels. He forced his thoughts back to the phone call, wondering how much she'd heard.

"How's my dog?" Marcus asked.

"In heaven. He's on the floor with Holly and Kaycie. They're brushing him."

"Holly's there?"

"Yeah. She's thinking about moving back to town. She and Kay have been online looking at nursing colleges."

"She'd make a damn good one. Give her my love." Marcus hated not getting to see her. The fact she was even considering coming back to Dallas was a sign she was healing. "Diablo won't want to come home after she and Kay get finished with him."

"I'll warn them not to get too attached," Nate said.

"Works for me." Marcus disconnected and got to his feet. "Give me time to shower," he said to Chris. "We have reservations at seven."

He hustled his ass out of the room before she could ask questions. He'd been speculating with Nate. She hadn't stopped him, which he took as an indication that she hadn't heard his idea about dual killers. Nothing good would have come from scaring her any worse.

True to her word, Chris had sorted their purchases and placed his on the foot of the bed. Her things were nowhere to be seen. He grabbed his clothes and hit the shower. Within fifteen minutes, he'd shaved and dressed. Slipping on the jacket he'd bought to conceal his pistol, he opened the double doors.

His heart skipped a beat. She wasn't in the room. He'd left her alone for fifteen minutes, and she'd disappeared.

"Chris?"

"Yeah?" Her hand surfaced first, grasping the back of the small wet bar.

Marcus crossed the room and leaned over the counter. "What are you doing down there?"

"I dropped a cup." She tossed a piece of glass into the trash bin. "I'll ask housekeeping to get the rest."

Marcus offered his hands, and she took them both, allowing him to pull her to her feet. He had a choice to make. Drag her into his arms or step back. He released her and then quickly moved to the other side of the counter. It was best to keep some distance between them.

"I wouldn't go anywhere without you." Her eyes held questions. Like, why was he treating her as if she had the plague?

He shrugged. "I know. We'd better head to the restaurant."

Chris slipped the strap of her bulky purse over her shoulder. Marcus fought back a smile. He understood how naked he felt when he didn't have his Glock with him. She'd kept hers close by for a long time.

"You can leave that here."

She didn't speak or move for a few seconds. "I don't like not having my pistol with me."

"I've got you covered." He saw the question in her eyes. "Tell you what. Let me have your gun." He held up his hand to stop her from arguing. "We'll stop by the boutique in the lobby and pick up a purse that isn't so bulky."

The corners of Chris's mouth lifted. "Are you saying this handbag doesn't go with my outfit?"

Business be damned. He crossed to her and cupped her cheek in his hand. "I'm saying you're safe with me."

Her small hand covered his as she leaned into him. Her scent, her hair, her nearness sent blood rushing from his head.

"I believe that. You won't let anything happen to me. Will you?"

"No chance in hell." He leaned down and kissed her.

CHAPTER 15

Marcus gripped her lower back and lifted her onto her tiptoes. His lips were soft, yet strong, as his tongue swept into her mouth and painted erotic images with each stroke.

Her purse landed on the soft carpet with a thud. Her fingers trailed up his rock-hard chest to the back of his head.

He tasted of mint toothpaste. The subtle scent of his cologne drifted through her, turning on heat sources and sending fire licking through her blood. An alarm went off inside her head. If they didn't stop, they'd wind up naked and on the floor. Reluctantly, she slid her hands down to his chest and lightly pushed.

His gaze was dark, full of lust, and smoldering hot. He blinked once and then backed away, leaving her regretting her decision to end the kiss.

He ran the backs of his fingers down her cheek. "We'd better go," he said. His words were thick and husky.

"Yeah." She picked up her purse, removed the gun, and handed it to him.

So many emotions coursed through her. Matched only by the number of questions. What did this attraction mean? A fling for the duration? A growing, evolving relationship?

The ride down the elevator was silent. Both she and Marcus seemed to be lost in thought.

"Let's buy that purse," he said, guiding her into the boutique.

Chris sorted through the small evening bags, mentally fitting her pistol into each one. A small silver one looked perfect. "This will work."

Once they were in the hallway, Marcus pulled her in front of him and took her new purse. It was much heavier when he handed it back.

"Feel better?" His hand rested at the small of her back.

"I do. Thanks."

Dinner was quiet. Neither of them seemed to know what to say or how to act. Chris vacillated between ignoring the elephant in the room and initiating a conversation. After a delicious steak and two glasses of wine, she was much braver.

"Marcus, we need to—"

His cell, which he'd placed on the corner of the table, buzzed. An omen she should keep her mouth shut?

His eyebrows drew together. "It's Nate. Can't be anything good, because I just talked to him."

Marcus answered the call. "What's up?"

His eyes close briefly. The nerve in his jaw jumped as he listened. "I guess you're right. It could be a ploy to get us back to the office."

Chris's mind raced in different directions. He disconnected, his broad chest rose and fell in a big sigh, and then he picked up his drink. The glass looked small in his hand as he swirled the whiskey, watching it dance in a circle.

He lifted his gaze and met hers, sending a chill racing up her arms. The fact that a smile played at the corners of his lips made him even scarier.

"I'm afraid to ask." She ached to reach across the table and take his hand.

"Bastard blew up my car." Marcus's voice was calm, monotone. He might as well have been reading the phonebook.

"But Nate was driving your car." A knot formed in her heart. "Are they okay?"

"Yeah. Luckily, he left mine on the lot and drove his pickup home." Marcus lifted a shoulder in a way-too-casual manner. "It's not unusual for Nate and Kay to have both their vehicles at the office."

"None of you are safe. Not as long as you're helping me. What are we going to do?"

"We're going to sit right here and enjoy ourselves."

"How can you even suggest that?" He'd lost his mind. If that had been her car, she couldn't have turned off her anger so quickly.

"Nothing we can do about it tonight."

"But—" She pressed her fingers into her temple, trying to stem the brewing stress headache.

"My day will come. And when it does, that asshole will regret that he terrorized you and torched my house and car."

Chris folded her napkin and placed it on the table. "I'm exhausted. Are you ready to go upstairs?"

Their waiter appeared at Marcus's elbow with the bill. He signed for dinner and requested their appreciation for a great steak be delivered to the chef. Marcus walked around and held her chair for her.

"Don't forget your new purse." His voice and demeanor were so calm it unnerved her.

They rode up the elevator with a pleasant older couple who'd come in from Florida for their granddaughter's wedding. Marcus chatted casually with them until they reached their floor.

Nobody maintained their cool after losing their home and car. He'd barely closed the door to their suite when she whirled on him. "Who are you? Does nothing agitate you?"

The corners of his mouth lifted into that little half smile. "I get agitated."

Marcus advanced toward her as if he were a big cat stalking dinner. She braced herself for a lecture. He took her purse from her hand, set it on the table, and then moved further into her space. When her breasts almost brushed his chest, he stopped. His gaze, steamy and full of lust, locked on hers. Chris swallowed hard. God, she wanted him to touch her. More than any man she'd known, he stirred a desire in her, a deep aching need that only he could soothe.

"Some people get agitated over anything and everything. I like to pick and choose. On the other hand, I do get excited from time to time."

"Marcus," she growled. "If you're going to kiss—"

He slid his hands around her waist, fisted the back of her blouse, and then pulled her tight against his chest. "Oh, I'm going to kiss you all right."

He lowered his head. This wasn't the hard, take-no-prisoners kiss they'd shared before dinner. Instead, this was a slow and sensual awakening. He moved her head, angling for better coverage. His tongue swept inside her open and willing mouth. Chris relaxed into the growing need, the pulsing craving between her thighs. He tasted every inch of her mouth, while teasing her, encouraging her to join him.

Chris dissolved into his arms. Pent-up desire she'd held at bay exploded. She rose up on her tiptoes, buried her hands in his hair, and met his tongue, pulling it deeper into her mouth. The hard line of his erection pressed against her, sending moisture south in anticipation. Marcus kissed down the side of her face to her neck.

He lifted his head and pinned her with his gaze. "I want you. But the decision is yours." He seemed to be waiting for her answer. "Be sure this is a good idea." His gaze, deadly serious and clouded with lust, rested on her face. His desire was so honest. So gorgeous.

"It's not a good idea," she whispered. At the same time, she began unbuttoning her blouse. "It's a great idea."

His hand stilled hers at the second button. "No. That's my job."

Marcus worked quickly, and soon, her blouse hung open and loose on her shoulders. He ran his fingers up the lapels, barely grazing her skin, blistering their way to her collar and sending chills racing across her flesh. With a flick of his wrists, her top slid to the floor, leaving her bare except for a thin lace bra.

"Jesus, you are beautiful."

"You're staring." Heat rose up her chest and face from his approving reaction.

He lowered his head, kissing the skin just above the lace on both breasts before taking her nipple into his mouth. Chris's back bowed, offering her body to him. With one hand. he unhooked her bra and shoved it to the floor on top of her blouse.

"You're quite accomplished in that maneuver."

He lifted his head but never took his gaze off her naked breasts. "A guy learns that in his early years. It's a pity, because we're way too young to appreciate the gift beneath that slip of material."

His hands, strong yet gentle, skimmed across her body. She trembled, her nipples reacting to his touch, and a soft moan escaped. He cupped her swollen breasts as if they were china.

"I need to see more."

"But I'm the only one half-naked."

"I can fix that." He unbuttoned his shirt then tossed it aside.

She swept her hands up the hard, lean muscles of his arms and over to the hair sprinkled across his chest. She flexed her fingers against the shapes and contours of his body. She leaned over, took his nipple into her mouth, and sucked gently. He hissed, prompting her to be even more aggressive. She scraped her teeth over the tip.

"Enough." Marcus scooped her into his arms and carried her to the bed, setting her on the edge. He knelt in front of her and removed her shoes, slacks, and then panties. His gaze journeyed across her skin, blistering furnaces as they glided back to her face.

"Your turn." Chris reached for his belt.

Marcus caught her by the wrist, reached back, and removed his gun, setting it on the nightstand. He kicked off his boots, pants, and then underwear in record speed. He grabbed his wallet, fished out a condom, and then placed it on the nightstand.

It was her turn to stare. Naked, he was magnificent. He had broad shoulders and a narrow waist, and his hips framed an erection that sent her heart racing. The word "mine" raced through her thoughts. He lifted her to the middle of the bed.

"I could look at you forever." He sat next to her. His gaze slid across her body. "Does this make you uncomfortable? It shouldn't. Your body is perfect. You were made to be worshipped."

"It should, but it seems I have no shame with you. I can't be embarrassed when all I want is you inside me."

"Not yet." His fingers circled her ankles, skimming and then massaging her calf muscles. He continued up her thighs and stomach to her breasts, taking his time and occasionally leaning forward to nip her skin or trail his tongue over a curve.

Slowly, he lowered his head, took control of her lips. Hard and soft, his tongue slid in and out, pushing her, driving her until she writhed under him. He moved to her breasts and hungrily pulled one nipple into his mouth before moving to the other side, leaving her chilled at his absence. His hand slid down her body, fingertips deftly massaging her stomach, lingering to trace a pattern.

Every nerve in her body silently begged for more, for release, for this pleasure to never stop. Heat spiraled downward between her thighs. His hand found her wet and wanting as he inserted a finger, dipping it in and out.

"Finally," she moaned. She opened wider for him, baring herself and wanting more. Her hands raced over his body, lingered as his muscles quaked. Glorious, him touching her, her touching him. Her thoughts were of nothing but desire and need. The need to touch and be touched. The need to caress and be caressed. Every inch of her skin burned, as if on fire, and cried out for his attention.

"Watching your expression of pleasure could drive a guy over the edge."

She smiled. "You should be on the receiving side and feel what I do." She lifted her hips, offering herself to him.

"I'm happy right here for now." He moved down the bed and wedged his shoulders between her thighs. She rose up on her elbows and watched as his head moved lower down her body. Chris widened her legs, giving him free access to her most private parts. He worked his way past her navel, raining kisses as he went. She trembled. He was so near. So damn near her needy core.

While keeping his gaze locked on her face, Marcus spread her folds and kissed between her legs.

"More," Chris begged. She dropped her head back and relished the sensations. She was lost as his tongue, warm and probing, slipped inside. He took his time, increasing the pressure and pushing her to the verge of climax. Just as she thought she couldn't take anymore, he'd slow down and let her cool off.

His thumb and finger found her clit. He rubbed in a circle for a minute before pinching softly. The rumbling started way down deep inside her. Gathering steam, rolling and getting larger, until all she could do was plead with him not to stop. She dug her hands into the bedcovers and held on for fear she'd fly off the bed when her orgasm hit. Her body quaked and trembled as stars exploded behind her eyes. Marcus didn't let up. He pushed his tongue deep inside, drawing out every last drop of her climax. He leaned forward and kissed her, mingling her juices with the taste that was uniquely Marcus.

"I need to feel you inside me." Her hand dropped to his burgeoning erection.

He slid to the edge of the bed. The muscles in his back rippled as he rolled away to cover himself. Then he was above her, kissing her again. Hard and soft. Deep and long. Reawakening her desire. His erection pressed at her entrance, and he breeched her slowly.

"You feel so good around me," he whispered.

A piece of her heart shifted as if a section now belonged to him. He moved her with his unselfish giving, but she couldn't allow herself to hope for more than what they had now. She'd lost a lot in the past few years, but losing him would be the worst.

****

Marcus buried himself deep in Chris's warm and welcoming body. He stopped for a second to let her adjust to his size, then he lifted her legs and hooked them over his forearms. Slowly, he slid out until just the tip of his erection was inside her. Damn, he wanted to slam home and pound into her until nothing existed except the two of them, but he held back. This would be nice and easy until he could bring her to the edge with him, and she surrendered everything.

She lifted her hips, pulling him deeper. Again, he pressed deep inside her body and again, he withdrew. Next time, he went a little deeper. Good Lord, she was tight, hot and wet, ready to take him all the way inside. He thrust once, seating himself all the way in. Her eyes flashed wide, and she smiled.

"So good," he whispered into her lips.

Her fingernails dug into his ass. "Marcus, I'm not going to break. Make love to me."

"My pleasure."

They moved in unison, quickly reaching a rhythm as if they'd been intimate many times. Her hands clutched his shoulders, and she met him thrust for thrust.

He increased his speed, pumping in and out, faster and faster. His climax roared to the point of explosion, but he tamped it back and concentrated on her orgasm. Her long fall of hair had spread across the pillow, so he tried counting the different shades of blond. He reached between them and massaged her clit.

"Marcus," she cried.

"I'm right here." He aimed for that spot that would give her the most pleasure. A tidal wave had headed to the surface, gaining strength until he fought his orgasm with each stroke. Her eyes fluttered closed.

"Look at me, baby," he said. Her eyes opened, and she locked on to his gaze. The passion on her beautiful face pushed him close to the end. "Come with me."

He sped up his movements. Faster. Harder. He pounded into her, pulling her climax to the surface. "Come for me. With me." Urging her on, he lowered her legs, and then slid his hands under her hips. Lifting her, he continued to thrust.

"Oh, God," she moaned.

Her inner muscles contracted. Her eyes fluttered and then closed. Witnessing the look of ecstasy on her face, he lost it. While he was buried deep inside her, his spine stiffened for a split second, and then he exploded. Saying her name, he emptied himself to the rhythm of her tremors.

Sweaty but satiated, neither spoke for a few minutes. A dull ache started in his heart the second he rolled away to dispose of the condom. He turned back to her and propped himself up on his elbow. He leaned over and kissed her. Her lips were so very soft and swollen from his kisses.

"Hair mussed, lipstick gone, and sleepy-eyed, you're the most beautiful woman I've ever seen."

"Thank you." She smiled and stifled a yawn. "For everything."

"Can you reach the light?"

"I can." She turned off the bedside lamp, rolled over, and nestled her head on his chest. The darkness was a good thing. No way could he explain the silly grin on his face.

"You're beautiful, too," she whispered.

"No more sex for you. It makes you delirious," Marcus said on a chuckle. "You'd better get some rest."

"Not delirious," she said behind a yawn.

Marcus lay in the darkness and tried to analyze why he'd let this happen. Did he want this thing between him and Chris to be real? Could he leave the past buried and start again? In his line of work, he couldn't even guarantee he'd come home at night. Sex with Chris would have to be a short-lived affair, nothing more. Besides, there'd be no reason for her to stick around once the killer was behind bars.

Chris shifted and pushed hair off her face. Her breathing said she was still awake.

"You're thinking too much." He smoothed his hand up and down her spine. "Stop trying to analyze what just happened."

"You don't know what I was thinking," she said.

"I can guess. And you're wrong. I don't regret making love with you," Marcus said, surprising himself by saying it out loud. In fact, he felt good.

"Neither do I."

"Then what's got your neck and back tied in knots?" He walked his fingers down her tense muscles, while he waited and wondered if she'd tell him.

"When you spoke to Nate earlier, you sent someone named Holly your love. Who is she?"

Marcus smiled to himself at Chris's question. A long time had passed since anybody had been the least bit possessive of him. Somebody caring felt damn good. "Are you jealous?"

She lifted her head, propping up on her elbow. "I'm sorry. I had no right to ask."

The overhead light in the outer room cast a shadow across their bed, but the embarrassment in her eyes was easy to see. He cupped her cheek, pulled her back onto his chest, and then kissed the top of her head. "Hey. I'm flattered. I don't mind you asking. I'll tell you anything you want."

She popped back up on her elbow. "Really? Mr. I Play My Cards Close to the Vest is willing to answer any question?"

He leaned up and kissed her. Damn, she tasted sweet. So he kissed her again. This time she joined in, making it difficult for him to remember the question.

Chris broke the kiss, then went back to her position on her elbow. "Is she an old girlfriend?"

"No. But I do love her. Holly Hoffman used to be a close friend of Kay's. Now, she's more of a family member to all of us at Lost and Found. Holly was our first rescue as a team. We didn't get to her in time to keep her from getting abused and beaten."

"Is she okay now?"

"She's dealing. The whole thing traumatized the hell out of her. I think she quit her job and moved to Hill Top because being around us served as a constant reminder of everything she went through. She's the assistant librarian at the Hill County Library and teaches night classes in English as a second language. Nate was telling me she's moving back to Dallas. She's apparently looking into becoming a nurse."

"I'll bet Kay missed their friendship."

"Yeah. It's all good between them now. Holly was working for Child Protective Services with Kay when she uncovered a human-trafficking ring. The bastards tried to kidnap Kay a couple of times. They failed, so they took Holly and offered to swap her for evidence. She took some rough treatment before we got to her."

Marcus went on to explain that their college friend, Jake Donovan, who they'd thought had been killed in Afghanistan, had turned out to be alive and working for the criminals. A tumor on Jake's brain had robbed him of his memory, and his boss had given him the name Johnny Darling. "Holly touched something inside Jake, restoring at least part of his humanity. He kept her from being raped and killed."

"She must be quite a woman to have survived such an ordeal. Her story makes me feel like a whiner."

The compassion in Chris's voice touched a place deep in Marcus's soul. He picked up a long blond curl off her shoulder and wrapped the silky threads around his finger. "You're one of the strongest, bravest women I've ever known. You haven't whined one time."

"You're being kind. Learning your friend Jake was alive had to have been a shock."

"For sure. His helicopter had been shot down, and we'd heard everyone on board had died. But he'd been flown to a military hospital where they patched up his injuries, but also found a growth on his brain. He was delusional, convinced the doctors were going to kill him, and so he ran. After he was arrested, the military took him back to the hospital, where they removed the tumor. Kay says he'll be released soon. We'll make sure he has a place to go and people to care for him."

"You really are a tight-knit group," Chris said softly. Her words were slurred and thick with sleep.

"We go way back. But we're not an exclusive club. There's always room for more." He'd almost added her specifically, but he'd caught himself. Instead, he buried his face in her hair, breathing in the scent of her shampoo.

He'd been right when he'd told her an affair would end badly. Right now, she was in need of that white knight on his fiery steed to protect her. He wasn't a knight, but he'd die trying to keep her safe. The two of them came from different worlds. She might not know it now, but when the case ended and she could think straighter, she'd go back to her affluent lifestyle. That's how it should be, and he was fine with that. Or he would be.

****

Marcus stood in the doorway, holding two cups of steaming coffee. Damn, he hated to wake her. Naked as the day she was born, she'd pulled up the sheet and covered her luscious breasts. Her beauty and strength were proof enough there was a god.

She rolled his direction. Opened her eyes. Her gaze strolled down his torso and back up, reminding him that he wore nothing but a towel.

"Good morning. Is one of those for me?"

"Sure thing." He sat next to her on the bed and handed her a coffee. He shifted his weight and then adjusted his towel, as it was dangerously close to falling off.

"Thank you." She held the cup under her nose, breathing deeply.

"My pleasure." He made an effort not to stare at her bare shoulders, opting to let her drink her coffee.

Much to his disappointment, she pushed herself up, taking the sheet with her, and adding his pillow behind her head. "You're awake early. What have you been doing?"

"Showered and shaved, but mostly I watched you. You're beautiful when you're asleep, almost angelic." She hadn't been an angel during their lovemaking. In fact, she'd surprised him by being aggressive, so he added, "Unlike last night."

Her eyes widened. One hand grabbed the sheet and pulled it under chin. She grinned mischievously, and her cheeks flushed. "Oh. Right. Last night."

Marcus set his cup on the nightstand and moved closer to her. He tugged the sheet from her grip and pulled the cover back, stopping at the edges of her nipples.

"I'll be damned. You do blush all over."

"An affliction I wish I could control. I hate blushing so easily." The soft skin at the top of her breasts colored as she spoke.

"I wondered how far it went."

"So that's what last night was all about. A fact-finding expedition?"

"Exactly. Since we have a few hours, I have a few more places I want to explore." She was so beautiful that he had to touch her. He swept her hair across the pillow, fanning it out with his fingers.

"It seems we have a lot of ground to cover." She tugged his towel loose and jumped out of bed. "You had your shower. Now I want mine."

She took off at a run to the bathroom with him right behind. He stopped directly behind her at the glass shower door, slid his hands around, and took her breasts in his hands. She reached back, grasped his butt cheeks and tugged him closer, pushing his erection into her flesh.

"That's a strong grip you have." He rolled her nipples with his fingertips. They pebbled, growing hard under his touch. Her body reacted perfectly every time.

"Hmm." She moaned, reaching in to turn on the water.

His phone chirped from the other room. "Not answering it."

"Good." She stepped inside. She raised one eyebrow, pushed her hair back over her shoulders, and extended her hand. "You coming?"

He chuckled at the double entendre. "I'll make sure that I don't too soon."

He stepped under the warm spray and took her in his arms. Looking up at him with mischief in her eyes, she was the very definition of sex. How had he gotten lucky enough to be in the shower with the most beautiful woman he'd ever seen?

Chris slowly sank to her knees, dropping kisses on the way down. She wrapped her hand around his erection, stroking back and forth, before taking him into her mouth. She braced one hand on his thigh for balance as she pulled him deeper, her tongue making circles around him. He'd just told her he wouldn't come too soon, but much more and he'd explode. Jesus, he hated to stop her.

"You better stand up." He caught her under the arms, pulled her to her feet, and then turned her back to him. "Hand me the soap."

He lathered his hands and started with her shoulders, rubbing and massaging down each arm and back up. Slowly, he soaped every inch of her, enjoying the sighs as he washed her breasts, belly, and between her legs. He kneaded, stroked, and smoothed her body, committing her soft skin to memory. The delicate curves and valleys of her body molded perfectly with his. The only word that came to mind was perfection.

He hated to release her, but it took two hands to get the top off the small bottle of shampoo. Burying his fingers in her hair, he scrubbed her scalp. Her sultry moans were almost more than he could take.

"Turn around. Let's rinse your hair."

She moved slowly, smiling up at him. "Thank you," she whispered, leaning her head back under the running water. "Much more of this, and you'll have to carry me back to bed."

"I'm happy to oblige."

CHAPTER 16

Chris had never been so pampered. Never been ministered to with the tenderness Marcus was showing. Never been so insanely turned on.

She finished rinsing her hair, stood on her tiptoes, and then kissed him. Deep and hard, she delivered the message. "Make love to me."

One corner of his mouth lifted. "I thought you'd never ask."

Marcus held her hand as she stepped onto the rug by the shower. He slid a soft terrycloth towel over her body. She closed her eyes and let him take control. As he dried her, he trailed soft kisses on her skin. He circled her nipple with his tongue, and she buried her hands in his wet hair, holding his head in place. "More," she whispered.

His cell phone rang again. "Damn it."

"You better answer it." She pushed his shoulder, indicating he should go.

"Don't start without me." He wrapped the towel around his hips, walked to the table next to the bed, and then picked up his cell. Frustration clouded his face. "It's Nate. I should take the call."

Chris nodded, knowing their time alone had ended. Reality had reared its ugly head. She gathered her clothes and returned to the bathroom. She slipped on her new linen slacks, a short-sleeve blouse, and then went to work on her hair. The hotel dryer and her brand new brush were different from the ones she had at home, but she was thankful to have them. For the first time in days, she didn't look like she'd stuck her finger in a light socket. A swipe of lipstick, a little mascara, and her new flats had her ready for the day.

Marcus was still on the phone, speaking so softly she couldn't understand what he said. He'd slipped on his jeans and stood with his back to her, looking out over the city.

He turned toward her, and her heart jumped into her throat. His eyes flashed cold, sending her stomach plummeting. When he saw her, his expression mellowed too late. The reality check had been received. She got it. Marcus had returned to work. It was his job to keep her alive, and it was time they got busy finding the killer.

Chris crossed to him. God, she wanted to wrap her arms around his waist. She refrained, not knowing how he'd react now that their personal time was over. Instead, she rubbed the heel of her hand over her chest, hoping to ease the dull ache in her heart.

"We'll meet you at the office." Marcus disconnected and shoved the cell into his pocket.

"What happened?"

"The bastard left a message for us on the office phone. Kay found it when she and Nate opened this morning."

"More signs of aggression."

"Yeah. They're becoming more frequent. We'll give Kay back her car, and then I'll call that rental place that brings your ride to you."

A loud knock sent Chris reaching for her purse. It surprised her that she'd completely forgotten her gun, because for a long time, it had never been far away. Her fingers wrapped around the grip, its cool handle giving her comfort.

"I ordered breakfast. It's room service." Marcus checked the peephole, opened the door, and directed the young man to put the tray on the bar. He signed the check and locked up after the guy left. "Come eat before these eggs get any colder."

"I'm not sure I can keep food down."

He uncovered the plates, filling the room with the scent of bacon. Chris's stomach rolled, but he extended his hand, and she couldn't refuse. She joined him and perched on a barstool.

"You strike me as an orange juice kind of girl." He set a glass in front of her. "Am I right?"

"Yes." She took a bite of toast, and it tasted surprisingly good. So she took another. And another. Pausing to take a drink of juice, she discovered her plate was almost empty.

"Good thing you weren't hungry." Humor danced at the corners of his sensuous mouth.

"You're humoring me. What did the guy say in the phone message that made you angry?"

"I was trying not to worry you, at least not until you'd had a chance to eat." Marcus leaned back in his chair. "The call came in around midnight. Nate said the guy was either drunk, stoned, or so pissed he couldn't talk straight."

"What did he say?" She sighed, and he instantly picked up on her impatience.

"His message was that people who break promises deserve to suffer and then die."

"Promises?"

"Whether real or perceived, he believes you've broken one."

"What about the women he's killed? Did they break a promise, too?"

"I think we need to separate you and your sister's case from the other victims. We have no idea if they'd been stalked, but he's damn sure stalking you. Maybe he stalked Chelsea, too. Nate and Kay will locate some of her friends. They'll ask different questions than the police did during their investigation."

Marcus's words were like a bucket of cold water thrown in her face. "You really believe he's someone we know."

"It's one possibility. If we operate under that assumption, we try to figure out where you came in contact with him."

"How do we do that?"

"We dig into your past."

"That's already been done."

"We'll redo it and dig deeper. If necessary, we'll go all the way back to the time you were in an orphanage."

His logic escaped her. Chris couldn't think that opening those files could help. Still, if he wanted to take a look, there was nothing in there to hide.

"I was seven. How could this be remotely related to back then?"

"I understand. It's like trying to catch smoke. What have we got to lose?"

"Nothing. Texas adoption records are sealed, but since my parents and biological mother are dead, there shouldn't be a problem getting the court to release them. I can call the law firm my dad used."

"That's okay. We've got one we use."

"Then I'd like to go listen to the entire message." Not waiting for his answer, she rose and went to the bedroom.

In the bottom of the closet sat the suitcases. She understood why Marcus had bought two. Inevitably, they'd go their separate ways. This way there'd be no sorting or dividing. They'd each just grab their bag and go. That thought wrapped a blanket of sadness around her shoulders. Had she fooled around and become attached to a man she'd known only a few days? So they'd made love. She had to remember that this was nothing more than two people who were sexually attracted to each other.

Chris quickly folded her belongings, filling maybe half the suitcase. She scooped the toiletries into her arms and dumped them next to her new pair of tennis shoes. If she could keep it together until they checked out, she'd be fine. It was just the next few minutes that she had to pretend nothing more than sex had happened between them.

"Chris," Marcus said, using that husky tone.

If he was expecting female theatrics, he was in for a surprise.

"I'm ready when you are." She popped the handle up and pulled her belongings past him. "I'll wait in here."

His hand shot out, catching her and spinning her around.

"Chris," he said again.

She really needed him to stop saying her name that way. "Don't give me the speech. Okay? I'm a big girl. We had a good time, but now it's time for Alice to leave Wonderland."

He tilted his head and stared at her. "You call it whatever you want. Truth is, a lot more happened here than a 'good' time."

Before she could react, he jerked her against his chest, cupped the back of her head, and covered her lips with his. She sighed and leaned into him. Hard and unrelenting, he ravaged her mouth with his tongue. Chris's knees wobbled, and she surrendered, matching his passion with a strength she hadn't known she had.

His hands moved to her shoulders, and he stepped back, separating them. Dark, stormy, brown eyes pinned her in place. She should walk away, but try as she might, her feet would not respond.

"If it wasn't important that we get moving, I'd—"

She stopped him by placing her fingers on his lips. "You're right. We have work to do." She prayed her rubbery legs would hold up as she shouldered her purse and walked to the door.

****

DaVinci turned his head away from the brain-piercing bright light. That simple movement set off explosions inside his brain. Maybe he'd keep his eyes closed and go back to sleep.

A stench assaulted his senses and made lying dormant impossible. Now that he was awake, he not only needed to take a leak, he had to figure out what smelled so horrible.

He forced his eyes open, moaning at the sensation of dragging his eyelids across sandpaper. Last night slowly came into focus. At least part of it. He remembered the owner of the restaurant insisting he and Michelangelo take a cab home. God, it hurt to move. How much wine had they consumed after they'd returned to his place? Had he and his mentor actually gone out again?

Fuck! He'd called that private dick's number. What had he said? Between the liquor and anger, he was sure he'd gone off the deep end. He sucked in a breath and sat up on the side of the bed. His mouth opened, but no sound came out. A scream gurgled in the back of his throat. His knuckles were raw and swollen. The skin was actually busted open. His hands, shirt, and pants were covered in dried blood. A quick scan determined it wasn't his, so where'd it come from? Whose was it?

He had no memory of killing anyone. Think. They'd drank a little more, but the rest was a blank. He forced himself to his feet and stumbled to the bathroom, passing on the way his six-hundred-dollar shoes that were spattered with blood. He flushed the toilet, stripped off the filthy clothes, and then crawled into the shower. Pain shot from his fingers as he held them under the warm water. He gagged at the sight of red swirling around his feet.

He had to remember. Had he killed someone? Had Michelangelo been with him? Many times they'd talked about working together again, but had never actually done it.

Too many unanswered questions rattled around in his aching head. After he'd carefully cleaned the shower, he dried off, dressed and went to the kitchen. Once a cup of coffee was brewing, he located his cell and dialed his friend.

"It's too early to talk," Michelangelo mumbled.

"Wake up. This is important. Besides, it's almost noon."

"Shit. I have things to do. I'll call you later."

"No," DaVinci insisted. "Why did I wake up covered in blood? What happened?"

A muffled laugh sent shivers up his spine. "You don't remember. Do you?"

"No. I tried, but it won't come."

"It will. Relax. We had great fun."

"Who was she?"

"A hooker we picked up off a street corner."

DaVinci's knees gave way, and he slid down the wall. "Where is she?"

"Sleazy motel down on Trellet Avenue. Shitty, roach-infested dump where she had a working arrangement with the manager."

"You should have stopped me." Panic had moved into the driver's seat, allowing his imagination to run wild.

"Stop you? I wasn't about to interrupt you. I thought we'd do her together, but you were out of control. My biggest disappointment was I didn't get to fuck her."

"What? We never sexually touched any of those whores."

"People change. I discovered many ways to use sex as a punishment. You should try it."

"The very idea is repulsive."

"You don't know what you're missing. Taking them by force is almost as much fun as killing them. I never thought of you as gay, but if you are, you should have said something. I don't care one way or the other."

Darkness circled DaVinci. He gripped the top of the breakfast bar as his vision faded until he saw only a faint light. Memories of his youth pulled him toward madness. Images of being held down and violated flipped through his brain in slide-show fashion. The pain of being beaten into submission and forced to do unspeakable things sent scalding hot tears flowing down his cheeks. He stopped himself right before he slipped into the abyss.

"Hello? Did we get disconnected?"

"I'm here." He found it difficult to speak. The question had almost silenced him. In all their time together, sexual orientation had never come up. In fact, he'd been leery of Michelangelo when they'd first met. More men than women had hit on him when he'd lived on the streets. That he'd had to submit to them to have money to eat still made him sick to his stomach. "No. I'm not gay. But never in a million years would I have sex with one of those filthy creatures."

"Well," Michelangelo said with a chuckle. "That explains why you flipped out on me when I suggested we get naked and have a three-way. You kicked her to the floor and started pounding with your fists. If I hadn't given you my knife, you'd have beaten her to death."

"You should have stopped me." DaVinci stared at the proof. His knuckles, part of his most-precious hands, looked as if he'd put them through a meat grinder.

"I see no need for you to be upset." Michelangelo hissed out the words. "I guess you don't want to hear that you referred to the whore as Christine while you were pummeling her face."

"No," he moaned.

"Oh, yes. Her mother wouldn't recognize her."

"We are so fucked. My DNA is everywhere on her. What if somebody spotted me walking into this building with bloody hands?" He was screeching, out of control, and completely unable to calm himself.

"Now you're insulting me. I took care of everything before we left. Unfortunately, I didn't think to take a picture before I put her on the bed and set fire to the mattress. And it was late when we got to your place. Nobody saw you."

"What about the security cameras?"

"I've taken care of that. They were out of commission for a few hours last night."

"You paid somebody, but that person saw the tapes."

"And he's dead."

A chill raced across DaVinci's back. Just how many people did Michelangelo have on his payroll? "This could ruin everything." He shouldn't have called Christine yesterday. Shouldn't have let that private detective get under his skin. Shouldn't have made the second call... DaVinci dropped his head in his hands. Had he? Or had he dreamed it?

"I just told you, we have nothing to worry about. I have an appointment in Fort Worth, but we'll meet later today. Over coffee," he said, with an emphasis on the word coffee.

"Fine." DaVinci had no argument left in him. All he wanted to do was crawl back to bed and forget how stupid he'd been last night.

"I have people on my payroll who, for a price, will do anything I ask. You and I will work out an acceptable plan that allows you to deal with your Christine. Whatever you have planned, forget it. I have the perfect place for you to take her."

"Fine. But first I've got to destroy these clothes."

"Cut them to shreds, soak them in bleach, and then pack them in small trash bags. Casually toss them in dozens of dumpsters. Hit the far corners of the city. Oh, remove the buttons."

"Dallas is a big town. Maybe I'll burn them."

Michelangelo's sigh was audible even over the phone. "And where will you do that without drawing attention? Pull yourself together. More than your feelings are at stake here. You fuck up, and we'll be on death row together."

"I need sleep. Food and water. Maybe then I can think better."

"Then go to bed. I'll call you when I get back from Fort Worth."

DaVinci stayed on the floor, propped against the wall. He hadn't told his mentor about the call to the detective agency. Had he dreamed leaving Christine a message? Had he revealed too much?

CHAPTER 17

During the drive back to the office, Marcus fished around in his head for something to say to Chris. She was confused. Hell, he was confused as to where their relationship was going or if it would go anywhere. Regardless, he felt compelled to salvage the situation. Try as he might, the right words just would not come. Crap, he hadn't been this tongue-tied in grade school.

Truth was, he'd taken advantage of her at a vulnerable point in her life. For the life of him, he couldn't make himself feel bad about it. She'd felt right in his arms, and he'd felt right inside her body. That in itself was a miracle. It had been years since sex had meant more than just release.

None of those thoughts could be shared with her.

So he refocused on her stalker. He asked for more information about her past, and she answered questions without hesitation. She'd lived a fairly reserved life. No bad or nasty breakups that might have left some guy wanting revenge. That fact didn't surprise him. Chris had been through hell, yet she was a warm, caring person. Being abandoned by her birth mother must have really hurt.

Someday she'd find a nice guy, marry, and devote her life to making sure her kids felt loved. For some reason, that thought was unsettling.

So far, she hadn't remembered anything that established a link to her stalker or her sister's killer. They'd keep digging. The reason was there. He just had to find it. Soon.

He drove into the parking lot at Lost and Found, stopping a few slots behind the charred area on the concrete that showed where his car had burned.

"I'm sorry." Chris sighed and shook her head. "I've told you that a lot in the past few days."

"The car can be replaced. I don't want you to worry about it." He did his best to sound reassuring, although he didn't think she'd buy in. "Stop saying it. Okay?"

"But you've lost so much because of me. Someday you'll resent me for it."

"Never happen."

"I hope not but wouldn't blame you."

He linked her fingers with his. The warmth of her touch and the cold, barren parking spot where his car had been parked sent a revelation to his heart that stunned him. Now if he could verbalize his feelings without sounding like a fool.

"You made me realize that things mean nothing. It's the people in your life, the ones you truly care about, they're what's important." A small smile and a sparkle in her eyes said she understood. He'd hung on to the past way too long.

"Thank you for telling me."

A hand pecked on the windshield, drawing his attention, and Kay's face appeared. Chris laughed a tight, nervous chuckle. "We have company."

"You guys coming in?" Kay asked. "I have a surprise."

Chris released his hand so fast his skin chilled without her touch. He'd probably said too much, which, until he'd met her, was out of character for him. He'd just have to ride this out with her and see where it went. If after the case ended, she returned to her old life, so be it. For now, he'd concentrate on keeping that sparkle in her eyes.

Marcus and Chris joined Kay, whose face was glowing like a kid with a gift card in a toy store. She linked her arms with theirs, wedging herself between them.

"You gonna tell us?" Marcus asked.

"Not yet." Kay smiled up at him. "I'm going next door to pick up sandwiches. Be right back."

Nate waited at the door. Marcus met him with an arched eyebrow. "Thanks for coming back last night and dealing with the cops and firefighters."

"I like having you owe me." Nate clapped his hand on Marcus's back. "You still have to call your insurance agent and go by the police station to fill out some paperwork."

Marcus looked around for Diablo. He was usually the first to greet him. "I'll do that later. Where's my dog?"

"Come on. My surprise is playing with him," Kay said, motioning for them to follow. Chris and Marcus followed.

The hair on the back of Marcus's neck stood up. The words *sientate* and *perro bueno* sent him barreling around the corner.

"Stop speaking Spanish to him," Marcus snapped.

Holly turned her head to face him.

"Diablo. Come. Heel," Marcus commanded, standing rigid until the dog obeyed. He leaned down and ruffled the animal's scruff. "Good boy."

"What did I do wrong?" Holly's mouth hung open, her eyes wide as she sat on the floor. "I told him to sit and then said good boy."

Instantly, Marcus felt like a dick for snapping at her. "I'm sorry. Just do me a favor. Only speak English to him. Forgive me?" He opened his arms, and she hurried into a hug.

"Always." As always, Holly was quick to forgive.

Chris caught his gaze then shifted from him to Holly. "You must be Holly Hoffman."

"And you're Chris Holland." Holly disengaged from him and shook Chris's hand.

"I've heard good things about you," Chris said.

"You can't believe everything Marcus tells you." Holly looked up at him. "Why is he an English-only dog? If he grew up in Colombia, it stands to reason he'd know the language."

"He was trained to respond to Spanish commands. The problem is that his specialty was to attack and kill. I've worked hard to make him forget those lessons."

"I'm sorry. I only said a couple of words to him." Holly held her hand out and let Diablo lick her fingers. "He's a beautiful dog."

"He really loves you women." Diablo wasn't a natural-born killer. He'd been trained to react to a command. Marcus would not let him down. He'd work until the last remnant of Colombia was gone from his memory. Diablo could never be allowed to revert.

Marcus wanted to hear the phone message from the killer before they played it for Chris. Instead, to keep from hurting Holly's feelings again, he stayed for a while. Not that anyone would've noticed him leaving. She chatted easily with Chris, telling her how Kay referred to Nate, Ty, Marcus, and Jake as her men or the Wolfe's Pack.

As Holly talked, Marcus caught a glimpse of the quick-witted and sharp-tongued woman who never used to let her diminutive stature slow her down. He was seeing signs that the old Holly was returning. One day soon, maybe, she'd shed the short brown pixie hairstyle and revert to her more flamboyant look of the past. She'd been such an original, always coordinating her outfit with a matching streak of color.

"Let's talk," he said to Nate, giving Diablo the hand signal to follow. Marcus stopped at his desk, grabbed the briefcase with the FBI files, and joined Nate in the conference room.

Nate closed the door behind them, turned a chair around backward, and then sat. Marcus walked to the opposite side of the table, motioning for the dog to follow.

"Down." When his command was followed, he added, "Stay." He patted Diablo on the head. "Good dog." Marcus pulled the desk phone to the center of the table. "You listened to the entire message last night?"

"Yeah. The bastard rambled on about how important promises were no matter how old you were. He repeated himself. Emphasizing that even if you were a kid you never broke your word."

"I have no doubt the son of a bitch is crazy. He's talking about kid promises. He proved my theory. He's someone from Chris's past."

"A vendetta or payback."

"Yeah," Marcus said. "If you're like me, you're thinking the fact her entire family is dead is worth looking at. We should look at the cause of death for her birth mother and her adopted parents' deaths. Were they accidents or natural causes? What if the killer has been working his way through relatives on his way to Chris for years?"

Nate's expression gave nothing away. Whether he agreed or not Marcus had to press forward. He opened the case and removed the files. "Dalton offered to help," Marcus said. "With his connections, he can get details on Chris's family."

Nate nodded. "We can't forget the other victims."

"I want to pursue my two-killer theory. Chris walked in during our phone call, and I couldn't continue."

"I figured," Nate said.

"We can start with the medical examiners' reports. Some of the women had been raped. But not the blondes."

Nate scanned the files for a few minutes. "You're right so far. None of the blondes showed signs of penetration, while the other women had evidence of violent vaginal abuse."

"More reason to think I'm right about two different killers."

Nate nodded. "I don't disagree. In fact, you may have hit on something big."

"We'll have to convince Dalton."

"I don't think that will be hard to do." Nate leaned back in his chair. "Two men working together but separate."

"We'll have the answer when we figure out why the killer didn't have sex with the blondes before he killed them." Marcus kept an eye out for Chris. All he had was speculation. For now, he'd wait until he had better news to tell her.

"This is a major break," Nate said. "Odd how the rape angle went unnoticed."

Marcus was pleased Nate agreed, but he wanted to hear the killer's message before Chris joined them. "Let's listen to last night's voice mail."

Nate punched in a number. For the next few minutes, they listened to a male voice ramble. His words were slurred, and often, he couldn't be understood. The gist of the message was clear. It was time for Chris to die. That no matter how old you were, promises had to be kept. Then a couple of words were too garbled to understand. Those two words had been followed by a maniacal laugh. Followed by a drunken belch.

Nate played the message a couple of times. Marcus jotted down any intelligible words. Movement caught his eye a second before Chris tapped on the glass door. Her eyebrows rose, questioning if she could join them.

He nodded but spoke to Nate. "She doesn't need to hear this crazy motherfucker puke up his threats."

Nate clicked off the machine.

Chris opened the door but didn't enter. "Kay's back with sandwiches. If you're ready to eat, we'll bring them in."

"Oh, hell yes," Nate said, scooping the files up and placing them back in the briefcase. "I'm starving."

Diablo's head had been resting on Marcus's foot. The minute food was brought in, the dog lifted his head and sniffed the air. Marcus leaned down and rubbed his ears. "I'm guessing he's not interested in a bowl of dog food."

"Of course he's not." Kay put a couple of sacks on the table. "I bought him a turkey on white bread, no lettuce or tomatoes."

Marcus groaned. "It's going to take me forever to wean him off human food."

Chris set four bottles of water on the table, joining Kay, who'd sat opposite him. "Where's Holly?" Nate asked.

"She had to get to work by one," Kay said. "I think she really came by to check on news about Jake."

Nate stopped salting his sub. "I'm not sure her getting involved with him is such a good idea."

"It's not like we have a say one way or the other," Marcus said, unwrapping Diablo's sandwich. "Think she's serious about a nursing career?"

"Yeah, I do. She sounded enthusiastic." Kay opened her husband's bottle of water and passed it to him.

Marcus held the sandwich down for Diablo. "Here you go, boy." The dog clamped down on the food without touching Marcus's fingers. Brown eyes never left his master's face. Marcus knew what he wanted. "It's okay."

Chris smiled as the dog padded out of sight and into a corner in the back. "Is your friend Jake coming home soon?"

"He's scheduled to be dismissed from the hospital in a couple of weeks. He had to square things with the military and the law." Kay went into detail for Chris, explaining the surgery had been a life-or-death event and that Jake had lost a chunk of his memory. "It's possible he'll regain the missing pieces. Nobody can say for sure."

"Otherwise, he's back to his old self?" Chris asked.

"He's older than his years, battle-worn, but inside, he's still one of us," Kay said with a proud tinge to her tone.

"The friend you mentioned last night?" Chris glanced at Marcus, who smiled and nodded.

"You got Marcus to open up enough to talk about the past?" Kay's eyes lit up.

Marcus's shoulder muscles tightened. He narrowed his eyes and glared at her, trying to warn her off. If she got the message not to play matchmaker, it didn't show in her expression.

"I wouldn't say he opened up." Chris shifted in her chair uncomfortably. "More like I pestered it out of him."

Nate cleared his throat. "Let's work through lunch. Okay?"

Kay grinned at her husband. "Y'all do that. I'll take my lunch to my desk."

"You don't have to leave," Marcus said.

"But I do. You two need a safe place to stay tonight."

"No more fancy hotels. Find somewhere that's isolated and easy to defend."

"You got it." Kay stopped in the doorway and gave Marcus a thumbs-up.

"Wait," Chris said. "How long can we keep this up?"

"Until you're safe," Nate said. "Right, Marcus?"

"Yep." Marcus had to try to talk Chris out of listening to the recording. "Before you listen to the phone message, I think I figured out some things that were missed."

Diablo trotted into the room. He stopped and scanned the room, no doubt looking for an easy mark. Chris held up her half-eaten sandwich. "Can Diablo have this?"

"Yeah." Diablo, having heard his name, looked up at Marcus. "Go see Chris."

She pulled the lettuce and tomato off then held the sandwich down for the dog. "Okay. Tell us what we missed," she said.

"I think we're dealing with two serial killers. Only one of them is fixated on you."

"Two? You found proof of two?"

"No. It's a hunch." There was no use keeping anything from her. "None of the blondes was raped. The other women were brutally assaulted. It's either two different men or one with a split personality. It's possible the blondes were facsimiles of you or Chelsea."

"Now I'm sure Dalton should dig into your past," Nate said.

"I told you to go ahead," she said. "There's nothing there."

Marcus hated to ask his next question. "An autopsy was performed on your parents. Right?"

"Not both. My father's body was in pretty bad shape when his car was found. His death was ruled accidental. My mother was autopsied, which I didn't understand since the empty pill bottle was found in her hand. Her death was ruled a suicide." Chris's eyebrows drew together. "What difference does it make? Why do you need to know?"

A band tightened around Marcus's chest. Damn, he hated to put her through this query. If he was right, it was just the beginning. "I'm sorry to dredge up hurtful memories. What if your parents' deaths weren't accidents?"

CHAPTER 18

Chris tried to formulate a response. She waffled between wondering if she'd heard Marcus correctly and telling him his question was ludicrous. A deep ache settled in her chest, cold as ice and heavy as a boulder. The pain was too much to deal with, so she took a defensive attitude.

"The problem with that theory is that my parents had no enemies. They were active in the church and community and had lots of friends." She caught Marcus's troubled gaze. He was trying to solve a puzzle. One nobody had been able to figure out. She softened her tone. "I suppose it's possible."

"If the blond victims' parents and siblings died under suspicious circumstances, we'll know if their deaths are related to Chelsea's murder and Chris's stalking. It will tell us if I'm on the right track or not. If I'm wrong, I'll drop this line of thinking. For now, it's all we've got."

Kay returned and gathered the lunch trash, stuffing everything into one sack. "I caught the last part of that. What can I do to help?"

"I'll know more after I speak with Dalton."

"Okay." Kay paused at the door. "In the meantime, I've got you the perfect place lined up for tonight. Do you want us to keep Diablo?"

"No, thanks. We'll take him," Marcus said.

Chris struggled to stay with the conversation. Her mind couldn't shake the bomb Marcus had dropped. What if her parents had been murdered? The idea just wouldn't compute inside her head. They'd been sweet and loving to her and Chelsea. Losing them had devastated her. To learned they'd been murdered, too? It was just too hard to fathom.

"I can help with research. Looking up death records online is easy."

Marcus tilted his head. The corners of his mouth lifted and for a second, all her troubles vanished. "I thought you'd zoned out."

"Why? What did I miss?"

"Don't let him tease you," Nate said. "I offered to lend you the company's extra tablet."

"Marcus is right. I wandered off for a minute, but I'm back. I appreciate your offer, but mine's in my bag."

"That purse must weigh a ton. No wonder it's so big." Nate laughed and stood. "Our tablets have certain programming loaded on them that will get you information a lot faster."

"Then I'd love to borrow it." Chris smiled as Nate left the room. "I'll be careful with the equipment."

Marcus walked around the table and sat beside her. "It's a lot to take in, and I didn't know an easy way to ask you about your parents' deaths." His gaze moved to the desk phone and back to her. "And then there's the message. You don't have to listen. I can give you the gist of it."

"The killer wanted me to hear what he had to say. I'll listen."

Marcus's eyes narrowed, squinting as if he disagreed with her decision. "I was hoping you'd let that slide."

"I can't."

He nodded and pulled the phone in front of them. "It's mostly rambling. Hell, it's gibberish. Shut it off any time you want."

"Okay." She held out her hand, and he wound his fingers through hers. With him holding on tight, she could face anything. "Go."

Marcus started the message. She leaned forward, paying close attention, hoping she'd recognize the voice. The killer's words were slurred and hard to understand.

He left sentences unfinished. The emotion, however, came through loud and clear. Venomous and full of spite, he poured out his contempt. His hatred had been directed at her, not at her family. The rambling ended abruptly.

Marcus hit the off button. "Words from a killer who probably wishes he hadn't lost control. He's unraveling, and now we know it." Marcus sounded so confident that she relaxed her grip on his fingers.

"I've never heard such hate and anger. I pride myself on having a good memory. Putting names with people's faces has never been a problem. You'd think if I'd pushed someone to the point of hating me, I'd know who and why."

"To an unstable mind, his interpretation of a hurtful act could be very different from mine or yours."

The guilt she carried multiplied, weighing her down and making it hard to breathe. If Marcus proved to be right, her entire family had been murdered because of her. As badly as she wanted to sink into the mire of self-pity, she couldn't allow it. Whoever this bastard was, she wouldn't give up until he was in prison. Or he'd killed her.

"Where do we start?"

"By leaving the office and moving somewhere secure. If we're being watched, the killer already knows we're here. We'll have two company tablets with access to background checks and records. Soon as we get situated somewhere else, we'll start digging." Marcus released her hand.

Nate returned, carrying a small bag, which he handed to her. "Here you go. Marcus can get you into all our programs." A broad smile lit his face. "We don't usually allow clients to work on their own case. Only two women have ever helped."

Marcus stood abruptly. His chair flipped back and would've fallen had he not grabbed the back. "Has Kay secured a vehicle and a safe house for us?"

Nate's grin only got bigger. "I can ask."

"If she has, we need to get out of here. It's too dangerous to you and Kay for us to hang around here. I'll leave it to you to explain my theory to Dalton and enlist his help looking into the deaths of Chris's parents."

"You got it."

When Nate was out of earshot, Chris had to ask. "What was that about? You reacted rather strongly to Nate's comment about two women."

Marcus glanced at the open doorway, as if waiting or hoping somebody would come.

"Is it a secret?" she prodded.

"No," he said. "Nate was being cute. Kay and Ana are the only two clients who actually worked hands-on with us."

"Ana?" A new name really stirred up Chris's curiosity.

"Ty Castillo's wife. Nate was scheduled to do a job for the government, but he'd been shot during Holly's rescue. Ty went to Colombia in his place. Ana was supposed to supply him with guns and explosives, but she'd been kidnapped by the cartel and taken to the very compound he'd gone to blow up. He went in after her and then blew the place off the map. Hardheaded son of a bitch finally met his match in Ana. They're married and live outside of Bogota. She's dedicated herself to the war on drugs, and Ty still works for Lost and Found."

"I see." Chris dropped the subject. Obviously, Nate had wanted to watch Marcus squirm by putting her in the same category as the other two women.

Nate stepped into view and gave them two thumbs-up. She stood, assuming Kay was ready with a new safe house location. "I'm ready when you are." Chris grabbed her purse.

"Then let's get started." Marcus picked up the briefcase and computer bag. "Diablo, come."

All smiles, Nate clapped Marcus on the shoulder as they walked to Kay's desk. "Just in case you need to take Diablo inside somewhere, I asked Kaycie to print you a copy of his papers. I figured the fire had taken care of the original set."

"You figured right. One big blaze, and pretty much everything was wiped out," Marcus said. "I'm glad you thought of it."

Nate bent down, scratched the dog's head, and then winked at Chris. "He's officially in training for police work."

"And if you get caught with phony papers, I've never met any of you." Kay removed pages from her desk printer. "Actually, this was Tomas's idea. We didn't want to lie and try to pass Diablo off as a service dog. It just didn't feel right. So we put him in a training program." She rolled her eyes while she slipped the documents inside a folder. She handed them to Chris and gave a set of keys to Marcus. "The car rental company dropped these off a few minutes ago. It's the beige SUV out front."

Marcus leaned down and kissed the top of her head. "Nate doesn't deserve you."

"You got that right." Kay came around from behind her desk and handed Chris a slip of paper. "My cell number. Call if you need anything."

"Thanks."

Nate and Marcus went to move the suitcases from Kay's car to the rental while Chris and Diablo familiarized themselves with the SUV. She settled in her seat while the dog smelled his way around the interior.

The sun heated the inside of the SUV, relaxing her and giving her a much-needed break from all the tension. This was her favorite time of year. For a few short months, Texas weather was warm in the daytime and cool at night. Soon, winter would arrive, bringing dreary, sunless days. She slipped the scrap of paper into her slacks pocket, leaned her head back and closed her eyes.

Her thoughts turned to Marcus. Her heart beat faster when he was near. That reaction had to be controlled. She couldn't allow herself to create a nonexistent relationship with him, even if he did give her world-class orgasms.

Marcus was a loner. Sure, he cared deeply for his friends, but he'd loved one woman with all his heart. She wondered if he could commit like that again. He'd said "things" didn't matter, and the people in your life were what's important. All she could do was wait to see if he believed in his own statement.

A cold, damp nose on her neck startled her. Diablo's soulful eyes studied her for a second. Then he rested his head on the back of the seat as close to her as he could get. "I can't imagine you as a killer. What a horrible life you must've had."

Marcus opened the back of the SUV, and he and Nate loaded the suitcases.

"Chris," Nate said. "I'll get in touch with Dalton right away. Things are moving slower than we'd like, but we'll figure this out. In the meantime, just know we're working hard and will use all our resources."

"Thank you."

"This may sound ludicrous, but try to enjoy the scenery at the safe house."

"I will," she said, knowing it was a lie. He waved and went back inside.

Marcus opened the driver's side door and slid behind the steering wheel. "That didn't sound too convincing." He ran the backs of his fingers down her cheek, wiping out all the instructions and warnings she'd given her heart. He'd rolled up his sleeves, revealing strong forearms.

"I tried," she said, leaning into his touch. She caught herself and moved back. He tweaked her chin and then reached over and scratched Diablo.

"Did you know that a dog's reaction to a person can be telling?"

"I did. Diablo's affection for you says a lot. What has he said about me?"

"Among other things, that you're a beautiful, warm, and caring person." Marcus's scent swirled around her, sending heat racing toward her lower belly.

Leaning closer, cornering her against the door, Marcus stroked her earlobe with his tongue. She hoped the dog had whimpered and not her.

"And do you agree with his opinion?" She thought it touching that he and Nate, while using different tactics, were trying to get her mind off the fact a killer may have been targeting her and her family for years.

"You'll have to wait to learn the answer." Marcus tugged her ear with his fingers and then moved back to his side of the car. Before she could blink, he'd buckled his seat belt and started the engine. "First, we have to get to the safe house and put these tablets to good use."

Had she been caught in a revolving door? One minute, the man was distant, and the next he had steam rolling off him. Whether he'd admit it or not, he felt something for her. Why else would he work so hard not to show it?

"Good. I need something to do. My mind is jumping all over the place. If all these killings were because of me, I don't know how I'll handle it."

"Don't start doubting yourself," Marcus snapped. "You're stronger and smarter than the killer. Together, we'll figure it out."

She didn't argue her point. Instead, she leaned back in the seat and stared at the scenery out the window. After a few miles, he exited the freeway and headed east onto a two-lane road. "We're pretty far out of town."

"About twenty miles. We're staying in a fishing cabin. Ty and Ana spent the night there before they returned to Colombia."

"Is there Internet coverage?"

"I'm sure there is. Nate knew we were bringing the tablets." Marcus turned off the two-lane and maneuvered the SUV down a winding farm-to-market road. Chris was almost convinced they were lost when he drove under a huge sign that read Camp Watson. For the next couple of miles, she thought for sure the SUV would bottom out in one of the deep ruts. Then the ground beneath them leveled out, and a bait shop and small grocery store came into view. A row of small houses lined the bank of a monstrous body of water.

"Welcome to Lake Watson. The third cabin is ours." Marcus drove past the main buildings, straight to the house and parked to the side.

"Won't we look odd, showing up without a boat and fishing gear?" Chris got out and walked to the porch. Marcus retrieved the keys from inside an old mailbox that was obviously there for decoration. He opened the door and then went back for Diablo and the suitcases and tablets.

"They'll think we're newlyweds or lovers sneaking off for some alone time."

Chris scanned the area, deciding the word isolated was an understatement. Marcus walked past her carrying their suitcases. "Sorry. I could have helped."

"Not a problem." He paused in the doorway. "Come in."

She and the dog followed Marcus into the house. He placed one suitcase and both tablets on the couch. "I'll put your stuff up in the loft."

The inside of the cabin wasn't too bad. Rustic would have best described the few pieces of mismatched furniture. Blinds and bright yellow curtains covered three windows. The couch had seen better days, but the place was clean, private, and quiet.

She and Marcus set the computers on the table and turned them on. Marcus took over, his oversize fingers moving smoothly across the small keys. His ability and dexterity didn't surprise her. He'd worked wonders on her body with those hands. The memory of him skimming across her bare skin set off that ball of heat that seemed to be firmly seated in her lower stomach.

"Ready?"

She nodded and took her place next to him. For a few minutes, they worked as teacher and student. He took one of the blond victims' files and demonstrated how to use the Lost and Found online access to records. They would start with the parents and siblings, pulling the records of those no longer living.

"You got this?" he asked.

"I think so."

He moved to the opposite side of the table and picked up a file. His cell buzzed, startling them both.

"It's Dalton." Marcus placed his phone between them and accepted the call. "Dalton. You're on speaker. Chris is here with me. You find something already?"

"Maybe. Chris, I'm glad you're listening. Kay sent me the names of your family members and the dates of their deaths. I started by pulling the police record of your dad's accident. Was he a heavy drinker?"

"No. He was a surgeon and always on call. He didn't consume alcohol of any kind. Why?"

"Without a toxicology screening, I can't be sure. The state trooper who found the wreckage made a note that he detected a strong order of alcohol in the car. It was one sentence, and nobody thought it significant enough to pass on to anyone. That there was no autopsy is ridiculous, because that one statement should've triggered an investigation."

"They swept it under the rug?" Chris couldn't believe her ears. Her dad had dedicated his life to helping others, and somebody had murdered him? She shivered even though the cabin was warm.

"I wouldn't say they covered it up. There could be any number of reasons the medical examiner didn't do an autopsy. Those Texas boys are usually better than this."

"So the first death you've looked at is suspect," Marcus stated.

"That's the key word. Suspect. Doesn't prove a damn thing except somebody overlooked the trooper's statement, but I didn't have to dig deep to find it."

"Now what?" Chris asked, hanging on to Dalton's words that he had no proof.

"I'm taking a few days off and coming to Texas. Nate has to leave on his next assignment in a little over a week, and we're going to put this to rest before he leaves."

Marcus's gaze held hers for a second. "Is it feasible to do an autopsy on the remains?"

That they were talking casually about her father's death pushed Chris's heart to the back of her throat. She understood the need to go over everything, but that didn't lessen the hurt. "Marcus, my dad died three years ago, Mom six months later, and then Chelsea." Chris swallowed hard. "Both my mother and father were cremated." Diablo must have sensed her stress. He abandoned the throw rug he'd claimed as his temporary bed, walked over, and put his head on her knee.

"I had to ask," Marcus said.

"Chris?" Dalton asked.

"I'm here." Stroking the dog's head helped, enabling her to speak calmly.

"Had your mother been taking tranquilizers long?"

"Her doctor prescribed something after Dad's death."

"Okay. I'll dig deeper into her records tomorrow after I get to Dallas."

"Thank you." She stood, walked to the back door, and pulled the curtain aside. A long wooden dock sat within steps of the cabin. The water rippled and danced under the bright sunlight. The movement was relaxing and peaceful.

Marcus's strong hands encircled her waist. His chin rested on top of her head.

She'd been so distracted by the lake that she hadn't heard the conversation end. She leaned against his rock-hard chest and breathed in his strength.

"I wish I could make this easier for you."

"Me, too."

"Think you should rest for a while?" he asked.

"No. My brain is working at warp speed. Resting isn't an option."

"Okay. I'm taking Diablo out. We'll be right out front by the tree. I'll leave the door open so you can see us."

Chris nodded and returned to the back door. The water gently lapping at the bank was mesmerizing. She should have gone with Marcus. Spending a few minutes in the fresh air might help her clear her head. She took her pistol from her purse, slipped it into the waistband of her jeans, and then stepped out onto the small porch. Before venturing any farther, she looked around. Either this was a slow time of year or everybody was on the lake fishing, because she didn't see a single person.

With a couple of steps, she stood at the water's edge. The lake, the trees, and the blissful quiet engulfed her, giving her a moment's peace.

A hand clamped over her mouth, and an arm grabbed her from behind. She was lifted off the ground.

A deep, angry voice said, "What the hell were you thinking? Oh, wait. You weren't."

"Put me down," she commanded, and he complied. Feet firmly on the ground, she whirled on him. "Why did you sneak up on me? I could have shot you."

Angry brown eyes stared down at her. "How did you plan to pull that off with your feet dangling a foot off the ground and your gun pressed into my belly?"

Chris backed away from Marcus's anger. "That was a dirty trick."

"Don't try to guilt trip me."

"You were right out front."

"And you needed to understand just how easily the killer could get to you. Granted, I'm fairly sure we weren't followed. But there's no guarantee." Marcus advanced two menacing steps. "You could have told me you wanted to walk out here. Hell, you'd have been safer if you'd brought Diablo. A stranger would be more reluctant to come near you with him along."

"I made a mistake. You don't have to get so mad."

Marcus's eyes closed, and he pulled in a deep breath. When their gazes met again, he smiled. "I'm not mad. But anytime you get careless, I'm going to be scared shitless."

He was right, and she knew it. She'd been foolish and could've put herself in harm's way.

CHAPTER 19

DaVinci fumbled with his fork, spilling rice on the tablecloth. The simple act of picking up an eating utensil sent pain shooting through his fingers. Scrubbing his swollen knuckles, applying ointment, and then wrapping them in gauze had been a painful experience.

"Would you like a bowl of soup?" Michelangelo asked. His patronizing tone grated on DaVinci's already frayed nerves.

"No." He motioned the waiter to take his plate away. "Why didn't you stop me before I injured my hands?"

"My boy. At the time, you were drunk and insane. I couldn't be sure you wouldn't lash out at me."

"When we talked on the phone, you mentioned you know people who'd help us with Christine. Exactly who are they and what do you have in mind?" DaVinci's patience was stretched tightly. His mentor's lack of concern that they might have left DNA or other evidence at the motel taxed his nerves even further.

"They are specialists in locating and eliminating people."

"And how did you come to be acquainted with this group?"

"Do you think I've been selling your faux masterpiece paintings to museums? This country has produced some high-class criminals with expensive tastes. They like to impress their friends and business associates while not paying the price of an original. You and I provide them with art pieces to furnish their private collections."

"Fine. I want to know where she's hiding, how many people are guarding her, and when it will be easiest to take her." Using Michelangelo's contacts meant if things went bad, he'd take the fall. Could DaVinci go it alone? "No one is to touch her. That includes you. Understand?"

"Customers are staring. Lower your voice before we're asked to leave."

DaVinci clenched his jaw to keep from shouting. "I don't like this side of you. Makes me wonder who you really are behind that cavalier attitude. We do this my way or you're out."

"My boy," Michelangelo said softly. "I haven't changed. You have. Your youthful enthusiasm has been replaced by an out-of-control, hate-driven fanaticism. No harm will come to Christine. You have my word."

****

Chris washed dishes while Marcus dried them. She'd peeled the potatoes for the home fries, and he'd handled the scrambled eggs, but they'd worked and eaten in silence. She could stay mad if it meant she'd exercise more caution. A sharp pain stabbed him in the heart if he even thought about her falling into the hands of the crazy bastard.

He tossed the kitchen towel onto the counter. "Diablo ate more eggs than either of us. I'd better take him outside."

Chris had gone back to her research when he and the dog returned. Diablo, belly full and body refreshed, trotted over to a throw rug and dropped like a rock. Marcus took out his tablet from the protective sleeve, turned it on, and resumed his search right where he'd left off.

"Want a cup of coffee?" Her voice relaxed the tension that seemed to have taken up residence between his shoulders.

He lifted his head, catching her gaze. The sparkle in her blue eyes was returning. "You buying?"

"Will it work as a peace offering?" A smile lifted the corners of her mouth.

The memory of kissing her until she sighed flashed through his mind, sending blood rushing south. Her lips were supple, giving, and so damn tasty. He could've kissed her for days, just exploring and enjoying her. The image of her taking his erection deep inside her mouth slammed into him. He blinked, hoping his thoughts weren't written all over his face.

"Well? Yes or no." She chuckled, reading his mind too easily. He knew it by the raised eyebrow and the darkening of her eyes. Lust on Chris was a beautiful thing.

"Yes," he answered. No way could he stand up without revealing the evidence that thinking about sex with her had left on his body.

Soon, the ancient coffeepot groaned and began to sputter fluid into the carafe.

"Locating these records takes longer than I expected." She returned to the table and opened the next file on the stack.

"Faster downloads would help," he agreed. "You can barely call this Wi-Fi. The pages couldn't load much slower."

"More speed would be good. That and a bigger screen. My eyes are crossing."

He wouldn't describe their small talk as interesting, but it qualified as an improvement over not speaking at all. So when the coffeepot beeped, he put down his tablet and fixed two cups. "Let's walk down to the end of the dock. An old bench sits on the far side of the gas pump. We can watch the sun set over the water."

"Should we take Diablo?" she asked.

"He'll never forgive us if we don't." He looked down at his dog. "Come on, boy." Marcus adjusted his Glock and followed Chris outside.

The walk down the dock felt good. His hand itched to slide around her shoulders and pull her closer. Instead, he thoroughly scanned the camp. The breeze was light, and for late afternoon, the cove was quiet. The angle of the sun banked off her face and hair, giving her an unnatural glow. He liked Chris, probably too much.

"So, you're not mad at me anymore for scaring you?" He sat on the bench, stretching his legs out in front of him.

She joined him, sitting close with their thighs touching. "Hard for me to be mad, since I was in the wrong. I let myself get caught up in the beauty of the lake. It was a dumb move, and you reminded me this wasn't a weekend getaway."

Marcus put his arm around her. He wanted to tell her that after this was over, he'd bring her back for a vacation if she wished. That thought ended when she slipped off her shoes and climbed down to sit on the edge of the dock.

"I have to dip my toes in." She scooted even closer to the edge of the dock then stuck her feet in the lake.

"You probably shouldn't wiggle your toes too much," he teased as he moved behind her. He spread his legs, placing her between his thighs. Diablo trotted to the end of the dock and drop down like a log.

"Why not?"

"This lake is known for monster catfish. I'd hate to have one think you were dinner."

"Stop it. I'm not afraid of a fish." She leaned against his chest and sighed.

Marcus kept their surroundings in mind, but at the same time, he memorized the sound of her sigh. When this was over, and she was safe and at peace with the world, he might never hear it again.

They stayed until the sun dropped out of sight. "I hate to be the bearer of bad news."

"We need to go inside."

"Yeah." He stood to help her up just as Diablo ran straight past them and took a long leap into the water.

Chris squealed with laughter as water splashed on them both. "He's a water dog," she said in between peals of laughter.

"News to me." Marcus joined her laughter as Diablo discovered the water was shallow. He jumped on every leaf that drifted past. After a few minutes, Marcus picked up her shoes and guided her back to the front of the dock. Diablo came bounding out of the lake, stopped and shook water everywhere. Marcus caught him by the collar and said, "Grab a towel and toss it to me."

Chris did better than toss a towel. She returned with two and helped dry the big mutt. She knelt and even wiped the dog's paws.

"I hope he appreciates you." Marcus found himself laughing again when Diablo rewarded her with a face lick.

"He knows who loves him."

She was wet, muddy, and radiant looking up at him. The sun had almost disappeared, but Marcus felt the sunshine in his soul. "Now you're the one with wet feet." He scooped her into his arms.

"Marcus," she whispered against his neck. "Look at me."

He turned his head toward her, and she kissed him. Her hands filtered through his short hair and her fingers gripped his head, holding him to her. All rational thought abandoned him. He took control, exploring the sweet taste and warmth of her mouth.

How they managed to get themselves and Diablo inside would forever remain a mystery, but Marcus closed the door, locked it, and then turned her to straddle his hips. Her legs wrapped tightly around him.

"Am I always going to be the one who makes the first move?" She nipped at the corners of his mouth, driving him crazy.

"You talk too much." He took the towels from her and tossed them into the kitchen sink. Then he caught the corners of her blouse and lifted the soft material off her, dropping it where they stood.

All that separated him from her lush, full breasts was a flesh-colored bra. He considered ripping it off. She laughed and quickly removed it, adding it the growing pile on the floor.

"You're a mind reader, too?" he asked, lowering his head to stroke her nipple with his tongue.

"Maybe." Her voice had deepened, lusty and short of breath.

"Then what am I going to do next?" Before she could answer, he slid his hands under her bottom and lifted her up so that her nipple was within his reach, pebbled and ripe for him. He sucked the tip into his mouth, rolling and nipping. When she moaned, he swapped to the other breast. Jesus, the woman smelled and tasted like heaven.

"You're going to put me down," she whispered.

"I don't think so."

"I can't undress you until you do." She relaxed her legs.

"You're going to undress me?"

"I am."

"Hold that thought." He swung her back into his arms. The sun had completely disappeared, so he snapped on the kitchen light and then carried her up the stairs to the only bed in the house. He slipped his hands under her arms and slowly slid her down until her feet touched the floor.

"That gun was in the way while my legs were wrapped around you. Why don't you put it on the nightstand?"

"Done." He did as she requested and then reached for her, wanting to get back to enjoying her beautiful breasts.

Chris took his arms and pushed them to his sides. "No touching while I'm at work." Her tone was firm, but her eyes sparkled with fun. "Okay?"

"Okay, but I've never been into the master and submissive lifestyle. So if you think you're going to spank me, you should know that I'll spank back."

"I might be bossy, but I'm not into pain." Her small hands slipped under his shirt and up his chest. She caught his nipples and tweaked them. She lifted his shirt over his head, one inch at a time. "You're a gorgeous man, Marcus Ricci."

"We've had this conversation. You've cornered that market."

"You really don't know." She raked a fingernail across his nipple. "I like that."

"How much longer do I have to stand like a kid waiting for the principal to tell me I can move?"

"Such impatience." She went to work on his belt.

His erection had been pushed against his zipper far too long, and he sighed with relief as she pulled his jeans down. Standing with his hands to his sides proved to be more difficult than he'd imagined. Chris, naked from the waist up, was like setting a glass of water in front of a man dying of thirst and telling him he couldn't have a drink.

"Sit on the bed so I can get your boots off."

He complied and considered letting her try to remove them. Instead, he toed them off then smiled up at her. "You didn't say I couldn't use my legs or feet."

With that, he wrapped his legs around her and pulled her on top of him. She landed with a squeal.

Laughing, they forgot her mandate. He rolled her under him, sat back on his knees, and made quick work of the rest of her clothes. He stopped and feasted his eyes on her. Marcus trailed his hand across her creamy skin, pausing at her core. She lifted her hips, enabling him to easily slide a finger inside her wet heat. Her gaze dropped to watch him. Damn, he wished he was better at saying the sexy stuff she probably wanted to hear. Instead, he went with the truth. "It should be against the law to cover this body with clothes."

"You talk too much." She turned his own words on him and then cupped his face with her hands. "I need you to make love to me. Now."

"But—" There was so much more he wanted to do for her.

"Now."

"I try to never argue with a lady." He quickly covered himself and returned to her. "You're the boss. Remember?" He pulled her astride him.

Chris rose above him, grasped his erection, and guided him to her body. Slowly, she lowered herself until every inch of him was seated deep inside. Her eyes closed, and her head tilted back. For a few seconds, neither of them moved.

She leaned forward. Brought her lips to his. That one simple movement of her hips sent him barreling toward the edge. No way was he coming too soon. He'd count backward, study the pattern on the curtains, or repeat his license number in his head. This was about her pleasure.

She rocked back and forth, her hips undulating slowly at first. She moaned and picked up speed, giving Marcus the cue to move. He caught her hips in his hands and met her stroke for stroke. Her hair swung free and her eyes closed as she lost herself in pleasure. Pleasure he could give her.

"Marcus," she whispered, bearing down on him, her contractions pulsing around him.

Her spasms broke his restraint. He tightened his grip and pounded into her until nothing existed but the two of them. His groan filled the room as he exploded. She collapsed on top of him, as both of them gasped for breath.

In the silence, they were one.

It had happened too fast. Next time, he'd make love to her nice and slow.

Diablo's growl brought Marcus crashing back to earth. The loft gave him the perfect view of the cabin floor except for the back door. The dog was on his feet facing that direction. He didn't have to tell Chris to stay quiet. She'd slipped off the bed and moved out of the line of vision of anyone on the lower level. Marcus slid on his jeans quietly and palmed his Glock.

"What is it, boy?" No way did he want the dog involved in a fight. He'd worked too hard to wipe those ideas from Diablo's mind. He walked to the railing but saw nothing. "I'm going down."

Whatever had disturbed Diablo had to be outside. The cabin was one big room with no place to hide except the bathroom. He jogged downstairs and looked around. Nothing. "Chris," he said. "I'm going out."

"Hang on. I'm coming." She hurried down the stairs to join him, grabbing her gun from her purse after handing off his things.

"Come," he called Diablo to his side. "We'll be right back." A trip around the cabin then down the dock and back revealed nothing. The dog didn't sense danger, so they went indoors.

"No telling what he heard. I didn't see anything."

"Might have been the cat I saw up at the store."

"Could have been." Marcus's gaze locked on her chest. She'd obviously pulled a T-shirt from her suitcase without paying much attention. The outlines of her breasts and nipples made his mouth water.

"I like it when you look at me like that," she virtually purred the words.

"I'd like it if you never put that bra on again. Would I sound crude if I say that I can't get enough of your body?" His zipper dug into his growing erection.

"Interesting." Her gaze dropped to the bulge in his jeans. "I was thinking the same thing."

"We really should work on the files." He closed the distance between them, slid his hands under her shirt and lifted her breasts in his palms. "Perfect fit."

"You think?" Her hands slipped around his shoulders.

"We'll work extra hard later." He started to pick her up again, but she slid her hand down the front of his jeans. She found plenty to hold on to, because he was hard as a rock again.

"Where were we?" she asked.

It occurred to him, in a fleeting thought, that he couldn't remember feeling this strongly about a woman in years. She'd found a tiny opening in his heart and had walked right in, bringing fun, humor, and gut-wrenching need back into his life.

She nipped the tip of his nipple, snapping his attention back to her. "I'm trying to seduce you. Focus."

"I'm focused." He glanced at Diablo, who'd gone back to sleep. "Focused on keeping you awake all night."

CHAPTER 20

Chris woke to the aroma of coffee brewing. The bedside clock read seven fifteen, making her wonder how long Marcus had been up. Had he rested at all? She'd slept like a rock, having been thoroughly satisfied and weak. She stretched her arms overhead and pointed her toes. She discovered a few sore places that hadn't been there before last night. Marcus was an inventive and voracious lover. A grin spread across her face. He wasn't the only one who'd been brazen. Somewhere around midnight, she'd lost count of the number of orgasms she'd had.

Marcus might be quiet in public, but in bed, he held nothing back. How would he act toward her after last night? The first time they'd made love, he'd reverted to the stoic private investigator. It was as if he'd hidden behind the job. He wasn't the kind of man who hopped in and out of bed with women. Could she give him the space to figure out how to move on?

The only way to find out was to join him. She showered, braided her hair into a rope hanging down her back, and dressed.

She met him coming up the stairs. "Good morning." She'd worked hard not to deliver that sentence as a question.

"It is, for a fact." He kissed her, put a cup of coffee in her hand, and then led her down the steps.

A heavy rock floated off her shoulders. Her heart relaxed. His brown eyes had a twinkle in them this morning, replacing the hard edge they usually wore.

Different aromas mingled and filled the air. What better combination could a girl have to start the day than fresh coffee, Marcus after a shower, and frying bacon?

"Hungry?"

"Starving," she answered.

"Come sit down. It's just about ready."

Chris did as he said, watching as he divided the eggs and bacon. Wearing jeans and a white T-shirt, he could have been a model. Not so much for a high-fashion magazine, though. Marcus was stunningly handsome in a masculine way. His movements, the self-assured way he walked shouted that this was not a man to screw with. His incredible biceps, so large she couldn't wrap both hands around one, served as punctuation marks to his body language.

Diablo appeared at her side. She dropped her hand and scratched. He rested his head in her lap and stared up at her. "Are you hungry?"

"Starving," Marcus said. He turned, holding a plate in each hand. "I should've known by the tone of your voice that you were talking to the dog." He chuckled at his own joke, set her food in front of her, and then moved to the other side of the table. "Diablo had his scrambled eggs first."

"I can't lie. He's stolen my heart."

"I'm glad. When this case is over, I think we should talk more about who has stolen what and from whom." With a wink, he lifted his fork.

She was dying to ask exactly what he meant, but she'd already discovered that you didn't push Marcus into talking if he wasn't ready. Instead of prying, Chris dug into her breakfast. "You're a good cook."

"Yeah. If you're willing to eat breakfast or grilled steaks for the rest of your life."

"Sounds like a balanced diet to me." She finished breakfast, stood, and gathered the dishes. "You fixed everything. I'll clean up."

He nodded. "It's a deal. I can be finished with this last file by the time you're done."

"How? We didn't get halfway yesterday."

"I was up early."

Chris turned off the water and took the four steps to stand next to him. "Did you sleep at all?"

"I rested after I worked through the rest of the victims' families." He turned in his chair, pulling her to stand between his thighs.

"Then you didn't sleep at all. There was a lot left to do."

"I'll sleep when this is over." His hands slid under her shirt and stroked her bare skin. "You'd better finish the dishes, or we won't be leaving at checkout time."

"Why can't we just stay here?"

"Company policy." He laughed when she raised her eyebrows. "Seriously, we keep a client moving. It's too easy to get comfortable, even complacent, if you stay in one place." His fingers walked up and down her spine.

A simple touch of his skin to hers, and her knees were weak. She leaned down and kissed him tenderly on his forehead, the tip of his nose, and then his lips. "I won't be long."

She went back to the dishes but had to ask if he'd uncovered anything helpful. "What have you learned?"

His gaze lifted from the tablet and met hers. "Nothing that gets us any closer to the killer. Most of these victims' families are still alive. One's dad never returned from Vietnam, but was declared dead years ago."

"So we didn't find a connection in the families, which in reality means we learned a lot. Everything points to the fact that my family is the only one who's been wiped out."

"Looks that way. I'm sorry."

"I'll make an appointment with my lawyer so I can ask him to facilitate getting my birth records."

"It's a good idea. I can get that done through Lost and Found's attorney. It might be faster. No appointment necessary."

Chris had tried to accept the facts. Tried to block out the pain and anger. How could she not have figured it out? She put away the last of the dishes and went upstairs to pack. When she came down, carrying her suitcase, Marcus shoved his cell in his pocket.

"The attorney moved our request to the top of his list. There's nothing to keep you from getting your birth records. He has some papers for you to sign giving him limited power of attorney to act on your behalf."

"I didn't expect it to be this easy."

"The fact that your birth mother and your adopted parents are deceased removed any and all obstacles."

Chris glanced around the cabin. "Can we stop by the attorney's office on the way back to Dallas?"

"His assistant is expecting us." He studied her for a second, and she steeled herself against telling him that she hated to leave.

"Come here a second." He met her halfway, pulling her into his arms. "I know this is frustrating, and it seems like we're not making any headway. The process of elimination can be maddening sometimes."

"Then we'd better go."

"Of course, you're right." He hugged her tightly and kissed her forehead. "I'll bring you back here someday."

"It's a date." Chris swallowed. The lump in her throat stayed put. She stood on her tiptoes and kissed him lightly.

Less than ten minutes later, their stuff had been loaded, Diablo had been taken to the nearest tree, and Marcus had parked outside the little store. With a promise to be right back, he carried the keys to the cabin inside and dropped them off.

Chris could see a glimmer of hope for a relationship between her and Marcus. If it ended badly, she'd walk away, knowing they tried. A pinch in her heart issued a warning as to just how painful that would be.

****

DaVinci opened the door and stepped back to allow the sexual sadist to enter. He hadn't been able to get past Michelangelo's revelation that he enjoyed raping women before killing them. The idea was repulsive to DaVinci. Long ago, he'd accepted the fact he was asexual. Intimate physical contact with either gender didn't appeal to him. The violence he'd endured in two different foster homes had been more than enough to turn him against that kind of degradation.

Michelangelo made himself at home. He lounged on the couch, stretching out his long legs and crossing them at the ankles. "So how are your knuckles today?"

"Swollen but not as sore." This wasn't why his mentor was here. He'd brought news about these so-called friends he'd hired to find Christine. "What have you learned?"

"I have people watching her home and the detective's workplace. No one could locate them last night, but they will stay on it until she's located."

"I want her alone."

"That won't be easy. You said her bodyguard is always with her."

"He won't be if he's dead."

"I thought you'd say that." He smiled as he pulled out his cell phone and placed a call. The conversation lasted only a minute or two. "My boy, I just underwrote the cost of killing this detective. I expect to be reimbursed."

"Of course, as long as they follow instructions and don't harm Christine." The image of Michelangelo brutally raping a woman flashed through DaVinci's mind. The time to end their relationship was near, and a plan was forming on the best way to end it.

"DaVinci, you keep drifting away. I worry about you."

"There's no need. My nerves have been a little raw." DaVinci was open for a lecture.

"You've always been inclined to exaggerate, but that was a huge understatement."

"If we're not extremely careful, our creating and competing will be over."

"It has to end eventually," his mentor said casually. "I'd prefer it happen before the police link us together."

"Then it's important that you use my nickname when you refer to me around these people you hired. I've always thought the use of the aliases was childish, but now I see the value."

"If that's how you want it." Michelangelo stood, crossed the room, and attempted to put his arm around DaVinci's shoulders.

He shuddered, wondering if his mentor had ever had sexual thoughts about him. "That's exactly how I want it."

"Stay close to your phone. The minute Christine is located, you'll get a call. It's imperative you reach my hunting cabin as quickly as possible. As soon as my men are comfortable, they can take down the bodyguard and secure Christine, and we'll move. I will bring her to you myself."

"You'll make sure she's not harmed?"

"Of course," Michelangelo said. "She is yours to kill."

"As long as you remember that, we'll be fine."

"My boy." Michelangelo's back stiffened. "You try my patience."

"So you've said," DaVinci joked.

Michelangelo handed over a single key and removed a piece of paper with a hand-drawn map from his coat pocket. "Put the past behind you. I bought this place for its privacy and only use it on occasion. No one has ever left there alive except me. I expect you to clean up after yourself and bury her in the woods before you leave."

DaVinci walked him to the door. "When I'm finished and back in town, we'll have dinner, and I'll reimburse you for expenses."

"Excellent. I can't wait to see pictures."

He closed the door and wandered through his apartment. How many graves were in the woods? When had Michelangelo started killing in secret? He'd made a stupid mistake saying that no one had ever left his hunting cabin alive. DaVinci knew who would be buried out back with Christine, and it wouldn't be him.

****

Dalton Murphy sat at Ty's old desk with his back turned to Marcus. The FBI agent was bent over a stack of paperwork. He had his cell held to his ear. He seemed oblivious to the fact that Marcus and Chris had arrived. Marcus decided to wait until the phone conversation ended to interrupt.

Diablo, on the other hand, felt the need to investigate. He swung wide and stopped about four feet in front of Dalton. Marcus watched closely, relaxing when the dog turned and trotted to the break room. Dalton ended the call and turned to face him.

"The dog looks good. He must've decided I was one of the good guys."

"He certainly wasn't disturbed by your presence. That desk fits you. Ever think about leaving the bureau?"

"Every day." Dalton laughed as he stood and shook Marcus's hand. He turned to Chris, took her hand but held on instead of shaking it. "It's good to see you. I'm glad you took my advice and came to see these guys. They're good at solving puzzles."

Marcus huffed out his disagreement. "We've gotten nowhere. Not one bit closer to finding who this killer is than the day Chris walked in here."

"Tell me what you decided after sorting through the victims' backgrounds." Dalton paused. "Sorry, I forget I'm not in charge here. Think we should round up Nate before we discuss the case?"

"I'll get him," Chris said, extracting her hand and going up front.

"Is she responsible for the gleam in your eyes?" Dalton asked Marcus.

"I don't know what—"

"Don't try it. You failed the test."

"What test?" Marcus asked, adding a snarl to the end of the question.

"You didn't like that I hung on to her. You never took your eyes off her hand the entire time. The longer I held it, the deeper you scowled."

"I'll have to remember you're also a behavioral analyst."

Dalton grinned wide. "You didn't answer my question."

Marcus considered telling Dalton to butt out, but didn't. "I like her. A lot. But my lifestyle and hers are too different. I work for a living, and she's from old money. I can't blame her for going back to the right side of town when this is over. It'll have to be her decision."

"You're giving me the runaround again. I happen to know you're part owner of Lost and Found, Inc. You're inventing excuses."

Thankfully, Chris returned with Nate and Kay in tow. Marcus ushered everybody into the conference room.

"You guys got the ball rolling on Chris's adoption papers?" Nate asked.

"We did. Chris gave the lawyer her information and the power of attorney to act on her behalf. His office will call Kay when they're in his possession."

Dalton leaned forward on one elbow. "I wasn't aware you were adopted."

Chris gazed at the ceiling. "I can't understand everyone's interest in that fact. I've explained that my life began the day the Hollands took Chelsea and me home with them."

Marcus slid his hand under the table and patted her on the knee for reassurance. "We'll take a look at Chris's birth records and let everyone know what we find. Dalton, what's your take on the deaths of Mr. and Mrs. Holland?"

"The results are inconclusive. The medical examiner's report on Mrs. Holland indicated enough diazepam in her system to easily have caused her death. Plus, police found an empty prescription bottle in her hand. All fairly bland information until you consider that she didn't leave a note, was wearing her housecoat, and was found sitting in the living room."

A pain slashed through Chris's heart. They were discussing the woman who'd raised her, played with her, sang songs to her, and nursed her when she was sick. This conversation reminded Chris that the sense of loss never really went away.

"You want to take a break?" Marcus asked.

"No." Chris rejoined the conversation. "We just got started. What's wrong with the way my mother was dressed?"

Marcus sensed the tension rolling off Chris. He wished he could spare her the pain of revisiting her mother's death, but Dalton had something on his mind. They had to hear him out.

"A large percentage of females who commit suicide leave a note," Dalton continued. "They either apologize or try to put the blame on someone else, like a cheating husband. 'You broke my heart, and I can't go on,' that sort of accusation. They usually dress for death, and they're normally sitting in the living room with the TV on. Before you jump to conclusions, remember I said some women, not all."

"My mother was very fastidious. She would've put on her best Sunday dress, plumped up the pillows on her bed, and then lay down." Unsure she could bear to listen much longer, Chris rubbed the back of her neck. "Why didn't I notice that she hadn't dressed?"

"For the same reason the police didn't," Marcus said. "They weren't looking for a homicide."

Nate stood and started pacing. "We have a bunch of nothing."

Marcus held back a frustrated growl.

"Does anyone know a hypnotist?" Chris asked.

All heads turned her direction, Marcus's included. "What questions do you want answered?"

The room was dead quiet for a second.

"I've toyed with the idea since I blanked out Chelsea's killer's face. To be honest, I've been a coward, afraid to let someone take control of my thoughts. There's so much of my childhood that I don't remember. If there's something buried besides the description of the killer, I want to know."

"Couldn't hurt, as long as we use someone we trust," Dalton said, breaking the silence. "I'll check with the agency office here in Dallas. See who they recommend."

Marcus gripped Chris's shoulder. "It's strictly up to you."

"Can we do it today while we're waiting for my adoption records?"

Dalton stood. "I'll make the call."

Kay patted the chair next to her. Marcus smiled as Nate followed her unspoken request. She was the only person in the world who could exercise that kind of control over him. A sharp pain hit Marcus's chest. Jealousy? Not of their happiness. Envy? Hell, yeah.

"Dalton will find someone you can trust," Kay said.

Chris nodded. Her braid had slipped over her shoulder, and she absentmindedly shoved it back. "If there's something I've repressed, I want it out in the open."

Dalton returned with his cell phone still at his ear. "You said today?"

Chris nodded.

"Yeah," he said to the person on the phone. "Great. Marcus Ricci will be with her."

"Thank you," Chris said.

Dalton waved off the gratitude with a dip of his chin. "We got lucky. Gayle Stern has agreed to see Chris over lunch. I've heard of her. She's a well-respected psychologist." Dalton handed Marcus a piece of paper. "Her office address. She's expecting you within the hour."

"I'm ready," Chris said

"Better leave the dog," Nate said.

Marcus shook his head. "I don't like it. Last time I left him, I came back and Holly was speaking Spanish to him."

"We'll make sure that doesn't happen again," Nate said, turning to his wife. "Are you going to tell them the news before they leave?"

Kay's smile could've lit up a football stadium. "Jake will be here in a few days. He's going to live with us for a while."

"You'll take good care of him." Marcus remained unsure how he felt about the situation. Which Jake was coming home? The man who'd busted his ass to become a helicopter pilot so he could fly wounded soldiers to safety? Or the one who'd helped kidnap teenage girls and had supervised their sales?

On his last mission, all the passengers on his flight had died, which no doubt weighed heavy on Jake's shoulders. Even though the surgery had solved his medical problems, he'd struggled to forgive himself. Would he ever fully come back?

A cold nose pushed its way under Marcus's hand, and he glanced down at Diablo. Trusting brown eyes stared up at him. The dog had been given a second chance at life, so why couldn't Jake get one, too?

Marcus understood guilt. He'd be there to help his friend.

"If you two are going to make it to Dr. Stern's office, you'd better go," Nate said. "Diablo will be fine until you get back."

"We left this number with the attorney. If he gets his hands on Chris's adoption paperwork and can't reach us—"

Nate nodded. "Kay or I will go after them."

Marcus knelt down and scratched Diablo's ears. An odd feeling rolled around in his belly. He didn't feel right leaving him today.

Chris was waiting, so he patted Diablo on the back. "Stay with Kay," he said. "Be a good boy."

Not one person commented on the fact that he'd spoken to the dog as if the dog understood. Which was a good thing.

CHAPTER 21

Being hypnotized was a little scary, but Chris wanted any buried secrets to surface. This perpetual fear was eating away at the lining of her stomach and had to stop. Yet, the closer they got to the doctor's office, the more hesitant she became. The idea of handing over control made her feel extremely vulnerable.

Marcus must've sensed her tension, because he reached across the car and rested his hand on her knee. "You comfortable with Dr. Stern getting inside your head?"

She attempted a laugh, but it sounded more like she'd choked. "I will be if you stay in the room with me."

"If you want me there, that's where I'll be."

"I don't have anything to hide, especially from you." Trying to lighten the mood, she added, "You already know your way around my body, I might as well let you prowl around inside my head."

"Every time I touch you, it's a new and wonderful exploration." He glanced at her. His eyes sparkled with humor.

"What a nice thing to say." Heat sizzled between them, crawling up her arm and circling downward.

This was a different Marcus. A more relaxed and at ease Marcus. Had they passed a juncture in their relationship that she'd missed? Dare she hope he'd moved past his wife's death?

"I like watching you squirm." He released her hand and placed his on the steering wheel. "Thank you for trusting me with whatever secrets might be revealed in your session."

She did trust him, not only with her body but also with her mind. Could she extend that trust to her heart? "Have you straightened everything out with your insurance company?"

"I called yesterday morning while you were still asleep. They're sending a check for the car, which of course they totaled, and they'll pay for the damage to the house, minus the deductible. No doubt, I can kiss those policies goodbye."

"You can replace the car, but inside your house...well, those were personal belongings. Those things were important."

"You're important. Stop worrying about things in the past. When this is over, and I'm sure you're safe, we're going to talk about what's essential and what's not. I promise. Normally, I'm not one to postpone things, but in this case, I think we should catch our killer first."

Slam. The door had closed on the subject. Chris didn't want to wait, she wanted to tell him she cared, but she could also see his point. People were dead and dying. If she and Marcus were going to have a future, the killer had to be stopped.

One thread still held him to the past. For Marcus to move forward, he'd have to completely release his dead wife.

She pulled down the visor, flipped open the small mirror, and stared at the mess in the mirror. Her actions had a double purpose. One, she wanted to change the subject, and two, she had to try to look presentable. Sheesh. Her braid was a mess. This morning she'd applied a dusting of makeup and had dressed in slacks and a blouse. Still, she felt underdressed to enter a psychologist's office. One she'd never met.

Her mother's words came back to Chris. Mother had always preached that first impressions were how people remember you. Chris's heart folded. All this time, she'd believed her mother had committed the ultimate act of selfishness and had taken her own life. No way would she have done that.

Chris fished her bag from the back seat and unbraided her hair. With a brush, rubber band and a clip, she swept it back and rolled it into an acceptable knot. A swipe of lipstick would have to do, as would her clothes.

"The doc's office is in the Palmer Building. Should be the next exit." He turned on his blinker, changed lanes, and then glanced her way. "You look great."

"Thanks."

The Palmer Building stood forty floors high and was one of the city's hallmark buildings. She'd been inside many times. When Marcus parked, she got out and walked ahead of him.

"I like what they've done with the landscaping," she said, keeping the topic generic.

"You've been here before?"

"My father's attorney is, or was, on the twenty-seventh floor. A sweet older man. He held my hand through three funeral arrangements, court appearances to file documents, and the transfer of ownership on everything my mother and father owned. He planned to retire soon after the estate was settled. His son was a partner."

The glass exterior of the building presented a cold and distant feel. She'd never been comfortable there. Maybe it was because none of her trips had been for pleasure and nothing to do with the man she'd visited. Nothing had changed in that regard. They stopped by the wall of names and suite numbers, verified where they were going, and then headed for the bank of elevators.

"Do you want to stop by on our way out? We'll make time if you'd like to check on him."

"No, I'm sure everything is different now."

The doors swooshed closed behind them. Marcus stood directly behind her. He slid his hands around her waist and rested his head on top of hers.

"I meant what I said about talking soon. I didn't mean to come across as harsh earlier. Right now, your life is more important than anything else is. I can't ask you to make any decisions until this case is closed."

"You're right about one thing. My life is plenty screwed up." The ache in her chest eased a little. "When it comes to relationships, I've never been lucky."

"That's hard to believe. I'll bet you had boys lined up outside your door."

"Nobody worth remembering." It was time for her to shut up. Before she blurted out what was really on her mind. The time had come too reel in her emotions because she was teetering on the edge of falling in love with him.

Marcus followed her down the hall and into the doctor's office. A young woman behind an oversize desk had a sandwich and chips spread across her blotter. They'd interrupted.

"I apologize if we ruined your lunch," Chris said.

"Think nothing of it." The woman dropped her napkin over her food. "You're Ms. Holland?"

"Yes."

"The doctor is expecting you." The woman stood.

"Don't you have some paperwork for me to fill out?"

"Only the doctor handles her patients' information." She turned to Marcus. "Would you like a cup of coffee while you wait?"

"He's coming with me," Chris said firmly. She wasn't budging on that point.

"Not a problem. If you'll follow me."

Chris's hands were suddenly clammy. The second they'd stepped into the quiet office, her adrenaline had spiked, and she wanted to run.

The warmth radiating from Marcus as his hand rested on her back helped calm her. He'd keep her safe while she was virtually unconscious. She wiped her hands on her slacks right before being shown into the doctor's private area.

Dr. Stern stood. She smiled, adding another layer of wrinkles, but at the same time, warming an otherwise formidable face. Her cream-colored linen suit looked to have been tailored to fit her robust figure. The jacket she wore complemented her peach blouse.

Chris's knees stiffened. Marcus stepped forward and shook the doctor's hand.

"Thank you for seeing us so quickly." He handed her a folder. "Special Agent Murphy thought you might want to look this over."

"Thank you. Your office emailed me the file. It won't hurt me to skip a meal. I try to accommodate the FBI when I can." Dr. Stern came out from behind her desk, shook Chris's hand, and then waved her toward a chair. "Come sit down."

"Thank you." She mustered a weak smile.

Dr. Stern leaned against her desk. "I've never lost a patient. Based on your expression, you might be the first."

The doctor's demeanor and gentle voice went a long way toward easing Chris's tension. The joke was appreciated. Still, she took the chair closest to Marcus.

"I understand there are a couple of areas you'd like to explore. Your early childhood and your sister's murder."

"You got all that from an email and committed it to memory? I'm impressed," Chris said. "And jealous."

"Don't be. I have total recall. Most of the time it's a blessing." Dr. Stern walked back behind her desk and sat. "Let's make sure you understand what's going to happen. There are lots of myths and misunderstandings about being hypnotized."

Chris listened intently. "Will I remember what was said?"

"Absolutely. You won't be unconscious. In fact, you'll be aware of everything. Understand that I can't make you do anything against your will or force you to tell me anything you wish to keep a secret. Clinical hypnosis is an altered state of awareness, a highly relaxed state. Your mind will be able to concentrate and will be highly focused. Most of my patients remember everything that's said, but there are no guarantees."

Chris scooted to the edge of her chair. The unknown scared the wits out of her. What if she'd suppressed something, a memory she might not be able to handle? She reached for Marcus's hand. "Is it all right if he stays?"

"That's fine." Dr. Stern stood, moved across the plush gray carpet, and opened a second door. She turned to Marcus. "I ask that you remain silent. Sit where Ms.

Holland can't see you, and if you think of something I need to ask, write it down and hold up the piece of paper. I'll come get it."

"You got it."

****

Sit still and shut up. The doctor hadn't used those exact words, but Marcus got her meaning. They had moved into a smaller area, which he thought looked more like a living room. A small couch and two chairs had been arranged facing each other. End tables flanked each one. The overhead light was a normal setting, which surprised him. He'd expected a softer glow to help relax the patient, but then what did he know about hypnosis? Dr. Stern started to move a chair out of the way, but he took it from her.

"Right there is fine." She indicated a spot, and he followed the doctor's orders.

"How do we do this?" Chris's voice had lost some of its strength, making her sound wary.

"Have a seat." Dr. Stern directed her to a chair. "If you're wondering, I don't swing a watch in front of you and ask you to follow its movement like they used to do in the movies. In fact, I don't use any equipment. We're going to take it nice and slow. I'll talk to you in a quiet tone and help you calm down. That process will continue until you're in a state of relaxation."

Marcus listened to Dr. Stern's words, thinking her low and monotone voice would put anybody to sleep.

"What do you want me to do?" Chris sounded a little more comfortable.

"Close your eyes and take a deep breath. Now let's start at the top of your head, relax the nerves and muscles. Now work your way down to your face and neck."

Marcus had never been hypnotized, and he intentionally tuned the doctor out. He pulled a small pad and pen from his pocket. The doc might be able to recall everything perfectly later, but he had to take notes.

Dr. Stern wandered through Chris's past jobs, boyfriends, school mates, and even teachers. Chris's words were pleasant, and her memories were good ones. She'd fallen in love with Mr. and Mrs. Holland the first time they visited the home.

Chris's tone of voice changed as they discussed her years before the adoption. She was a frightened little girl who didn't understand why the bad people had taken her mommy away. She wanted her mother to come get her.

The doc switched back to the day Chris's adoptive parents took her and Chelsea home with them. Chris began to cry. Her arms extended toward someone. Then she clutched her arms to her breasts as if holding on to something tightly.

"Who is there with you?" the doctor asked.

"We're leaving the home, but Charlie's not coming with us."

"Who is Charlie?"

"My brother. He's upset."

Another sibling? Marcus leaned closer, listening for the next revelation.

"Talk to your brother. Why is he upset?"

Chris was silent for a moment. She extended her arms and shook her head. "Yes. I won't forget. I promise. Yes. I swear." She struggled to pull away from something that held her back. Her sobs filled the room.

Marcus wanted to intervene. Chris's sorrow was gut-wrenching. His heart ached for her, but they couldn't stop now. He scribbled on his pad, and then passed the note to Dr. Stern.

"Chris, I want you to relax. Let's talk about your sister's death."

She stopped crying on the spot. Marcus was amazed how the mind could turn scenes off and on. He listened carefully, not wanting to miss a thing, as the doctor calmly walked Chris through the incident.

"Okay, Chris. You're inside the house. I want you to remember that you are just an observer today. The attacker can't hurt you."

"I don't want to look at Chelsea."

"You don't have to. We're only concerned with the person who killed her."

Chris frowned. "It happened so fast. He choked me."

"What color is his hair?" the doctor probed.

"Blond."

"Lighter or darker than yours?"

"About the same. He is tall and has blue eyes." Chris fidgeted.

"Stay calm and relaxed. He can't hurt you."

"He's so angry."

"Chris, do you know this man?"

"No. Yes. Something about him is familiar."

"That's enough for today. You'll remember everything we talked about, but you'll wake calm and relaxed." The doctor reached over and touched Chris on the hand. "Chris?"

She opened her eyes and let out a long breath. Marcus knelt in front of her. He grabbed her hands, rubbing hard because they were ice cold. "It's over. The doc and I are right here."

Her blue eyes widened as they searched his face. "I remember," she choked out the words.

Dr. Stern caught Marcus by the arm. "Come sit down. Let me chat with Chris for a minute." Her tone reminded him that she was the doctor.

He gritted his teeth and reluctantly followed instructions. She couldn't possibly realize that Chris had revealed a very important memory.

"Chris, I want you to take a few deep breaths." The doc waited a few seconds. "When you're ready, let's talk about what upset you."

"I have a brother." Chris sounded calm, but he wasn't buying it. She shuddered. "How could I have forgotten?" Her voice caught, and Marcus knew the tears had returned. The hell with standing behind her. He knelt next to her chair where they could see each other.

"If his existence was never mentioned, it's understandable that you'd forget him. Leaving him behind was a traumatic experience for you, too. You were a child and couldn't keep your promise, so you suppressed his memory to protect yourself from the pain."

"I remember my birth mother."

"Do you?" the doc challenged. "Or do you remember what you were told again and again over the years?"

"I'm not sure anymore."

"What did you promise him?" Marcus had to ask.

Chris frowned. "I promised I'd come back for him."

"Who was the oldest of you three?" Marcus pushed.

Chris's head tilted to the right. Her gaze focused somewhere only she could see. "Charlie was two years older than me." She dropped her head into her hands. "How could my mother and father have been so cruel as to split us up? Why?"

"The answer may stay buried with your adoptive parents," Marcus said. Chris's tortured expression ripped at his soul.

"Oh my God. The killer looked a lot like an older version of Charlie."

Pieces of the puzzle had started to drop into place. "Your description of the blond, blue-eyed killer brings a lot of answers to light."

Dr. Stern stood and glanced at her watch. "I'm expecting a patient in a few minutes, but if you'd like to dig deeper into your past, we can schedule an appointment."

"I'd like that, but let me call back with a time," Chris said.

Marcus helped Chris to her feet. He put his arm around her waist to steady her. Together, they followed Dr. Stern back down the hall to her office, where she checked her computer.

"I'm free between ten and twelve tomorrow. Call my assistant if you decide to come in."

"Thank you," Chris said. "I appreciate your help. I can't believe I'd blanked out that period of my life."

"You're welcome. One other thing you should be aware of, now that you remember your brother, more of the blanks in your past may come back on their own."

Marcus shook the doc's hand and then followed Chris to the elevator and outside. He called Nate while they walked to the car and quickly filled him in on everything she'd remembered. He slid behind the steering wheel. "Nate says our attorney has your adoption records. Kay's gone after them. They will be at the office by the time we get there."

"I'd rather go to the Miriam Waters Home for Children in Fort Worth. Maybe somebody there can tell us something. Surely, they keep records forever."

"We can try. Maybe they'll share information without you asking for a court order."

"Only one way to find out." She leaned her head back and closed her eyes.

"That's my girl. I told you before that your strength is amazing. I meant it."

"Why do I feel as if I've just run a marathon?"

"This is just a wild guess, but maybe it's because you just relived years of your life?" She smiled, and the weight of a brick house lifted off his shoulders.

"Can we make it to Fort Worth before the children's home closes?" she asked.

"I don't see why not."

"I have to know more about Charlie." Her fingers gripped Marcus's arm. "He's a monster. But why? He was a sweet little boy. What happened to him?"

"We'll find out. I'll let Nate know where we're going." Marcus fired off a text, started the rental car, and drove out of the parking lot. A few seconds later, his cell vibrated. "Nate must have questions." Marcus accepted the call. "What's up?"

"Dalton's with me," Nate said. "He has some questions for Chris about her brother."

"You got it," Marcus said. "Hang on." Marcus handed the cell to Chris. "Nate and Dalton. Go ahead."

"What was your last name before you were adopted?" Dalton asked.

"Shelby."

"And Charlie is two years older than you, right?" Marcus added.

"Yes. He'd be thirty-four now."

"You hear that?" Marcus asked Nate.

"Yeah. While you're in Fort Worth, Dalton and I will shake the bushes. See what we can learn about Charles Shelby."

"Good. How's my dog?"

"He gets petted more than I do. What does that tell you?"

"He's easier to love?"

"Could be." Nate laughed. "Kaycie just took him out back. Do you want to speak to him?"

"Cute." Marcus disconnected the call. "You getting thirsty or hungry?"

"No. I don't think I can eat." Chris wasn't sure she'd ever be able to hold food down. Charlie had butchered his own sister and tried to choke Chris. She could almost feel his hands on her throat.

"Hey," Marcus said. "You're going to get through this. I'm going to make sure you do."

"I could've saved Chelsea."

"You don't know that."

"I wasn't very nice to her the last time we spoke. Chelsea had been kicked out of another rehab center. She'd come home and was staying with our mother. I stopped by there one day and caught her berating our mother, trying to get money from her. I lost it. Accused her of being a selfish brat. She left and never came back."

"That wasn't your sister you were talking to. It was the drugs. The narcotics had taken over her every waking thought."

Marcus had been watching a van behind them. It had changed lanes with him twice. There had to be hundreds of white vans registered in Dallas County, but he wasn't taking any chances with Chris's safety.

CHAPTER 22

Chris grabbed the armrest to steady herself as Marcus crossed two lanes of freeway and shot down the off-ramp. She fought the urge to turn and look behind them. "Is someone following us?"

"I'll know for sure in just a minute." Marcus made a U-turn, swerving around the tight curve at a high speed. Just as the car leveled off, he pushed the gas pedal to the floor, slinging her back against the seat. Every nerve in her body tensed. Thank God, he hadn't let down his guard.

He glanced at the rearview mirror. "The white van came with us. Hang on."

With the skill of a race car driver, he wove in and out of traffic. This time she did turn to check behind them. She held her tongue, hoping he had shaken their tail.

"Nobody is behind us now," he said.

Chris's heart pounded against her rib cage. She tried to wet her lips, but her mouth was desert dry. "That was a wild ride."

"Son of a bitch must have picked us up when we left the office. I don't know how, because I watched carefully."

A sudden sinking feeling washed over Chris. She closed her eyes, hoping it would go away. Instead, she felt as if she were falling down a black hole. Her flesh and blood was responsible for all those murders. She'd studied the pictures and the reports. Those women had died horribly. They'd suffered because of a promise she'd made as a child?

"I can't get past Charlie doing those horrible things." An ache rushed through her entire body. Her seat belt seemed to get tighter, choking the breath out of her. "His voice has changed, but I should've recognized him on the message. 'Promises have to be kept no matter what your age.'"

"I still believe he has a partner. Could've been him who called." Marcus was no doubt trying to ease her pain. Who'd have thought that when she'd walked into the Lost and Found office, she'd meet someone like him?

He drove into a grocery store parking lot, put the car in park, and then unhooked his seat belt. His hand cupped her cheek. She knew better than to look into his eyes. She wasn't the strong person he thought her to be. He was much tougher than she was. Much more able to rein in his emotions. Much less likely to lose control.

"Don't be nice to me right now. I'll fall apart."

"Go ahead. I'll catch you." His thumb stroked her skin.

"I didn't want to believe my brother would actually kill me. I guess the van following us hammered everything home."

"He's not the same person you remember."

"You're right. But I can't help wondering what must've happened to him to turn him into this monster." She turned her head in his hand and kissed his palm. "We'd better get going. The home will close for the day around five. I think we want to talk to the first shift."

"How do you know what time they shut down?" Marcus drove to the freeway and blended in with the traffic.

"I have no idea. Maybe Dr. Stern was right about bits and pieces of my memory coming back."

****

DaVinci dropped the paint brush into a container of cleaner and hurried to answer his cell.

"Yes?"

"We've located her and her friend," his mentor said.

"And?" he asked.

"Her driver took evasive action and lost our lead tracker."

He didn't want to hear excuses. "Then why the hell did you call me?"

"I said the lead tracker lost visual contact. We have more than one car following her to prevent such occurrences." Michelangelo went on to explain that she and her bodyguard had gone to the Palmer Building, but a confrontation there in broad daylight hadn't been feasible.

"Where is she now?"

"On I-30, headed west toward Fort Worth."

"Stay with her. I want to know the minute they get situated for the night. I'll be dressed and ready." He disconnected, not waiting for a response.

****

Chris stopped at the bottom of the steps. Standing in front of the Miriam Waters Home for Children sent her memory into hyperdrive. Tiny pieces of her past flashed like a slide-show presentation, moving too fast to fully understand. She fisted her hands against the light-headed feeling pushing its way to the surface.

"You're not going in there alone." Marcus wrapped his arm around her shoulder. "If you'd rather, I'll come back by myself tomorrow. You'll be safe with Dalton and Nate watching your back. Not to mention Kay. She can kick ass when she has to."

Chris appreciated his offer to spare her and his attempt at humor. This visit wasn't a job she could shift onto his shoulders. "I have to do this. I want to."

"It could dredge up even more upsetting memories."

"Funny, standing here in front of the place, different emotions are flooding my brain. I recall crying for my mother late at night. An overwhelming sense of loneliness had wrapped around me. Along with an irrational fear of the dark."

"I imagine those feelings are normal for any child who'd been taken from her mother or who'd been abandoned."

She leaned against Marcus, drawing on his strength. "My fears went away when a new mommy and daddy took me home with them. I have to know how long Charlie was here. Was he adopted? Or did he get lost in the system?"

"Hey," Marcus said.

She turned to look at him, and his soft lips covered hers. This wasn't passion, it was comforting and connecting. It was his way of saying, "I'm sorry for all the sad days you had." And she loved him for it. Hopelessly loved him.

"If you're sure." He smiled down at her and swiped his thumb across her bottom lip. "Then let's do this."

"Okay."

Walking up the steps and into the building wasn't as daunting as she'd expected. The front desk still sat just inside the big double doors, which weren't all that large now that she was grown. She scanned the waiting area, noticing the softness of the decor, the pale-colored walls and a couch with two chairs facing it. No doubt, the space provided a place for adults to discuss which child to adopt or not.

"Chris," Marcus said, snapping her attention back to the front desk.

"Sorry, I was taking it all in."

A striking brunette was heading straight toward them. She wore navy slacks and a crisp white blouse. Her thick-soled flats spoke to the many miles she probably walked every day. She smiled, and her compassionate eyes sparkled.

"I'm Joyce Waters. You look a little lost. Can I help?"

Chris introduced herself, offered her hand, and Ms. Waters clasped it tightly. Chris relaxed a little. "I lived here twenty-five years ago."

"An alumni. Welcome back."

"Thank you. This is Marcus Ricci. He's helping me locate my brother."

Marcus handed his business card to Ms. Waters. "Nice to meet you," he said, shaking her hand. "We're looking for information on Charles Shelby."

The woman picked up a pen off the front desk and wrote Charles's name on the back of the card. "That long ago, you should speak with my mother. If you'll wait here, I'll see if she's available." Ms. Waters turned and walked down a hall.

Chris fought back the crushing feeling in her chest. "What if she refuses to help us?"

"Then we'll find another way. I don't know Texas law when it comes to situations like this. We may need a court order."

Ms. Waters didn't return quickly. Chris's nerves got the best of her and she paced, hoping to learn more about the past.

"Here she comes. Are you ready?" Marcus asked.

"Yes."

Ms. Waters motioned Chris and Marcus to follow. "If you'll come with me."

She ushered them into a small office and introduced them. The woman who rose and shook their hands didn't look familiar to Chris. She tried to remember something, anything, but failed. Once they had been seated in plain but functional office chairs, she stopped trying.

"Forgive the wait. I wanted to pull up your files. My daughter said your name is Christine Shelby and you're searching for your brother Charles?"

"That's correct. My sister, Chelsea, was here with us, also."

"You're trying to locate both of your siblings?" The older Ms. Waters brushed a hand over her salt and pepper hair. Maybe in her late fifties, she was attractive, but her eyes held a sadness.

"Just my brother." For a second, Chris debated whether telling the truth would help or not. "My sister and I were adopted, but for some reason our adoptive parents didn't take him. It's important that I learn everything about him that I can."

"I pulled up the archives. Some things came back to me as I read. I'm happy to share those memories." Her fingers moved to the collar of her blouse, patting it as if it had suddenly become askew. "Unfortunately, I can't be a lot of help."

"I'm going to excuse myself," the younger Ms. Waters said. "You're in good hands."

Marcus stood, shook her hand, and then returned to his chair. He leaned forward. "It's really important we locate Charles Shelby."

Ms. Waters leaned back in her chair, her friendly demeanor shifting to that of sympathy. "Charles is in trouble, isn't he?"

"We think so," Chris said, deciding lying would serve no purpose. "Do you remember him?"

"I do. And I wish I had better news."

"Can you tell us what happened to him?"

"I can share some personal memories. After you girls were adopted, Charles became destructive and disruptive. We thought if we quickly relocated him with a family, he'd settle down. More than one set of foster parents returned him because he was too unruly. One couple said he was downright cruel."

"I don't remember him being mean."

"He was an angry little boy when you children arrived." Ms. Waters stared at her computer screen for a minute. "Another family tried to channel his anger. They got him interested in oil painting. According to their statement, your brother had an extraordinary talent."

"So they kept him?" Chris took a second to absorb that fact. Even though raised apart, they both painted.

"No. The mother got pregnant, and they felt Charles's behavioral problems would be a risk to the baby."

Abandoned again, Chris thought while Ms. Waters scanned and scrolled. How could any child be expected to understand being dumped and rejected over and over? Chris ached for all the times he'd been rejected.

Ms. Waters opened her mouth then closed it. Color flooded her cheeks.

"Please don't hold back. I have to know," Chris pushed.

"Charles ran away a few times, but he was always found and returned to us. He vanished from his last foster home. No one ever heard from him again."

"How old was he?"

"Fifteen." Ms. Waters chewed on the corner of her bottom lip. "I can share this information with you because it's an open case with the Fort Worth Police Department. They came here looking for Charles. They wanted to question him regarding a murder and mutilation. The foster parents' son was found dead the same day your brother disappeared from their home."

Dots swam in front of Chris's eyes. Marcus reached over and squeezed her hand as if he understood she was struggling with such horrible news.

"So the police never located Charles, and he never turned up here?" Marcus asked.

"I can't tell you more than what I have." Ms. Watered folded her hands and rested them on her desk. "Names, addresses, that kind of information is kept private. Check with the police. They can tell you if he was ever arrested."

"Something horrible must've happened to my brother."

Ms. Waters moved to the chair next to Chris. "I've probably told you more than I should've. I'm sorry I can't give you the names of the foster homes your brother was in. That order would have to come from the court."

"You've told us what we needed to know. I appreciate your time and help." Chris stood. "We'll show ourselves out. Thank you for your help."

"You're welcome. Come again. The children love it when alumni stop by and spend time with them."

Chris and Marcus walked outside and down the stairs without speaking. She turned and studied the home one last time. "Maybe I will come back. This is the perfect place to offer financial assistance."

"I think you're right."

The wind picked up, and a chill raced along her arms. "When I think about the wonderful life I had as a kid and then consider what Charlie must have endured, it makes me ill. I don't remember him being destructive or mean. The little boy who keeps surfacing in my memory was an almost too-sweet, innocent child."

Marcus guided her to the car. Once she'd buckled her seat belt, he leaned over and kissed her forehead. He closed her door, walked around the car, and got in. "I'll grant that he went through hell. I hate to sound harsh, but your brother is a grown man, and he's responsible for some heinous crimes. Every second of the day, you have to remember that he killed six women that we know of, one of them being one of his sisters. He's committed to seeing you dead."

"I understand. Nothing justifies his actions." A quick blast of exhaustion hit Chris. How long could she keep hiding from Charlie when he seemed so determined to make her pay?

Marcus dug his cell out of his pocket. "Nate and Dalton need to hear what we've learned." He hit a speed-dial number then handed her the phone. "It's on speaker. We'll both talk."

The call went as expected. Marcus navigated afternoon traffic while both men on the other end of the line listened to her.

"We're running his name through the databases," Dalton said. "That's a fairly common name. More than one have had a brush with the law, so we'll take a look at each of them after we narrow the list using his age. He could be using an alias or he's stayed under the cops' radar. I'll run him through the federal database."

"So you're on board?" Chris asked Dalton.

"That we're looking for your brother? Yes. Your conversation with Ms. Waters convinced me. Experience tells me that he was abused, probably mentally, physically, and sexually. He believes everything that happened to him as a child is your fault. None of it would've happened if you had gone back for him."

"What the hell kind of statement is that?" Marcus snapped off the question. Chris watched his knuckles tighten on the steering wheel. "Sounds like you're blaming Chris."

"Hold on," Dalton said. "I'm telling you what I think is going through his mind."

Chris smiled, reached over, and tugged Marcus's hand off the steering wheel. Winding her fingers through his, she commented, "We'd figured that out. It doesn't matter that I was a child, too. I promised him I'd come back."

"Exactly," Dalton said. "He hung on to that like a lifeline. Eventually it became distorted, gave him an excuse to lash out."

"We'll be there in a few minutes to pick up Diablo." Marcus abruptly changed the subject. "Nate, did Kay line up a place for us to stay tonight?"

"Yeah. I'll give you the address when you get here. See you in a bit."

Marcus ended the call.

"That was abrupt."

"Sorry. I was pissed. Dalton could've worded that a little better."

"Thank you for defending me, for having my back at the psychologist's office, and for holding my hand at the children's home. If we weren't on the freeway, I'd reward you, even if your anger was misguided."

"What makes you think I won't pull off on the shoulder of the road to collect this 'reward'?" He glanced at her, and even his eyes smiled.

"Hmm, let me think. Could it be that you don't want to get arrested for indecent exposure?"

"Don't push me," he said, and he broke out in a full-blown grin.

"It's good to see you're human."

"It's good to see you let go of today's round of bad news and horrors. I'm proud of you."

"Well, thank you." The thought of another night alone with Marcus appealed to her, but would it go on forever? Would it end with both their deaths? "Are we being followed?"

"I don't think so." He checked the rearview mirror. "Did you see something?"

"No. I had a thought."

"I'm listening."

"We can't hide forever. So set a trap using me as bait."

CHAPTER 23

Marcus took a second before he responded. That Chris had again offered herself as a lure to entice a showdown ranked somewhere between heroic and insane. He'd known women who would've crumpled under the weight of the murders and the realization her brother was behind it all. Not her. She'd proved to be a real trouper. Intelligent and courageous. He liked and respected those qualities about her.

"Are you thinking my idea over? Or are you ignoring me?" She reached across and tugged his earlobe.

"I was ignoring you." He added a smile to let her know he was joking. Anything to get her to forget such a dangerous idea. "Intentionally putting you in jeopardy would make me crazy. I won't do it."

"That's the nicest thing you've ever said to me." She released his earlobe and stroked his neck with her fingers.

"Really? Then I need to get better at complimenting you." Jesus, she was like a runaway horse with the bit in its teeth. "I get that you're tired of running, hate hiding, and want this to be over. But I won't gamble with your life. Ask any cop and he'll tell you that most cases aren't solved by good police work. They're solved because the case is approached in a logical and analytical manner."

"My offer stands. Use me, if or when you feel it's time."

"End of discussion. Lost and Found does not use their clients as bait. And you're more than that."

"I am?" She punched him in the arm.

"You are if that counts as a compliment."

"I haven't decided."

Marcus hated to push, but he needed to know if she'd remembered anything else. Know your enemy was a good practice in any walk of life. That someone like Chris, who would never hurt anyone, was being stalked, not to mention all the women Charlie had apparently killed, pushed Marcus's temper right to the edge. Although he'd prefer the state of Texas put a needle in her brother's arm, Marcus had no qualms about killing the bastard if necessary.

"You're not listening." She touched his arm, snapping him out of his thoughts. "Where were you?"

"Hoping the state takes care of ending your brother instead of me."

"I understand you don't want to kill him. Neither do I."

"Just so we're clear, if the situation presents itself, I have no problem taking his life. But he is your blood, and once, a long time ago, you loved him."

"You think I'd be angry with you for killing him to save my life or yours? Never. I hope it doesn't come to that."

"It might."

"I know. But I can't help thinking about Dalton's profile of Charlie. He must've endured a lot of things we know nothing about. I understand he's insane and has to be stopped."

Marcus breathed a little easier. "Anything else about Charlie come to you?"

"Bits and pieces. His hair was blond like Chelsea's and mine, but he never had the curls we did. People thought he was adorable, which makes it even odder that Mom and Dad didn't adopt him, too."

Marcus drove off the freeway and checked the rearview mirror. There was too much end-of-the-day traffic to say they hadn't been followed. He pulled the rental car between Nate's car and Dalton's rental and parked. Most of the businesses had closed for the day. The detective agency and the sandwich shop were the only buildings still open. Overhead lighting gave off a bright glow, but Marcus didn't like being out in the open. Too much had happened. He'd be extra cautious crossing the parking lot with her.

"Let's get Diablo, find out where we're sleeping tonight, and call it a day." Marcus unbuckled his seat belt and turned to face Chris. She did the same, only she leaned across the seat and kissed him.

"Thank you," she whispered into his lips.

"Don't thank me yet. We haven't caught your brother and turned him over to the cops."

"Not for that. Thank you for being there for me. The children's home wasn't an easy trip for me, and I appreciate your support. You're a special man. A rare breed of good guys."

Marcus squirmed in his seat. Unused to flowery compliments, he was at a loss for a second. "At least you didn't tell me I was beautiful," he joked.

"That's for when you're naked." She opened the car door.

"Wait. Don't get out." Marcus scanned the lot as he walked around to her. He extended his hand. "Come on." With her directly in front of him, they walked into the building.

Once inside she glanced over her shoulder and grinned. His heart did a weird flip as she turned the corner and went to the conference room. So this was how Nate felt when Kay tossed him a sexy look?

Marcus had forgotten the feeling of excitement that caring about another person gave him. He'd blocked it out. Hadn't wanted to run the risk. Hadn't believed he deserved another chance. He shook his head. Now wasn't the time to lose focus.

He lifted a slat on the window blinds, scanning the almost empty parking lot. Traffic was light, but he watched the street, noticing as a plumber's van, a taxi, and a beat-up truck drove by. None of the vehicles' occupants looked toward the office.

Where was their tail? No way had the crazy bastard given up. Like a copperhead, he was lying low, waiting for the right time to strike.

He felt Diablo lean against him. Marcus dropped down on one knee and buried his hands in the soft fur. The dog had quickly warmed to affection, lapping it up as if he'd never been petted before. He was slowly forgetting all the bad habits he'd been taught. Diablo tilted his head and licked Marcus on the chin. When he stood and walked to the conference room, the dog followed.

Nate, Kay, and Dalton were leaning back in their chairs, chatting with Chris, who stood in the doorway. Marcus had the feeling she was waiting for him. They both sat and collectively took a deep breath. This day was over. They'd share information and head somewhere quiet. First, Chris was asked to share her conversations with Dr. Stern and Ms. Waters. She did so with a minimum of words. She'd learned a lot today and needed time to digest it all.

"Did you uncover anything helpful? she asked Dalton.

"Nothing yet. We could narrow it down if you remembered a middle name," Dalton said to Chris.

"I have no idea." Chris's eyes closed for a minute. "I don't even know if my middle name is the one my birth mother gave me. And I sure don't remember Charlie's."

"We'll weed through the records," Dalton said. "Single out individuals about the right age."

"If there's nothing else, I think we should all call it a night." Marcus scooted his chair back.

Kay stood. "Let me get you tonight's address. It's not fancy, but it's nice."

"Just as long as there's a hot shower, I'll be happy." Chris followed Kay to the front of the office.

Dalton looked up from his laptop. "We don't have a lot to go on."

Marcus leaned to the side and watched until Chris was out of sight. "Charles Shelby stayed in this area. He lives here and hunts here. Think about it. Proves my theory that he has a partner, one who doesn't give a damn what color hair his victim has."

"I agree. The partner is an unknown, and that makes him even more dangerous. We have nothing on him, which is why we need Shelby alive," Dalton said pointedly.

"I'm not going to kill him." Marcus didn't try to hide his annoyance. He might want to beat the bastard to death, but he understood the law wanted to question him. "Not unless he forces my hand, and if he does, it will be my pleasure to end his sorry life."

Nate stood and strangled out a cough. "If you'd like me to stand guard duty tonight, I'm ready. If not, let's take this up tomorrow."

"Chris wouldn't sleep a wink if she knew you were out there. Hell, she'd be in the car with you."

"If you change your mind, let me know. We won't tell her."

"I could use your help when we leave," Marcus said. "I didn't spot a tail on the way back from Fort Worth, but I'd appreciate backup for a few miles until we're clear."

"You got it," Nate said.

Dalton closed his laptop and stood. "I'll work on this from the hotel. I'll have the list narrowed down by morning."

"I can't believe the FBI hasn't outfitted you with a tablet," Nate said. "They're a lot easier to carry around."

"It's an option." Dalton lifted a shoulder. "But I prefer my old laptop."

"Good enough," Nate said.

"See you," Marcus said as Dalton waved and headed for the door. "And you," Marcus said to Nate. "I'll check in later."

"You okay?" Nate's hand came to rest on Marcus's shoulder.

"Yeah. Why?" Marcus thought it was an odd question, especially coming from Nate.

"I don't give advice often, but you're emotionally involved with Chris." He cut off a response from Marcus by holding up his hand. "I'm not saying that's a bad thing, but if something happens to her, how are you going to handle it?"

"Nothing's going to happen."

"I've seen the way you two look at each other. Today it was even clearer." He held up both hands this time. "Hang on. The sermon is almost over. I'm your friend, and I worry about you."

"I appreciate your concern. But I'm a big boy. Let me worry about myself."

"I'll try, brother. I'll try." Nate clapped his hand on Marcus's shoulder. "Let's get out of here. Kaycie and I will follow you for a few miles. If somebody's on your tail, I'll call the cops. If we can trap him, we'll either have Shelby or someone who can lead us to him."

"Works for me." Marcus and Nate walked to Kay's work area. She was handing a thick manila envelope to Chris, who folded it to her chest.

"My adoption papers."

"Thanks." Marcus winked at Kay.

"No problem," Kay said. "With everything you've learned about Chris's brother, I'm not sure the information will help." Kay handed a document to Marcus. "Paperwork you need to sign from the builder. He's started on your house and needs your okay on something."

Marcus scanned the work order, signed on the dotted line, and handed it back. "My insurance agency check should show up here, too. Then I can turn in the rental and buy myself a car."

"I'll let you know when it arrives."

"You ready?" Marcus asked Chris.

"Yes. I have a lot to absorb and think about."

"We're all calling this day done, too," Nate said.

On the walk to the car, Marcus explained to Chris that Nate was going to follow them for a while. "He'll spot a tail if there is one."

"You guys are really close. I envy you that bond."

"Yeah. We've been like family for a long time. Funny how we went our separate ways after college, but when we teamed up ten years later, it was as if we'd been together the day before." Marcus waited until Nate and Kay were inside their car before he pulled onto the freeway and blended in with traffic. He didn't have to look to know Nate was right behind him.

"Where are your parents?" Chris asked.

"Like yours, they're gone. Dad retired from the Air Force. He'd been a pilot for years and went straight to work for an airline. When he retired, he couldn't keep his feet on the ground, so he bought a single-engine plane. He and Mom flew all over the US. A sudden storm blew in, he lost power, and couldn't keep the nose up. They both died in the crash."

"I'm sorry." Her hand touched his arm.

"Me, too."

"The affection in your voice tells me that you miss them."

"You're right. Dad always talked about how he was going to spoil his grandson. He was so afraid the name would die."

"What if you end up with all girls?" she asked.

The smile in her voice prompted Marcus to play along. "Heaven forbid." He laughed. "Actually, he'd have been thrilled just to have a grandbaby, male or female."

"I can imagine," she agreed. "But denying the world a little boy who looked exactly like you would be unfair."

"I don't know about that." His cell buzzed, and he passed it to Chris. "Read that text from Nate for me. He's probably heading home."

"He says there's a black pickup that changes lanes every time we do. It also speeds up and slows down with us. We're supposed to stay on the freeway. Nate decided to get Dalton involved. He got a quick response from the cops."

Marcus gripped her knee and squeezed. "Text him to make sure the cops come in silent. We don't want to scare this guy off."

"Marcus?" She only said his name, but fear had put a tremble in her voice.

"We'll be fine. Trust me."

Marcus pressed the gas pedal to the floor, pushing the car's speed just to the posted limit. The rental responded nicely, allowing him to easily move into the outside lane.

"When will the police get here?"

"Shouldn't be long now."

Chris jumped when his cell buzzed. "Want me to read it?"

"Yeah."

"Nate says we should slow down. Let black truck get closer. Takedown in five." She sucked in a breath.

"The car between us and the truck is getting tired of going this slow, he's passing. Hang on." Marcus slammed on the brakes just as Nate pulled beside the truck and moved into his lane, forcing the black vehicle to the shoulder. A black and white slid in behind the pickup. "Got the bastard."

Marcus had barely uttered the words when the truck lurched forward. "He's making a run for it."

Marcus had nowhere to go and there wasn't room for their car and the pickup. He swerved as far into the center lane as he could safely. The truck barely missed the rental as it rushed past. Chris ducked toward the center console. Her eyes were squeezed closed.

The truck's oversize bumper guard clipped the edge of a bridge abutment. It spun out of control, flipped onto its side, and then rolled down the grass embankment into the traffic below. The crunch of metal and shattering of glass didn't bode well for the driver.

"Son of a bitch." Marcus shook his head, maneuvering the car all the way off the road onto the shoulder. Nate parked directly behind Marcus. He and Kay hurried down the embankment.

"We have to go help." Chris reached for her seat belt.

"I'm sorry, but it's too dangerous for you to be outside."

"I know you're right. But if it's my brother..."

Her voice trailed off. She didn't finish the sentence, and he didn't push. "Nate will let us know something as soon as he can."

A couple of ambulances came and left, but from where they were parked, Marcus couldn't see who the EMTs carried to the hospital or if the passengers were even alive.

Chris fidgeted in her seat until Nate and Kay walked up the embankment with a police officer at their side.

"Now we can get out," Marcus said, barely getting the words out before Chris had opened her door.

The officer asked for their identification and checked it against something written in his notebook.

"I referred DPD to Dalton. Figured he could vouch for us," Nate said.

"The driver of the pickup?" Chris asked as Kay moved to stand next to her.

"He died before the firefighters could cut him out." The officers passed Marcus's and Chris's driver's licenses back to them.

"It wasn't Charles," Nate said.

"Do you recognize this man?" The officer handed Chris a driver's license.

"No. I've never seen him before," Chris said.

Marcus looked over her shoulder and studied the young man's picture. "He's just a kid."

"Barely twenty-two," the cop confirmed. "At this point, while we think he was following you, there's no proof. But he sure didn't want to be questioned. We'll check his family and friends. See if we can find out why."

"Was anyone else hurt?" Chris asked.

"Not seriously," the cop said. "A man and woman were transported to the hospital, but their injuries weren't life threatening. A few minor scrapes for the other two drivers involved."

"So we can go?" she asked.

"Sure thing. We have names and phone numbers." The officer slipped the dead man's license into his notebook and walked back down to his patrol car.

"He was well informed," Marcus said.

"I called Dalton. He talked to someone at DPD. Interesting to see how smooth things go when we have the FBI working with us. When you drive away, a patrol car will follow you to the motel." Nate walked over and put his arm around his wife. "I'm taking Kaycie home. You two should get off the highway."

"Talk with you soon." Marcus held Chris's door for her, walked around the car, and then got behind the wheel. He checked his rearview mirror and then slowly filtered the car into the still slow-moving traffic. In the distance, a black and white followed. Nobody knew for sure if the danger of being followed had been removed. How many thugs had been hired to keep tabs on Chris?

He couldn't lose sight of the threat. Failing wasn't an option. No way could he let her down.

****

Chris couldn't shake the visual of the crashed black pickup. The sound of metal crunching, the noise of the sirens, and the news of the young man's death would stay with her for a long time.

She had closed her eyes, laid her head back, and tried to keep the images at bay. Anything that might help calm fear that tried to take root and grow. She had to keep it together. Too many people were working hard to ensure her safety. She had to be strong for them.

Her cell buzzed, startling her. "Very few people have this number." She fished the phone out of her pocket and checked the screen. "It's Melanie, one of my Little Sisters. What am I going to tell her if she wants to take in a movie or something? It's too dangerous to have physical contact with either of the girls."

"Talk to her. If you have to, tell you're going out of town but can be reached by phone."

Chris answered, chatting with the young girl who'd been removed from her parents' custody because of their drug use. When the call ended, Chris felt better.

"Your side of the conversation was upbeat. I'm guessing all is well."

"It's great news. Melanie made the school's debate team. She's got great foster parents. They're supportive of her activities. All I do is offer a little praise. Sometimes a friendly ear means a great deal to a foster kid."

"Speaking with her certainly helped your mood."

"It did. I'm supposed to be helping them cope, but I think it's the other way around."

"I'd say you and the girls are lucky to have each other."

Chris studied Marcus's profile. In her opinion, he was stunning. The lines of his face, the determined set of his jaw, his deep-chocolate eyes that could look into your soul, gave him a look of confidence. Yet, he had no idea the effect he had on people.

She'd teased him that the world shouldn't be denied a little Marcus. Truth was, the idea of him fathering a child with anyone but her had her stomach tumbling. It just wouldn't be acceptable.

Realization smacked into her. She'd done exactly what she feared most. She'd fallen in love with him. Hopelessly and forever, gushy words and all, in love with him. And that just wouldn't do. Not until she was sure how he felt about her. She'd read that in crises some people turned to each other for comfort. Even after a death in the family, sex could be an affirmation of life. Chris knew her heart, and that didn't apply here, and Marcus was used to working in crisis mode. He cared for her. How much was the question.

"Hey. You look like you're going to open the door and jump." Marcus's tone was heavy with concern. "We're safe for now."

Chris realized she had a death grip on the armrest and her seat belt. She made a big show of uncoiling. "Just a little aftershock. So many questions keep running through my mind."

"For instance?"

"Is Charlie following us? What are his plans? Does he plan to torture me like he did those other women?" She'd lied to Marcus, but no way would she admit she was thinking about him.

"No. He won't make it past me." The finality in Marcus's words scared her.

"I'm guessing he plans to kill you first." She had no doubt Marcus would sacrifice himself to keep her safe. It was who he was.

"If he gets to you, I will be dead, but I don't plan on getting killed."

Marcus pulled up to a stop sign. Chris hadn't realized they'd traveled so far or that they'd left the freeway. "We're on the outskirts of town. Are we almost there?"

"Yeah. I'm double checking that nobody followed us."

They sat in silence for a few minutes while Marcus watched the road, and then he made a U-turn and got back on the freeway. A few seconds later, he pulled into the lot of a motel and parked close to the entrance. "Not as fancy as the other night, but Kay picked a place where all the doors into the rooms are from the inside. Plus, there's a restaurant on site."

Chris couldn't imagine being hungry. She waited next to her door while Marcus got out and took the suitcases from the trunk. His gaze was intense as he scanned the area. Dalton had to find Charlie. She couldn't bear the thought of Marcus dying because of her.

"Once we're settled, I want you to tell me what really upset you."

She opened her mouth but had no argument. Instead, she smiled and allowed him to guide her inside. Again, he placed his body between her and the street.

Marcus checked in, making sure the room Kay had reserved was on the first floor.

"Does it matter?" Chris asked, keeping her voice low.

"Yeah." He grinned down at her. "If I have to toss you out a window to run for safety, I'd rather do it from the ground floor."

"Oh," she said. "Got it." She fell in step beside him and together they walked down the hall. He stepped inside the room, looked around, and then let her enter.

No matter what happened she'd always be grateful to Marcus. If he cornered her about their relationship, she'd look him straight in his eyes and lie. No way could she tell him how she felt. The next move had to be his.

She flipped on the light, vowing to make the most of her time with him.

CHAPTER 24

Chris dropped down on the couch, slid off her shoes, and looked at the manila envelope containing her adoption papers.

Marcus placed the suitcases on a stand and sat on the edge of one of the beds. "You just going to stare at the outside? Aren't you curious?"

"Why am I reluctant to open this? There can't be many surprises left."

"You'll have to look and see."

"Sit with me?"

He joined her on the couch, reached over and lifted her feet onto his lap. Strong thumbs applied pressure to her arch, and she sighed. "You go ahead," he said. "I'll entertain myself."

She dumped the contents in her lap and started reading the first document. There was more information than she'd expected. "Interesting. My mother left us at the home but hadn't actually given us up for adoption. When the Hollands came, they intended to foster a couple of children. Apparently, they changed their minds and decided they wanted to adopt. Before that could happen, my birth mother had to legally relinquish her maternal rights to us. She made us wards of the court. She literally gave all three of us away."

"Yet, the Hollands took only two of you."

Chris couldn't imagine her mom and dad leaving Charlie behind. She'd never known them to be cruel, but that single act was beyond her understanding. She read on. "Holy crap. This is important."

"What is it?"

"Charlie's last name was different than mine and Chelsea's. It says so right here in the document our birth mother signed for the state. Christine Shelby, Chelsea Shelby, and Charles Bridger. Dalton is checking out men with the wrong name."

"I can fix that." Marcus called Dalton and gave him the news. "I'd better tell Nate, too."

Chris read on, half-listening to Marcus's conversations. His tone softened, and she assumed Kay had answered the phone. "Yeah. Bridger." He spelled the name out loud. "Tell Nate when he gets out of the shower."

Chris handed him the papers. "There's nothing else of interest here."

"What else did you expect to learn?" He leaned forward and rubbed her calves.

"I'll probably never find the answer to the one question that will haunt me forever. Why split up our family? Mom and Dad were brilliant, educated, and kind. Yet, they left a little boy behind. One who'd lost his mother and then his sisters." She blinked back the tears that threatened to fall. "In my wildest dreams, I can't imagine how he felt when we drove away. For a nine-year-old, the pain must've been unbearable." She swiped the back of her hand across her cheeks.

"I wish I could answer that for you." Suddenly, her feet were on the floor, and Marcus was next to her. He pulled her onto his lap and cradled her in his arms. "It's okay to cry."

Chris couldn't shake the image of a young Charlie from her mind. A vision of a broken and rejected child would haunt her forever. A child who'd endured all sorts of atrocities and had grown up seeking revenge. She had no idea how long Marcus held her or how long she cried, but his stomach growling pulled her back to the present.

"You're hungry," she said into his neck. Closing her eyes, she inhaled, soaking in his scent and hoping to absorb some of his strength.

"I'll eat later."

"I hardly ever cry. My dad believed shedding tears didn't create solutions." She brushed away the lock of hair that had fallen onto his forehead and kissed him. "Thank you."

"Anytime. Was this what had you so spooked in the car?"

"I was thinking how I hope no one else dies because of me."

"Chris—"

"No. It's true. I get that I'm not to blame. No way could I keep a promise to go back for Charlie. But somebody is responsible for what happened to him."

"I'm not trying to sound callous, but you have to keep your perspective here. Do you have any idea how many kids go through bad foster homes? Or how many suffer abuse from adults? Thank God, they haven't all snapped."

"Of course you're right. My Little Sisters are perfect examples. They will go on to lead productive lives, not because of me, because of something good inside them. But Charlie never had a chance." She slid off Marcus's lap and stood. "Enough. Let's figure out something for your dinner."

"Chris, I wasn't trying to upset you."

She scrubbed her hands over her face. "I know. And in my heart, I get it. My brother made his choices."

"You need to eat, too. How about I order pizza?"

"I'll do it." She went after her cell and looked up the nearest place that delivered. "What do you want for toppings?"

"Anything you eat."

Chris made the call, ordering pepperoni, Italian sausage, and bell peppers. "They're running behind. The pizza should be here in forty-five minutes."

"No problem. I'm going to take a shower." Marcus stood and walked toward the bathroom.

He'd tried to console her, made an effort to reason with her, and she'd responded badly.

"Marcus?"

He turned and said nothing.

"Is there room for two?"

The corners of his mouth lifted as he walked closer. "You bet."

All she could see was a sliver of his bare chest. Her hands itched to slide across the hard plane of skin, to stroke his shoulders and arms. Her mouth watered at the thought.

He walked into her until his entire body was flush with hers. He pushed her hair off her neck, kissed her behind the ear, catching her earlobe with his teeth. His hands covered her breasts, causing them to strain against the lace bra. Bolts of lightning couldn't burn any hotter than his touch. Chill bumps raced down her arms, while at the same time, liquid fire rushed through her blood.

Marcus's erection pressed into her, making it difficult for her to think of anything other than how wonderful he felt. "We don't have a lot of time, but we should probably rinse off."

They scattered their clothes one piece at a time, leaving a marked trail to the bathroom. Chris stepped onto the bath mat and held out her hand. Her gaze drifted across his body. Long firm legs, trim hips and thighs, but it was his chest that made her mouth water.

He held her grasp and pulled her into his arms. "You are so incredibly beautiful."

Chris pulled her gaze from his chest up to meet his. Beautiful wasn't a word she'd use to describe herself, but the way he looked at her made her feel like the most gorgeous woman on earth.

Lust had darkened his eyes to almost black. His mouth crashed down on hers, demanding entry. His tongue probed, warring with hers for position. He wrapped her hair around his hand and pulled her head back. Kissing his way down, he nipped her nipple then lavished attention on it with his tongue.

Chris's body was on fire. Her skin burned everywhere he touched and ached for him everywhere he hadn't. Need spun out of control.

"No shower," she managed to say. "Bed."

"Right." He flashed a bright smile, reached in and turned off the water.

Chris wasn't sure how she wound up on the bed amidst all the kissing and touching. All she knew was Marcus had a condom in his hand. Impatient to touch him, she reached over and removed the packet from him. "Let me."

She took her time, wrapped her fingers around his erection, and marveled as the velvety steel hardened even more at her touch. Slowly, she rolled their protection down his length.

"You're killing me," he hissed, pulling her down on the mattress.

His hand slid between her legs, but she stopped him. "No waiting this time. No foreplay. I need to feel you inside me. Now."

He wedged his hips between her thighs, and she opened her legs wider, offering him everything she had. He entered her, and she lifted her hips, taking him deeper. Chris was lost in the emotion boiling up from deep inside and the passion begging for release. For now, there was no killer. No mystery to solve. No end to her love for the man in her arms. She tried to memorize every inch of silky skin and every hard muscle underneath.

Marcus stopped and lay very still, watching her face. Then he began a slow and steady movement. Claiming what was already his.

****

Marcus, spent and sweating, knew he had to be crushing Chris. Knew he should at least roll off to her side. They might have just had the shortest lovemaking session on record, but his orgasm had to have registered on the Richter scale. Somewhere along the way, his heart had left his body. He was fairly sure it had taken up residence next to hers.

"Sorry," he mumbled into her neck. "I'll move." He tried to push up on his forearms, but Chris locked her legs and arms around him.

"No. Don't go. Stay where you are for a few more minutes."

Shit. He distinctly heard tears in her voice. The last thing he wanted to do was hurt the woman he'd fallen in...really? Really. He loved her. When this was over, he'd figure out a way to convince her they should be together.

The knock on the motel room door made both of them jump. The pizza.

Marcus tossed the condom in the trash and quickly slid on his jeans. He grabbed his gun from the nightstand. "Where's your pistol?"

"In my purse on the coffee table. Do you think—?"

"You can never be too safe." He went to the door, bent down, and then looked through the peephole. "No pizza. It's the desk clerk."

Chris had slipped on her jeans and was buttoning her blouse. He fished out her gun and handed it to her. The knock came again, only this time louder.

"Yeah?" he called out, without opening the door. "Anybody gets past me, you shoot the son of a bitch." He pointed to the bed, waiting until she stood next to it out of the way.

"You got a message to call Nate," the voice from the hallway said.

"Will do. Thanks." Marcus watched through the peephole as the guy shook his head and walked away.

Chris handed Marcus his cell. He sat on the couch and patted the spot next to him. "You might as well hear the conversation."

Nate answered on the first ring, "Answer your damn cell. You scared the shit out of me."

"Sorry, I was in the other room."

"Dalton ran the driver of the black pickup through the system. Local thug with a handful of arrests. Nothing big enough to warrant a lengthy stay in Huntsville State Prison. DPD will dig deeper and get back to us."

"We figured Chris's brother had help."

"I called Tomas. He'll get involved. Make sure the communication stays open. I wasn't worried, but I think he needs to stay involved."

"Maybe this is the break we needed."

"I hope so," Nate said. "Just as a precaution, I'm headed your way. Give me a call in the morning when you're ready to check out, and I'll follow you to the office."

"Bring Diablo. Let me know when you get here. I'll come out after him." Marcus ended the call.

A second knock on the door pulled Marcus to his feet. Once again, he checked the peephole. A man wearing a red-checked hat and shirt held a pizza box.

"Who'd you order the pizza from?"

"Pizza Pete's."

"That's what his hat says. Let's not get careless." Marcus pulled a twenty from his wallet. "Take your pistol and stand out of sight."

He cracked the door, leaving the safety chain in place. "How much?"

The aroma wafted off the pizza and into the room while the man pulled the ticket off the box and handed it to Marcus. "Sixteen forty-eight."

Marcus passed him the twenty. "Set the pizza on the floor and keep the change."

The guy looked at him as if he were crazy, but did as he was told. He stuffed the cash into his pocket and walked away.

"I'm starving," Chris said.

Marcus opened the door and reached for the box. A pop followed by a flash of color and the back of his head felt as if it had caught fire. Shit. He'd been shot. He staggered, stumbled, trying to keep his feet under him. Chris screamed his name. Another gunshot rang out. Darkness engulfed him.

****

Chris couldn't breathe. Something covered her entire head. She couldn't move her arms or legs. Her brain screamed. She'd been tied to a chair.

She forced herself to stop trying to gulp large quantities of oxygen into her lungs. Small inhales and exhales through her nose proved more productive. She twisted her head, trying to dislodge the encumbrance. The movement sent nausea washing over her. Please, no. She couldn't throw up.

Laser-like pain sliced through her at the memory of Marcus lying on the floor, the back of his head bleeding. The pizza man had stepped inside the room, aiming at Marcus's forehead. She'd fired at him, but her bullet had only clipped his arm. How could she have forgotten to keep firing? In seconds, the man had been on her, wrenching the gun from her hand.

"You killed him," she'd screamed.

"Shut up or you're next," an older man, dressed in a suit, said as he entered the room. Disdain had clouded his face as he looked her over from head to toe.

She'd run toward him, ready to pummel the life out of him, but he shoved her to the floor. An eerie calm had come over her. "Where's my brother?"

"We'll see how brave you are after he gets his hands on you." He'd grabbed her hair and slapped a rag over her face. "If you weren't so important to him, I'd enjoy killing you myself."

That was the last thing she remembered. Where had they taken her?

Pain rose like a huge wave, pulling her into the undertow. She couldn't move anything except her fingers and head. Bound tightly and still barefoot, she wiggled her toes against some kind of rug. Was she hearing crickets chirping? "Marcus," she moaned. "Where are you?"

"I'm afraid there's no one here by that name," a voice said from close to her ear. "He's dead, and you're all alone with no one who cares for you. How does that feel? Scary? Frightening? Now imagine if you were a child."

"Charlie, please."

"Don't call me Charlie," he screamed.

The bag was jerked off her head, ripping out a chunk of her hair along with it. Chris bit back a cry, counting on her ability to stay calm. She blinked, trying to adjust to the overhead light. At the same time, she pulled deep breaths into her lungs. Her vision cleared, and she looked into blue eyes filled with hate.

"Hello, Sis." He hissed the nickname. The venom in his tone chilled her to the bone.

"Why?" The moment she'd asked, the expression on his face made her regret the question.

He placed his foot on the chair and shoved. Helpless to stop the fall, she tumbled backward, landing on her back. Stars flashed behind her eyes as her head bounced on the wood floor.

"You don't get to ask questions," he said over his shoulder as he walked to a breakfast bar. He opened a black bag and began taking items out. "I've waited a long time for this. How does it feel to have nothing or no one to come to your rescue?"

Chris could only imagine what he was carefully lining up on the counter. She pushed her pain out of her thoughts and concentrated on controlling her rising panic. Marcus could not be dead. She refused to even consider that he wouldn't come for her. What would he want her to do until he arrived? First, he'd want her to know her surroundings.

A quick scan revealed a high-end, fully furnished, open floor plan. Hardwood flooring, leather furniture, and the tall, beamed ceiling hadn't come cheap. She spotted two exterior doors. If she could reach one, where would it lead? Did it matter? No. She'd run as hard as she could.

Over a large rock fireplace hung a knife display, carefully protected by glass. If she could get free, could she break the case and get her hands on the sharpest blade? Had he brought her to his hunting retreat?

The door opened, and the man who'd put the rag over her mouth walked inside. Dressed in a gray suit that shouted money, he glanced at Charlie and then down at her on the floor.

"I see you've started the party." He watched as Charlie polished the long blade of a knife. "Her resemblance to you is remarkable. She will truly make a masterpiece."

Charlie's shoe heels echoed as he walked across the hardwood floor. "Michel-angelo." Charlie's tone sounded almost sad as he pulled the man in for a hug. "Thank you for bringing her to me."

Chris couldn't see what was happening from her position, but Charlie's arm made a wide swing and the older man grunted. He stumbled backward. Both hands were on his stomach, and blood had already begun to rush from his wound. The man dropped down on his knees. Charlie caught him under the arms and dragged him over to a wall, where he propped him up.

"DaVinci," the guy said as blood bubbled from his mouth. "After all I've done for you."

"You never should have had one of your thugs take a shot at Christine. I warned you there would be consequences."

"I did it for you." The man coughed and blood ran from his nose and mouth.

"We knew it couldn't last." Charlie returned to the breakfast bar and continued lining up different instruments. "I just acted first."

DaVinci? Michelangelo? They were role playing.

The older man tried to push himself to his feet, but his arms gave out, and he fell to the floor. Charlie ignored him as if he hadn't entered the room.

Images of the murdered women flashed through her mind. Some had been eviscerated. Was that her destiny? She grasped at her sanity.

Charlie's face suddenly loomed over her. He grabbed the back of her chair and restored her to an upright position. The light reflected off the blade of the knife in his hand.

"Did you get a good look around? Work out an escape plan? This place belongs to him." His head jerked in the direction of the dead man. "I've never actually hunted anything. Well, except you." His blue eyes glittered with excitement.

"You hunted and butchered those women."

"Nonsense. They went willingly."

"You look so much like Chelsea." Tears threatened. "She didn't willingly allow you to do those horrible things to her."

"She did at the start. She thought I was a John who'd pay for her next fix." He shook his head. "If you're trying to postpone your death by trying to make me feel sorry for that tramp, it's not necessary. I plan on taking my time with you."

"How could you do it?"

He sighed as if her questions were tedious. "Why did you leave me? Did you even ask the Hollands to adopt me? I think not. Besides, I made sure Chelsea knew who she'd invited into her bed. What do you care why I killed her? Your arrival almost ruined everything."

Chris couldn't take her eyes off the knife he twirled in his hand. "I don't understand your hate for me."

"Sure, you do. You lived the good life, never thinking about what I was going through. Did you think I would forgive and forget?"

"I was a child." She couldn't tell him she'd forgotten he existed. "You can't hold me responsible for what happened to you."

"You have no idea what 'happened' to me." He walked to the dinner table, picked a chair, and dragged it across the room, the legs scraping across the floor. He placed it directly in front of her. "But now you understand what it means to be alone. To have no one to keep the monsters away. You know how it feels to be at the mercy of others. You get it now." His voice grew louder and louder. "Don't you?"

"Yes. I get it. But why torture those other women, especially your own flesh and blood?" Chris's mouth was dry, making speaking difficult. She had to keep him talking. Had to connect with him. "Chelsea was innocent. I made the promise. Not her. Why did you do those horrible things to her?"

An evil grin spread across his face. "That was for sport. A contest with Michelangelo." He pointed the knife at the dead man.

"Contest?" Her mind scattered. "I've seen pictures. I know what you did to them. A sane person wouldn't think of doing those horrible things. And you're telling me it was for fun?"

"It was something to keep me occupied until you'd lost everything and everybody." He grabbed her hair, and the blade silently swung toward her.

Chris cried out, but realized he hadn't stabbed her. He waved a long blond curl in front of her face. "Oh, God," she whispered.

"You'd do better to pray to me."

"You killed everyone I loved. Just get it over with."

Another swipe, and this time a huge chunk of hair hit the floor. "You'll do more than ask me to kill you before we're finished. You'll beg. And we have days to play. You ready?"

Fear and anger rolled from deep inside. "You're sick."

"And you're dying."

The knife flashed again, slicing through her jeans.

CHAPTER 25

Police cars, an ambulance and a fire truck, all with flashing lights, forced Marcus to keep his head turned away. Rage was building, and he was seconds from letting it surface. "Just put a fucking bandage on it," Marcus snapped at the EMT. The madder he got, the more the back of his head throbbed, but he didn't give a damn. He had to find Chris.

"He's right." Nate leaned around and checked the back of his head. "You need stitches." He patted the EMT on his arm. "Slap a bandage on it, because Marcus isn't going to the hospital. Give it up."

Marcus growled, "Hell, the bullet just grazed me." That it knocked him down and out pissed him off. That he'd allowed Chris to be taken was almost more than he could bear. He signed the waiver and joined Nate, Dalton, and Tomas, who'd set up a command post in the manager's office.

"Where's the clerk?" Marcus asked Dalton.

"He's fine. Being interviewed. He was bound and gagged behind the front desk."

"Where's Diablo?"

"I'll get him." Nate left and returned with the dog. He passed the leash to Marcus.

"What have you learned about Charles Bridger?" Marcus couldn't stand around and do nothing any longer.

"There's a few locals with the same name. Only one with the money it would take to pull something like this off. Kay might have been right when she mentioned the art gallery owner by that name."

"Yeah," Tomas spoke. "Take a look at this picture on file with the Department of Motor Vehicles."

"Son of a bitch." Marcus stared into blue eyes the same color as Chris's.

"I sent a squad car to his apartment. He's not there," Tomas said.

"Then we talk to his neighbors. Find out who works for him and question them, too."

"I've got the list on my tablet. I'll email it to you right now so you have a copy," Nate said.

"I'll take the gallery manager." Marcus scanned the room, spotted his gun, and picked it up. A drop of blood close to the door caught his eye. He knelt down to inspect it.

"Chris hit one of the guys." Tomas supplied the answer.

"One?"

"Yeah," Tomas said. "According to the desk clerk, a Latino came in, looked around as if to size up the place. He motioned to someone outside, and two men came in with guns drawn."

"One of them intercepted the pizza guy. He's dead," Nate said. "Tomas has men in the apartment building. Dalton and I were going to start on Bridger's employees."

"Do what you want. I'm talking with the gallery manager. That's usually the one person who knows everything."

"I'll drive you," Dalton said, patting the badge clipped to his belt. "People tend to be more cooperative when you're wearing one of these."

"Then let's go." Marcus lifted Diablo's leash, and the dog immediately stood.

"Don't you think you should put on a shirt?" Dalton closed his laptop, slid it in its case, and then stood. "And leave the dog."

"The shirt's a good idea. Diablo goes with me." Marcus jerked a pullover out of his suitcase and slipped it on as they walked to the car.

Nate and Tomas followed, stopping at the plain navy sedan that Dallas detectives drove. "Stay in touch," Nate said.

The drive across town was agony. Dalton pushed his rental car hard, weaving in and out of traffic. Still, it seemed as if time had slowed to a crawl. Time they didn't have to spare. Time Chris might not have to live.

Dalton had rented a car with navigation, and every now and then, a monotone voice issued instructions, breaking the silence. When the voice announced their destination was on the right, Marcus almost cheered.

The neighborhood consisted of almost identical rows of town houses. Dalton parked in front of number six eighteen and killed the engine.

Marcus turned to Diablo. The dog sensed something was wrong. He hadn't flopped down on the seat as usual. Instead, he'd been moving around. "Easy, boy."

"You leaving him in the car?"

"Never." Marcus and Dalton wasted no time getting to the door.

"Who is it?" a female asked through the closed door.

"FBI. Ms. Janet Kelly? It's important that we speak with you." Dalton held up his ID for her to see.

"Just a minute."

"Look," Dalton said to Marcus. "You're a scary-looking son of a bitch with the dried blood on your neck and the patch on the back of your head, not to mention the dog. So am I wasting my breath to ask you to let me do the talking?"

"Not at all. You're the expert. Lead off, but I may have questions."

The door opened, and a wide-eyed young woman blocked the entryway with her body. "What's happened?"

"We have some questions concerning Charles Bridger. I think you can help." Dalton took a step forward.

Her gaze stopped on Diablo. "He's harmless," Marcus said. "May we come in?"

"Of course," she said, letting a loud sigh escape. "I thought something had happened to my family." She led them into a small living room, picked up the remote, and muted the TV. "Please, have a seat."

Dalton sat, but Marcus was too edgy to park it anywhere. He and Diablo stood to the side. Her discomfort showed as her gaze kept drifting between him and the dog.

"Really, they're both harmless," Dalton said in an easy, joking manner. "A bullet nicked the back of his head."

Marcus wanted to scream at the top of his lungs. At this rate, the questioning would take forever. Then, he realized, she'd leaned back and relaxed, chatting away as if she and Dalton were old friends. When he asked about Bridger's close friends, she brightened.

"The only friend I know of is some old guy with a shit-load of money. He's an art dealer. Richard…let me think. Yes, Richard Franklin."

"Excuse us." Marcus took Diablo and hurried out onto the sidewalk, where he called Nate and relayed the man's name.

"You're on speaker. Tomas is already on it. I'll get back with you," Nate said.

Dalton walked out, followed by the young woman. "I hope Charles is all right. He's a good boss," she said, walking inside.

Dalton slid behind the steering wheel, pulled out his phone, and placed a call. Marcus's heartbeat had moved to his head. He put Diablo in the back seat and got into the car.

"We'll know something on Richard Franklin soon. I'm having him run the database."

"Tomas is running his name, too." Marcus checked his watch. Chris should be here with him, tucked in bed, and sound asleep. Where was she?

****

"Stop cutting me. Please," Chris pleaded.

"Okay," he said. "I am kind of thirsty." He set the knife on the coffee table and strolled into the kitchen area. "Hmm, red or white. What do you think, Sis? Red? Good choice." He opened a bottle of wine and poured a glass. He returned but sat on the couch this time. "I'm sure Richard won't mind me drinking vintage."

That her hair was scattered across the floor wasn't Chris's main concern. Even the acrid scent coming from the man he'd killed had stopped turning her stomach. The burning from her wounds and the pain in her shoulders made it hard for her to focus. She had to control the panic worming its way through her system, threatening to take over her mind.

Charlie had been running the knife blade along her arms and legs. Not slicing deeply, cutting just enough to cause pain and damage. Blood ran down her limbs and pooled on the floor. The slashes across her thigh had turned her jeans a dark crimson. At this rate, it would take a long time to die.

Charlie held the glass to his nose and breathed deeply. He took a sip, swishing the deep red liquid around in his mouth before swallowing. He didn't appear to be angry anymore. In fact, he seemed to be almost giddy.

"I can't feel my hands. Will you loosen the knot? Please."

"Let me think about it. You kicked me in the balls the last time we saw each other." He drummed his fingers on his chin. "You never worried about my well-being, so why should I care if you're tied too tight?"

"I'm your sister. And I'm sorry for everything that happened to you."

"Really? You gave up that right when you chose your new mother and father." He paused to empty his drink. After he'd refilled it, he hoisted his glass toward the dead man. "Excellent wine, Richard."

"You killed my parents, didn't you?"

"I told you. I took everybody from you. Figure it out." He smiled and appeared to be proud of what he'd done. "I wonder. Did you really suffer? After all, they weren't your real family."

"I loved them dearly."

"Did you? Then I'm glad I killed them." He picked up the knife, ran his finger along the side of the blade, smearing her blood as he went. He stood and advanced, still wearing that sickening smile.

She braced for him to slice her arm or leg again, but the knife pierced her right shoulder, sinking into her flesh. He jerked the blade out quickly. Chris cried out and tried to lean into the pain, but her shoulders felt as if they were being ripped from their sockets.

"Oh, stop," he said using a whiny tone. "None of these"—he stuck the blade into her abdomen and pulled it out—"are very deep. Are you getting weaker? I'd rather you not bleed out so soon."

"If you're going to kill me, do it!" She couldn't tolerate his insanity any longer. "Just know that you're not my full brother. You're my half-brother."

He sank to the chair in front of her. "Why would you tell such a lie?" The blade sank deep into her again. "First, you let those people abandon me and now you try to deny me."

"I saw my adoption papers today. Chelsea and I had the same father. His last name was Shelby. Your last name is Bridger."

The blade slid slowly across her forearm. "You think I haven't done my research? Who knows why our junkie mother put Bridger on the birth certificate? Probably to milk some poor bastard out of his money." He ran his hand over his hair. "All you have to do is look at me. We could be twins."

"Stop this now, Charlie. I'll get you help. Stand by you."

"It was fortunate that I met our friend over there." He ignored her comment. "He took me in. When I opened the gallery, I decided to use Bridger as my last name. You see"—he leaned closer and whispered—"Charles Shelby is wanted for murder."

"So is Charles Bridger."

The change in his demeanor was instantaneous. He dragged the blade down her arm, deeper this time as the blood didn't ooze, it ran. "They only know my name because of you!"

Darkness called her. A calm and peaceful quiet place where she could rest engulfed her.

****

They were taking a big chance driving this far away from the city. Marcus refused to entertain the idea they could be wrong. Time was running out.

No one had seen Richard Franklin, but he fit the description from the desk clerk. Dalton had learned that Franklin owned a couple of properties, and one was located outside Fort Worth in deer-hunting country. According to Tomas, none of the people in Franklin's apartment building thought of him as a hunter.

Marcus appreciated the clear sky, the stars, and especially the full moon, because they were miles away from such things as street lights. They'd parked the rental car and walked down the long, narrow, unpaved drive. Dalton hadn't suggested they wait for Tomas and Nate. Smart man. No way was Marcus delaying. If Chris wasn't there, they'd hit a dead end.

Why hadn't he protected her? He'd allowed her to be hauled off and turned over to a mad man. Letting her down had delivered a blow he didn't know how to handle.

They stopped when the cabin came into view. He and Dalton drew their weapons. Marcus gave Dalton the signal to circle the house from the right side. As soon as the fed walked away, Marcus and Diablo moved closer.

Lights were on in the house, but all the blinds had been drawn, making a visual inspection impossible. Marcus kept moving, listening for any sound from inside.

Diablo tugged at the leash. Agitated, he lunged, almost pulling out of Marcus's grasp. Chris was here! And Diablo sensed she was in trouble. Marcus dropped down on one knee and pulled the dog's head around. Once he had his attention, he gave the hand signal for the animal to be quiet.

Dalton stepped around the corner. Marcus motioned for Dalton to follow. They silently walked around back. Marcus handed Diablo's leash over to the fed.

Without a clean shot, Marcus had but one choice. He stepped up and kicked open the door. If he could get Charles to move away from her, Dalton would fire.

Marcus felt nothing but rage at the sight of Chris tied to a chair. Her brother held her by her hair, a knife at her throat. God in heaven, she appeared to be dead. Marcus's heart hit the floor.

"Look, Sis. We have company," the asshole said. "Marcus, I presume."

"That's right." Marcus inched forward. "Doesn't look like she can hear you."

Her chest moved, but he couldn't celebrate yet. "Which means I have nothing left to lose."

"You must have nine lives."

"How do you figure?" Marcus asked, circling to stay out of the line of fire.

"You're supposed to be dead. I thought it was you when I shot the cop. And my friend there"—he jerked his head in the direction a dead body—"was supposed to make sure you died tonight." Charles's eyes were darting every direction. He jerked Chris's hair, smiling when she moaned. "Put your gun on the coffee table or I'll slit her throat."

The tip of the blade pressed against her skin, and a drop of blood slid down her neck. "You son of a bitch." Fear and anger poured out of Marcus. He slowly walked to the coffee table. Dalton had to be poised to fire. Now to hold this crazy bastard's attention. "I will kill you with my bare hands if you don't move that blade away from her neck."

Diablo burst into the room. A dark blur, emitting a low growl, the dog never slowed down. He left the floor and landed on Charles with a force that surprised even Marcus. It happened so fast, Charles Bridger had no time to react. He threw his arms up to try to cover his face as he stumbled under the dog's weight and fell backward. The man's scream as the dog's teeth sank into his flesh was blood-curdling.

"No. Diablo. No." Marcus lunged for him. Would he listen? Had he reverted? His teeth were embedded in Bridger's right cheek and jaw. Marcus wrapped his arms around the dog. "It's okay, boy. It's okay."

Relaxing, the dog released Charles. Dalton appeared and, without checking the damage to Charles, flipped him over and handcuffed him. "I took his leash off, but didn't expect him to react like that."

"Chris," Marcus said, ignoring Dalton. "Diablo, down. Stay."

Chris's cry of pain when Marcus cut her bindings and her arms fell free sliced through him. Her pulse was weak but steady. But there was so much blood. Had he gotten to her too late? "Please say something."

Her gaze met his. She grinned and put her hand out for Diablo. Blood-covered muzzle and all, he ignored Marcus's command to stay and crawled on his belly to Chris.

"I love that dog."

"That's a damn good thing," he said as flashing lights lit up the night and sirens filled the air with sound. "Because he and his owner love you."

All the other problems they might face meant nothing. He and Diablo had been given a second shot at life. No chance in hell would they blow it.

EPILOGUE

Four weeks later

Marcus parked his new SUV as close to the Lost and Found office front door as possible. He killed the engine, hurried around the front of the vehicle, and then opened the door for Chris. Extending his hand, he asked, "You sure you're up for this?"

"I'm fine. You have to stop treating me like I'll shatter into a million pieces." Chris took his hand, got out, and then lifted up on her toes for a kiss.

"Get over it." Marcus accepted the kiss. Then he leaned down and rested his forehead against hers for a second. "Seeing you cut up and covered in blood almost did me in."

"Most were superficial cuts."

"The key word in that sentence being 'most,'" he grumbled to himself as he opened the back door and let Diablo get out. Truth was, Marcus was relieved and delighted that her brother hadn't inflicted permanent damage. Not that he hadn't tried.

"My range of motion is almost back to normal." She rolled her shoulder and lifted her arm, cupping his cheek in her palm. "Physical therapy is getting rid of the stiffness."

Marcus hadn't watched her demonstration. Instead, he'd kept his eyes on hers, searching for any sign of pain.

"You're not missing your friend's welcome home party on my account. If it's important enough to warrant Ty and Ana to fly in from Colombia, we can show up to support Jake." She took his hand and tugged him toward the door to the Lost and Found office.

Marcus stiffened, refusing to budge. "I'm not convinced this get-together is a good idea. What if he's not ready for a crowd? Kay may have missed the mark surprising Jake with a party. If it were me, I'd want to be left alone."

"He's not you." Chris's eyes warmed. "You have me now. Those days of you being left alone are over. I love you. Remember?"

"Yes, ma'am. I do." Marcus grinned down at her. "Are you gonna show them your new ring?"

"No." She held up her left hand and wiggled her fingers. "I'm going to wait and see who notices it first. Besides, today is about showing support for your friend."

Marcus pulled her into his arms and breathed deeply. How had he gotten so lucky? He hadn't done anything good enough to warrant having a woman like Chris love him. Somebody had been watching out for him. Had waited until he understood what love really meant before giving him a second chance.

"You're stalling."

The door opened, and Ty stepped into view. He headed straight toward Marcus and Chris, his long strides quickly covering the pavement beneath his feet. His clean-shaven head glistened in the bright sunlight. A smile slowly spread across his face.

"Down, Diablo," Marcus said, and the dog dropped to his belly.

Damn, Marcus was glad to see the man. Marcus stepped forward and gathered Ty in for a bear hug. Ty turned his famous smile toward Chris.

"You must be Chris."

"I am." She hugged Ty as if they were old friends, while Marcus stood back and beamed with pride.

"You having trouble getting this loner to come inside?" Ty raised a jet-black eyebrow.

"Looks like it," she said, holding her left hand out for Marcus to take. Sunlight reflected off the diamond in her ring. The sparkle caught in her eyes. "But he's not a loner any longer."

"No, I'm not," Marcus confirmed. He slid his arm around her waist and tucked her under his arm.

Ty's smile returned. "Then let's get inside before Nate gets back from the airport with Jake."

"Let's." She patted her thigh. "Come, Diablo."

Stay tuned for No Greater Hell, book four in the Lost and Found, Inc. series

ABOUT THE AUTHOR

Author of The Green-Eyed Doll, The Last Execution, Someone To Watch Over Me, and Hell Or High Water, and Cold Day in Hell, books one and two in the Lost and Found, Inc. series, my husband and I live in Texas with our rescue dog, Buddy. I write alpha males and kick-ass women who weave their way through death and fear to emerge stronger because of, and on occasion in spite of, their love for each other.

Get up to date information on new releases. Sign up for my newsletter at http://www.JerrieAlexander.com and connect with me on Facebook and Twitter.

If you enjoyed this book, please help me spread the word. Facebook and tweet your approval. A review on Amazon and or GoodReads would be greatly appreciated. Send me an email if you post a review, I'd love to thank you personally.

ACKNOWLEDGEMENTS

I would be remiss if I didn't acknowledge the following people. Their support, advice, and enthusiasm were invaluable.

To my editor, Joyce Lamb, your guidance helped me polish this story until it shone. For that, you have my sincere appreciation.

To Jackie Pressley, who critiqued my words, poked and prodded me when the story stalled, and offered encouragement every step of the way. This past year has been particularly rough on my family. You stuck by me, and I appreciate yours support more than I can say!

To my advisor on all firearms and tactical matters, a real American hero who prefers to remain nameless, thanks for sharing your knowledge and for your service to our country. Any mistakes are my own!

To my husband, who has always said I could do anything I set my mind to, and our daughter, who believes in me one-hundred percent. Thank you for your unwavering love and support.

Last but not least, thanks to my readers. You are why I write. Your emails make my day! I hope you enjoy this story as much as I loved writing it.

Praise for Cold Day in Hell

"The sexual tension and sizzling chemistry between Ty and Ana has the temperature rising even higher than the sweltering heat of the jungle, as they escape from the relentless pursuit of the cartel henchmen, who threaten their existence. "Cold Day in Hell" is an entertaining story filled with action, suspense, and romance, which will keep the reader enthralled until the very end!"
   - InD'tale Magazine

Praise for Hell or High Water

"This is only book one in Jerrie Alexander's Lost and Found Inc series but I personally can't wait to pick up book two, Cold Day in Hell. I can't wait to see what happens to Tyrell. Overall, this book was a wonderful blend of suspense and romance. For those who like romance you will be satisfied and for those suspense lovers you won't be able to put this book down either."
   - The Book Maven